THE OUTCAST

1957, and Lewis Aldridge is travelling back to his home in the South of England. He is straight out of jail and nineteen years old. His return will trigger the implosion not just of his family, but of a whole community.

A decade earlier, his father's homecoming takes a different shape. The war is over and Gilbert is demobbed. He reverts easily to suburban life but his wife and young son Lewis resist the stuffy routine, and escape to the woods for picnics, just as they did in wartime. Nobody is surprised that Gilbert's wife counters convention, but they are all shocked when, after one of their jaunts, Lewis comes back without her.

Not far away, Kit Carmichael keeps watch. Lewis's grief and burgeoning rage are all too plain, and Kit makes a private vow to help. But in her attempts to set them both free, she fails to predict the painful and horrifying secrets that must first be forced into the open.

THE OUTCAST

Sadie Jones

WINDSOR
PARAGON

First published 2008
by Chatto & Windus
This Large Print edition published 2008
by BBC Audiobooks Ltd
by arrangement with
The Random House Group Ltd

Hardcover ISBN: 978 1 405 64917 9
Softcover   ISBN: 978 1 405 64918 6

Copyright © Sadie Jones 2008

Sadie Jones has asserted her right under the
Copyright, Designs and Patents Act 1988 to be
identified as the author of this work.

British Library Cataloguing in Publication Data available

Printed and bound in Great Britain by
CPI Antony Rowe, Chippenham, Wiltshire

PROLOGUE

AUGUST 1957

There was nobody there to meet him. He stood in line behind three other men and watched them get their things and sign the papers and walk out, and they all did it just the same way, as if you couldn't choose how to do a thing like that after all the time you'd been waiting for it. It made the same man out of all of them.

When it came to his turn there were only the clothes he'd been in when he arrived and his wallet and cut-throat razor. They made him sign for them, and for the postal order his father had sent, and he was put to get changed in a side room. His clothes didn't fit him properly any more; the trousers were an inch too short and the arms of the shirt didn't cover his wrists.

He went back to the desk and put his wallet in his back pocket with the postal order inside it, and the razor in his other pocket, and waited while the doors were all unlocked again to let him through. He didn't look at the guards, but crossed the yard to the small door in the wall to the side of the big gate. The door was unlocked, and opened, and he stepped out into the street.

*　　*　　*

There was no sign of the men who'd gone before him, or of anyone at all. He kept a hold of himself and didn't feel too much about it. He had been in a state of waiting, but the waiting wasn't for his release, it was for his homecoming. Two years is not a long time, but maybe longer from seventeen to nineteen than at other times of your life.

It was the colours that struck him first, the colours and the very bright sunlight. His eye could see far away, down the street to where a small, pale blue car was turning a corner and disappearing.

He looked up and down the street and thought that he could stand there for ever in the clean air and look at the distance, and the bricks in the houses that were different shades of yellow and brown, and the bits of grass between the paving and the way there was nobody there. Then he remembered the prison at his back and wanted to get away from it. Then he thought that it was all he'd known for a long time, and he didn't want to get away from it, but he stopped himself thinking that and walked down the street, away from the prison and towards where the pale blue car had gone.

*   *   *

Lewis needed to cross the river to Victoria to catch the train home. He had to get to a post office to cash the postal order and he had to get to the station, then he decided he needed to buy something to wear because he felt foolish, and going home would be hard enough without looking stupid as well.

Getting from one place to another and having to speak to people he didn't know made him feel frightened and more like a convict than he had expected to, and when he got to Victoria he stood across the road from the station, trying to make himself go in.

There was no shade. He had bought two white shirts and a light-grey suit that came with an extra pair of trousers, and some cigarettes and a pack of cards and a metal lighter with a hot flame. He was wearing one set of clothes and the man in the shop had sold him a cardboard case to put the other things in, and now he put the case down, and took cigarettes from the pocket of his new trousers and lit one with his new lighter and waited to be able to go into the station.

He'd never bought clothes for himself before. It was odd that he could have done the things he'd done and not know how to clothe himself. His father had sent him enough money not to come home, but he hadn't asked him not to.

Thinking about what he'd done and what his father thought of him wasn't helping, so he watched the people on the streets instead. The colours were still very bright. There was a lot of blue sky and the trees on the pavements seemed marvellous and the women looked wonderful and he had to stop himself from staring at all of them. He felt the flicker of life inside himself, looking at them, and it was a bright flame and not a dark one and there was promise in the way the women walked and the lightness of them. He tried not to stare and was dazzled and hypnotised by every woman who passed him. Trying not to stare at women, but still looking at them as much as he could was a game, and a good way to stop his head from getting away from him, and made him feel alive again. He wondered if you could get arrested for staring at women for an hour outside Victoria station, and imagined the judge putting him away again the day he got out for picturing them under their clothes, and after a while he was able to cross the street and go into the station and buy his ticket.

*   *   *

The train had the same rhythm and the same sound and the same varnished wood as every other time he'd made the journey. The seats were hard, with parts of them worn to a shine. He had gone without thinking to the last second-class carriage towards the front, and sat in a window seat facing the back of the train so he could see the platform pull away from him.

*   *   *

Alice had been dreaming a lot about Lewis, knowing he was coming out, and in her dreams he was always very young and was being taken away, or being lost, and in some of them she was a child too and she wasn't sure if she was him or herself as a little girl.

She made sure Lewis's room was ready. She aired it and asked Mary to make up the bed and saw it was dusted and then she closed the door again, but she didn't know what time they would have let him out and he hadn't written to say if he was coming. If he didn't come, she thought, they wouldn't know where he was.

It was a hot summer and it had become a habit to leave the windows and the French doors to the garden open, and the inside was often as warm as the outside and the carpet felt hot from the sun coming in. Alice went to her room and checked her face and then went down to the kitchen and spoke to Mary about supper. Then she sat in the drawing room by the empty grate and tried to read, not knowing if she was waiting or not.

*　　　*　　　*

The platform at Waterford was as empty as the street outside the prison. Lewis walked down the steps from the platform without seeing anyone. The road had trees arching over it and sunlight came through the branches of the trees and dappled the road. Lewis walked with his head down and when he heard a car engine behind, he kept to the side, not looking.

The car passed him. It stopped. He heard it reversing and then it drew level.

'Hey you! I know you.'

He looked into the open-topped car, at the blonde girl driving. It was Tamsin Carmichael and she smiled at him.

'Hello, Tamsin.'

'I'd no idea you were back!'

'Well, just.'

'Hop in.' He didn't move. 'Are you getting in, or not?'

He got in next to her. The car was an Austin and Tamsin wore short white gloves and a pale summer dress. Lewis didn't look at her after the first look, but away and out of the car at the country going by.

'How's it feel?' she asked, as if he'd just scored a century in a cricket match. 'You've missed absolutely nothing, I can assure you. Caroline Foster got married, but apart from that, do you

ix

know, I don't think a single thing's happened. Home, is it?'

'If that's all right.'

'Not exactly what you'd call a detour.'

Tamsin let him out at the end of his drive and drove off, waving a gloved hand, and the sound of her car faded. Lewis didn't think she knew what it meant to him for her to be nice like that, but then he forgot about her, because his father's house was ahead of him and he was home.

He walked up to the house and felt as if he was doing it in a dream. When he knocked, Alice opened the door immediately, smiling very brightly.

'Lewis!'

'Alice . . . You knew I was coming?'

'We knew they were releasing you. Sorry. Hello.'

He went into the house and she shut the door and they looked at each other in the dim hall for a moment and then she kissed his cheek.

'You've grown,' she said. 'We just didn't know whether to expect you. You look so different. Your room's ready.'

Lewis went upstairs and Alice stood in the hall wondering if she should phone Gilbert and tell him Lewis was back, and if Lewis really looked as different as she thought, or if she had just remembered him wrongly.

It was like having a man in her house. A man she didn't know. He had been in prison and she had no idea what he'd been through there and he had never been predictable. She felt alarm and she waited in the hall, but Gilbert would have left his office already and there was no phoning him.

x

Lewis's bedroom was roughly the same size as his last cell in Brixton; a little bigger, maybe. That had been green and not white and he had shared it. He put his case on the bed and went over to the window and lit a cigarette and looked out at the garden.

There was a bluebottle crashing against the glass. It explored the edges, and seemed to search for an opening and then went straight at the panes of glass in a series of small assaults and then back to the edges again, and then it rested and then it went for the glass again, hitting itself, and it didn't stop, but carried on with it, trying to get out and not getting out and trying again.

*   *   *

The mantelpiece clock had a light, metallic chime and the sound of it striking six reached Lewis in his room.

Alice quietly started to assemble the ingredients for her jug of Pimm's, which would be ready at exactly six-thirty, just before Gilbert walked through the door. She made it slowly, and a small one for herself as a taster, to get the Pimm's and gin mix right. When she went into the kitchen for mint and apple and ice, she tried to make things better with Mary. Mary hadn't known Lewis was coming out; the first she knew of it was hearing his voice in the hall, and she was angry and she didn't want to be in the house with him. There had been a row and Alice had to beg her not to give notice. Now she found herself practically following Mary around the kitchen trying to ingratiate herself, and after a while she gave up and took her mint and her slices of apple and went back into the drawing room.

*   *   *

When Lewis heard his father's key in the door he went to the top of the stairs. Gilbert stood in the doorway with his briefcase in his hand, still wearing his hat. Alice came out of the drawing room and watched them. Gilbert took off his hat and put it on the straight-backed chair by the door.

'You're home.'

'Yes, sir.'

'Come with me.' He said it quietly, but with rage.

'Gilbert—'

'Come!'

Lewis started down the stairs to his father and followed him out of the house. They got into the car without a word.

*   *   *

Gilbert drove quite fast towards the village and Lewis didn't need to ask him where they were going. It was hard to be next to his father again and to have his presence filling the car up like that and Lewis tried to remember what he'd planned to say.

Gilbert pulled over and stopped and turned off the engine. Lewis found he couldn't raise his eyes, but stared down at his hands. He'd been going to make a promise. He'd been going to make his speech and his promise and reassure his father, but

xii

now he couldn't even raise his eyes from his hands and Gilbert said, 'Look, can't you?'

He looked, obediently.

The church was ahead of them, warm with evening sunshine and very quiet and peaceful.

'It's just the same,' said Lewis.

'Yes. We wanted it to be just the same. Lots of people chipped in. Dicky Carmichael helped enormously. It was very important to everybody that it be just the same.'

Lewis looked at the church and there was silence as he looked.

'Well?' said Gilbert, 'Do you have anything to say?' Lewis said nothing.

Gilbert started the engine and drove home without speaking to his son again.

*   *   *

The family sat in the dining room by the open window and Mary brought in the dishes and put them on the table before she left for the night. The sky was still light and the candles stood unlit. Lewis was distracted by the things on the table. There were holders and containers for everything; silver and glass and lace that were almost hypnotically diverting. He worked hard not to think about the wine that Gilbert was pouring for himself and Alice. He could smell the red wine as it was poured, mixing with the smell of the damp vegetables. The only talking was to do with the passing of things, and thanking, and Lewis wanted to laugh because he was nostalgic for the huge noise of the mass mealtimes in prison. It had been not unlike school, and quite relaxing, but this was just self-conscious and tense and everything he'd hated about home before. He thought there must be something really wrong with a person who would rather be in Brixton prison than their own home.

Gilbert made a speech about what was expected of Lewis; how he must behave and get a job and be polite and not drink and as his father spoke, Lewis kept staring at the things on the table, but he couldn't see them properly any more.

Alice stood up, pushing her chair back crookedly. She excused herself and left the room and Lewis and his father finished their supper in silence. Gilbert placed his knife and fork together and wiped his mouth carefully. He put the napkin on his side plate and stood up.

'Good,' he said.

He waited to see if Lewis would get up too, but Lewis continued to stare at the table. After watching him for a moment Gilbert went to join Alice in the drawing room.

Lewis waited until he heard his father say something to Alice, and then the sound of the door, closing. The wine bottle on the table was empty. He looked at the liquor on the sideboard. There was no gin. There was brandy and whisky, in decanters, and glasses next to the decanters. He hadn't had a drink since the night he'd been arrested. He could have one now. It wasn't as if he'd decided not to drink, he wouldn't be breaking any promise. He took a breath and waited and then got up and stepped out of the open window onto the grass and walked up the lawn.

*   *   *

The woods were dark already. The sky was pale and the house was lit up behind him, but there was dark ahead. Lewis looked into the trees and he thought he could hear the river—but he couldn't hear the river, the river couldn't have got closer. He felt a coldness go over him at the thought of the water coming closer to the house.

'All right?'

Alice was standing next to him and he hadn't realised and he hadn't heard her.

He looked at her and tried to pull his mind back to where they were.

'I wanted to say,' she began, 'I wanted to say—let's try and be friends, this time, shall we?'

'Of course.'

She looked so worried, he couldn't disappoint her.

'Your father,' she said, 'he missed you.'

It was kind of her to say so, but he didn't think it was true.

'Was it bad?'

He wasn't sure what she meant, and then realised she was asking him about prison. She didn't really want to know, though.

'There are worse things.'

'We didn't come.'

They hadn't come. At the beginning, when he was so frightened, it had been unbearable that they didn't, and he had written to them a few times, asking, but after that it was easier not seeing them and hardly hearing from them, and he'd forgotten about it—or nearly.

Alice let the silence go on as long as she could and then she tried again. She put her hand out, indicating his arm, stretching her fingers lightly towards it.

'No more silliness?' she asked.

He pulled his arm away and put his hand in his pocket.

'Right,' she said, 'right,' and she smiled again, apologetic this time. The grass was wet with dew and she had taken off her shoes to come out to him and carried them now as she went back to the house.

*   *   *

It was the same dream, and when he woke in darkness and sweat, and cold with the fear of it, he had to sit up and put his feet on the ground, and make himself keep his eyes open, and tell himself he wasn't there and it wasn't true, or even if it was, it was an old truth and he should forget it. He'd had the dream while he had been in prison, but much less than before and sometimes not for weeks at a time and he'd hoped it was leaving him.

He waited for the fear to drain away and to feel like he was breathing air again, and not water, and he kept his eyes open and looked for a moon outside the window, but there wasn't one. He thought of Alice, pointing at him like that, and his forearm reminded him of itself, like a separate thing making him look and, after a while, he did. It was too dark to see the scars, but he could feel them with his fingertips, both numb and raw; a feeling of wrongness.

He went to the window and tried to make real things from the shapes of the garden. He could see the apple tree and past it he could see the line of the woods meeting the sky. He made himself stand still, but it was very hard to be still and very hard to stand there, and he would have clawed out of his skin if he could, just to get away from himself. He told himself it was a luxury to be able to get up in the night without disturbing anyone and a blessing to be able to walk to a window if he wanted, and there to be no bars on it, and a garden beneath. He told himself all that, but it didn't mean anything.

PART ONE

CHAPTER ONE

1945

Gilbert was demobbed in November and Elizabeth took Lewis up to London to meet him at the Charing Cross Hotel. Lewis was seven. Elizabeth and he got onto the train at Waterford and she held his hand firmly so that he wouldn't fall when he climbed up the high step. Lewis sat next to the window and opposite her, to watch the station get small as they pulled away, and Elizabeth took off her hat so that she could rest her head against the seat without it getting in the way. The seat was itchy against Lewis's bare legs between his shorts and his socks and he liked the way it was uncomfortable and the way the train moved from side to side. There was a feeling of specialness; his mother was quiet with it and it changed the way everything looked. They had a secret between them and they didn't need to talk about it. He looked out of the window and wondered again if his father would be wearing his uniform and, if he were, if he would have a gun. He wondered, if he did have a gun, if he would let Lewis hold it. Lewis thought probably not. His father probably wouldn't have one, and if he did it would be too dangerous and Lewis wouldn't be allowed to play with it. The clouds were very low over the fields, so that everything looked close up and flat. Lewis thought it was possible that the train might be standing still and the fields and houses and sky might be rushing past. That would mean his father would be rushing

3

towards him standing in the Charing Cross Hotel, but then all the people would fall over. He thought he might feel sick, so he looked over at his mother. She was looking straight ahead, as if she was watching something lovely. She was smiling so he pushed her leg with his foot so that she would smile at him, and she did, and he looked back out of the window. He couldn't remember if he'd had lunch or what time of day it was. He tried to remember breakfast. He remembered going to bed the night before and his mother kissing him and saying, 'We'll see Daddy tomorrow', and the way his stomach had felt suddenly. It felt that way now. His mother called it butterflies, but it wasn't like that, it was more just suddenly knowing you had a stomach, when normally you forgot. He decided if he sat and thought about his father and his stomach any more he'd definitely feel sick.

'Can I go for a walk?' he asked.

'Yes, you can go for a walk. Don't touch the doors and don't lean out. How will you know where to find me again?'

He looked around, 'G'.

'Carriage G.'

He couldn't open the door; it was heavy and they both fought with it. She held it open for him and he went down the corridor, one hand on the window side, the other on the compartment side, steadying himself and saying under his breath, 'along-along-along'.

*   *   *

After Elizabeth had spoken to Gilbert on the telephone the day before, she had sat on the chair

4

in the hall and cried. She cried so much that she'd had to go upstairs so that Jane wouldn't see her, or Lewis, if he came in from the garden. She had cried much more than any time they had parted since he had first gone away and more than she had in May when they heard the war in Europe had ended. Now she felt very calm and as if it was normal to be going to see your husband whom you had been frightened might die almost every day for four years. She looked down at the clasp on her new bag and thought about all the other women seeing their husbands again and buying handbags that wouldn't be noticed. Lewis appeared through the glass, struggling with the door, and she let him in and he smiled at her and stood balancing with his arms out.

'Look—'

He had his mouth open with the effort of not falling over and his tongue to one side. One of his socks was down. His fingers were each stretching out. Elizabeth loved him and missed a breath with loving him. She grabbed him around the middle.

'Don't! I wasn't falling!'

'I know you weren't, I just wanted to give you a hug.'

'Mummy!'

'Sorry, darling, you balance.' She let go, and Lewis went back to balancing.

*   *   *

They took a taxi from Victoria to Charing Cross and they looked out at the buildings, and the big holes where buildings had been. There was much more sky than there had been and the gaps looked

5

more real than the buildings, which were like afterthoughts. There were lots of people on the pavements and the road was crowded with cars and buses. The weather made it look as if the broken buildings and people's coats and hats and the grey sky were all joined together in greyness except for the blowing autumn leaves, which were quite bright.

'Here we are,' said Elizabeth, and the taxi pulled over. Lewis scraped his calf climbing out of the taxi and didn't feel it because he was looking up at the hotel and seeing all the men going in and out and thinking that one of them might be his father.

*   *   *

'I'm meeting my husband in the bar.'

'Yes, madam. Follow me.'

Lewis held Elizabeth's hand and they followed the man. The hotel was vast and dim and shabby. There were men in uniform everywhere and people greeting each other and the air was full of smoke. Gilbert was sitting in a corner by a tall, dirty window. He was in his uniform, and greatcoat, and he was smoking a cigarette and scanning the crowds outside on the pavement. Elizabeth saw him before he saw her and she stopped.

'Do you see your party, madam?'

'Yes, thank you.'

Lewis pulled her hand, 'Where? Where?'

Elizabeth watched Gilbert and she thought, I should hold this moment. I should remember this. I will remember this all my life. Then he looked up and saw her. There was a moment of blankness

6

and then a smile and from then she wasn't on her own in her head any more, she was with him. He crushed his cigarette into the ashtray and got up and went over to her. She let go of Lewis's hand. They kissed, embraced clumsily, and then allowed each other to be very close, quickly.

'God, we can get you out of this bloody uniform—'

'Lizzie, you're here—'

'We'll burn it, ritually.'

'Don't be treasonous.'

Lewis looked up at his mother and father holding each other. His hand felt strange where she had let go of it. He waited. They stood apart and Gilbert looked down at Lewis.

'Hello, little chap!'

Lewis looked up at his father and he had so many thoughts in his mind that his face went blank.

'Aren't you going to say hello?'

'Hello.'

'What? Can't hear you!'

'Hello.'

'Shake hands then!'

Lewis held out his hand. They shook hands.

'He's been so excited, Gilbert. He's been full of things to ask. He's talked of nothing else.'

'We can't stand here all day. Shall we get out of this ghastly place? What do you want? What shall we do?'

'I don't know.'

'Are you going to cry?'

Lewis looked up at Elizabeth in alarm. Why would she cry?

'No. I'm not going to. We could have some lunch.'

7

'Well, not here. Come on, I'll get my things. Wait.'

He went over to the table where he'd been sitting and picked up his kit bag and another bag. Lewis held tightly to his mother. She squeezed his hand. They still had their secret, she was still with him.

*   *   *

They went for lunch and a huge fuss was made about the chops, which were small and brown, in the middle of a large silver plate. Lewis thought he wasn't hungry and ate enormously. He watched his parents talking. They talked about the housekeeper, Jane, and whether or not her cooking was tolerable. They talked about the roses Elizabeth had just planted and that there was going to be a big Christmas party at the Carmichaels'. Lewis thought he would explode with boredom and his insides would splash all over the walls and onto the waiter's white jacket. He tapped his father's arm.

'Excuse me, sir.'

His father didn't look at him.

'I'll get the train, I should think . . .'

Lewis thought he hadn't heard.

'Excuse me, sir . . . Excuse me.'

'Do answer him, Gilbert.'

'Lewis?'

'Was it very hot in the desert?'

'Very.'

'Were there snakes?'

'A few.'

'Did you shoot them?'

8

'No.'

'Were there camels?'

'Yes. Lots.'

'Did you ride on any?'

'No.'

'Did you shoot lots of people or blow them up?'

'Lewis, let Daddy eat his lunch.'

'Shoot them to death, or blow them up?'

'Lewis, nobody wants to talk about things like that.'

He could see that they didn't. He thought he'd stick to safe subjects.

'Do you like chops?'

'Chops are jolly nice. Don't you think so?'

'Not bad. Did they give you chops in the desert?'

'Not usually.'

'Jelly?'

'Talkative, isn't he?'

'Not always. He's excited.'

'I can see that. Eat your lunch, Lewis, and be quiet, there's a good chap.'

Lewis had already finished his lunch, but he obeyed the second part, and was quiet.

*   *   *

His room was dark. The curtains were drawn, but a little light came in from the landing and fell across the bed. He could hear the wireless downstairs and his parents' voices, but he couldn't hear what they were saying. He wriggled down further into the bed. The sheets were cold. He heard his mother's step on the stairs. She came in and sat on the edge of the bed.

'Good night, darling.'

'Good night.'

She leaned and kissed him. He loved her closeness and the smell of her, but the kiss was a tiny bit wet. He felt further away from her than usual, and not sure what to think about anything.

'Sit up,' she said.

She held him and hugged him hard. She stroked his hair. Her blouse was slippery on his face, her skin was warm, and her pearls dug pleasantly into his forehead. Her breath smelled familiarly of cigarettes and what she'd been drinking and her scent was the one she always had. He heard her heart beat and felt absolutely at home.

'All right?' she said.

He nodded. She released him and he lay back down.

'What about Daddy?' she asked.

'Now he's back we can be a proper family.'

'Yes. Will you try to remember not to go on at him about fighting and things like that? When people have had a difficult time they often don't want to talk about it. Do you understand? Will you remember, darling?'

Lewis nodded. He didn't know what she meant, but he loved her confiding in him and asking him to do something for her.

'Is Daddy going to come and say good night? I can't remember if he does or not.'

'I'll ask him. Go to sleep.'

Lewis lay down and she went away. He lay in the dark and listened to the voices and the music downstairs and waited for his father to come and then he fell asleep, quite quickly, like the light going out of a room when the door is closed.

'War over? There's still nothing to bloody wear and nothing to bloody eat!'

'Lizzie, the boy.'

'Oh he's used to bloody.'

'Lewis, run and play.'

Lewis had been watching them get ready for church. He had often lain on his mother's bed while she dressed before, but his father didn't like him in their bedroom so, in the two days he had been back, the doorway had become his in-between place.

'Lewis! Go.'

Lewis went. He sat on the top stair and picked paint off the banister. He could hear his parents.

'For God's sake, Gilbert. Church!'

'I was brought up with church.'

'Well, I wasn't.'

'No; you and your heathen mother more likely to be dancing around with druids.'

'How dare you—'

There was a pause, and a small laugh from his mother. They must have been kissing. Lewis got up and trailed down the stairs and out into the drive. He kicked the gravel about for a bit and waited.

The small church was brick and flint and the sky was low, and close to it, and full of clouds. The children ran around in the leaves, scuffing their Sunday shoes, and their parents met and spoke as they always had, but still, not quite as they always had, because every week someone else had come

11

home, and another family was altered, and added to, and showing itself again.

Elizabeth, Gilbert and Lewis left the car and reached the churchyard and Lewis pulled away from his mother and joined the children playing between the graves. The game was catch, the gravestones were safe, and you had to try to get to the tree. The rules kept changing and no-one ever said them out loud. Lewis was one of the smallest boys. There was a boy called Ed Rawlins who was two years older and Lewis raced him for the tree. Ed was 'It', but Lewis got away from him and stood against the tree getting his breath and looked down at the church.

He could see the girls playing near their mothers. He could see the Carmichaels greeting his parents. He knew they'd have to go in soon and the thought of the cold and the hard pews was practically unbearable. His parents were standing close together. His father saw him and gestured him over, and he took his hands off the tree to go to him and Ed rushed him from one side.

'Gotcha!'

'Didn't.'

'Did!'

'Anyway I'm not playing.'

'You are!'

He shoved Lewis sideways onto the ground, wanting to get him down, and then he looked around, waiting to be in trouble and to see if Lewis would cry and draw attention. Lewis got up and inspected his slightly grazed hand.

'Get off,' he said, and went to his father.

'Lewis, behave yourself. This is a churchyard, not a schoolyard.'

'Yes, sir.' He took his mother's hand.

'Hello there, Lewis!'

Lewis looked at the shiny buttons on Dicky Carmichael's blazer and didn't like him. He didn't see why Mr Carmichael got to stay home while his father was away in the war, and he didn't like that he got to be in charge of everyone, or that he was going to be father's boss again. Lewis thought his father should be everyone's boss.

'Good to have your father home?'

'Yes, sir.'

With a wink, 'Maybe we'll see you at church more often.' This was a tease directed at his mother and Lewis didn't say anything. Gilbert laughed loudly.

'Now I'm back, I'd better get my house in order.'

Lewis looked at his mother; she was smiling her social smile.

'No more Black Mass?' she said, 'What will I do?'

Dicky moved away with his wife Claire and they went into the church followed by their two girls, one big and one small, in their double-breasted coats and hats and patent shoes.

'Do you have to make such tasteless jokes?' said Gilbert.

'Yes, I really do, darling.' Elizabeth kissed his cheek and they went inside.

*　　　*　　　*

Church was as bad as it could have been. The only thing bearable was exchanging silly faces with his mother. It seemed to go on for ever and ever. Lewis thought he'd die and slither under the pew

13

in front and rot there. He tried not to fidget. He tried to count the beams in the roof and read his hymn book. He thought about lunch. He thought about the vicar's ears. He stared at the backs of the Carmichael girls' heads and tried to make them turn around, but Tamsin was nine and didn't notice and there was no point to Kit at all, she was only four and too young for anything. He thought about no cricket until the summer.

*   *   *

The low sky got lower over the church and a cold wind started and then fine rain on the wind, until the roofs shone with water. Beneath the roofs were Sunday lunches cooking, and fires built up to last until after church. The road into the village was curved and, along it, the driveways were lined with rhododendrons and laurel hedges so that the houses were hidden from each other. The Carmichaels' big Tudor house backed onto fairly deep woods and you could walk from there to the Aldridges' without going on the road if you wanted. Elizabeth had done it often when Lewis was smaller and Claire Carmichael was pregnant with Kit. There was a post office and a shop and the church was close to them, on the main street, but as you left the village the houses spread out and they were more disparate. Some of the houses were 1920s, like the Aldridges', and some of them were even newer, or were cottages that in the past had been attached to the Carmichaels' house.

The station, like a toy station, was a mile away, along a road of arching trees, and so many of the men worked in London that the road to it had been made wider in places so that the cars could pass one another. Now there had been the war, the station had taken on a new significance. There had been partings and reunions that had made the sound of the trains in the distance, as they were heard from the houses, invested with emotion, not just an everyday sound like before. Even though so many people had come back, it seemed there would never be a point where you could say it was over. There was a lot of talk about rebuilding and making fresh starts, but really it was an odd sort of victory after the first rush of it, because so many people were still away and the news they heard every day was not peacetime news, but full of death and emerging horror.

The rain stopped as everybody came out of the church and got into their cars or walked away through the village and Elizabeth pulled Gilbert to the car faster and faster, like running away, and made him laugh. At home they ate lunch without talking very much and not tasting anything particularly at all and the afternoon, for Lewis at least, was strangely flat and just difficult. He couldn't seem to do any of the things he normally did, and the sight of his father was still unfamiliar to him and disturbing. He was used to a feminine presence and he found his father's maleness oddly threatening. He was exciting, and to be adored, but he was foreign too, and he changed the balance of the house. Gilbert's uniform had not been burned, but hung in the wardrobe in the spare room, where he dressed, and Lewis should have liked him to keep wearing it and be distant and heroic instead of real and influencing Lewis's daily life the way he did. In his suits and tweed jackets he looked like a

15

father and more approachable, but it was deceiving, because he was a stranger, and it would have been easier if he hadn't looked like someone you might know very well and yet not be.

*   *   *

The night Gilbert came home it had been at first like he and Elizabeth had never made love before and then, suddenly, familiar and just like always. She had cried with gratitude and he had held her and said, 'What on earth is it?'—as if he didn't know.

'Is it odd to be home?'

'Of course it's odd. What do you want me to say about it?'

'I don't know. I think I want to know everything in your mind. I want to know what it's been like for you. I want to know what you're thinking right now and if you're happy. You never say anything.'

'All right then. I was thinking it's jolly nice to be on proper sheets.'

'You weren't!'

'I was.'

'And what else?'

'Oh, how much I enjoyed dinner.'

'Stop it!'

'Absolutely true. You can think me as superficial as you like.'

Elizabeth, giggling, 'No jelly then, in North Africa?'

'Actually we did have jelly at Christmas.'

'Why on earth didn't you tell him? He would have been thrilled.'

'Well, what about you? How's your war been,

16

darling?'

'Ha-ha.'

'Ha-ha.'

'I know I write dreadful letters, but everything was in them.'

'Just Lewis?'

'Lewis and being here and not going up to town much.'

'Not too lonely?'

'Of course lonely. But Kate came once or twice when she could get away from the boys. And Lewis is just a perfect companion.'

'You've been spoiling him.'

'I don't think so. It's not as if I indulge him.'

'With your time you do.'

'Jealous?'

'Of course not, but you ought to have had a nanny. I don't understand you. You could have had more time to yourself.'

'If I had any more time to myself, I'd drink myself into a stupor within about two minutes.'

'Lizzie!'

'You know I would. For goodness' sake, time to what? Visit Claire Carmichael, or Bridget Cargill? Or go up to town and most likely get bombed to buggery?'

'Your language is appalling.'

'Don't be so pompous.'

'He'll be off to school in September.'

'Yes. I suppose he will. Eight seems so little to go.'

'All the others will be eight too. You'll miss him.'

'He'll miss me, too.'

'It'll be good for him.'

'Probably.'

'Now I'm back, you won't be lonely and bored.'
'You'll be home every night.'
'Every night.'
'I can't really believe it.'
'I know.'
'If I fall asleep, will you still be here? Tomorrow?'
'Of course. And Lizzie, do you really want to know what I'm thinking? I'm thinking—just that—'
'Oh don't, you don't need to tell me if it makes you cry. Don't . . .'

CHAPTER TWO

CHRISTMAS 1947

Dicky Carmichael would have liked a double-height hall, as some houses have, and to have had space for a really tall Christmas tree. He made do with the hall he had, and the tree did look splendid to him against all the dark wood panelling, but that was the disadvantage of having an old house—it was never exactly what you wanted. He thought he might build a new one, and please himself completely. The Tudor house was long, with rooms going off one another, and most of the party would be in the drawing room, which had three fireplaces and mullioned windows down two sides. There were bowls of punch and cases of champagne and a buffet lunch laid out over tables in two rooms—even if it was what Claire called 'all gong and no dinner' because of rationing. Claire had hired two girls from the village to help the housekeeper and fires were lit in all the downstairs rooms.

The party was an annual event and a talking point; it didn't matter about New Year's Eve; this was the end of the year. Because it was a lunchtime party there were always a lot of children, and this was felt to be acceptable so long as they were mainly confined to the morning room and a room known as the pink drawing room, which was in fact red and had once been used as a dining room, being nearer the kitchen than the room they used now. There were nannies assigned to keep control of the children, but as the day went on the children broke free and went upstairs and played sardines or murder, and the nannies surrendered responsibility and sat by the fire eating leftover cake and holding the smallest children on their laps.

*   *   *

When everything was ready and the polished silver and bottles and glasses lay in perfectly arranged splendour, Kit Carmichael lay on her tummy in the hall under the Christmas tree. Occasionally a maid or her mother or Dicky would pass by, carrying something or instructing somebody about something. She was very uncomfortable in her smocked dress, the elastic of it itched, and she hated her hair, which was tightly plaited and dug into her scalp. Gradually the sounds stopped as the servants went into the kitchen to eat an early lunch. Her parents were in the library and Kit didn't know where Tamsin was; in her room probably, sulking about having to be with the children still, even though she was eleven. The best bit of the party was in the evening, when all the children had gone and been sent to bed.

Kit turned over on her back and looked up through the branches of the Christmas tree. She half-closed her eyes and pretended she was in a forest and could feel snow on her face. She imagined the very soft fall of it and how each flake would melt on her cheeks or eyelids. She imagined a small, hot campfire next to her and wolves waiting in the trees with the fire reflected in their yellow eyes. She couldn't hear anything now, except the crackle of the fire and the wind in the pine trees. Then there was a sound. It was the sound of a cry and a glass breaking, and then a thump.

Kit didn't sit up. Her forest and the snow and the wolves had all disappeared. She heard her parents' voices and then a sharp sound. She didn't move, except to slide a bit more under the tree; her father was hitting her mother and she didn't want to go and look.

Dicky often hit Claire, it was his habit, and part of the pattern of the family, and it wasn't questioned between them at all. None of them had ever, ever referred to it, but Kit got so angry it made her cry with rage. The crying was because of being six and not able to change anything. She used to imagine Dicky meeting God, and God saying, 'I know what you do to Mummy, you're a very, very bad man and I'm going to send you to Hell!', and Dicky would be so terrified he would beg, but it would be too late, and he would burn for ever. Kit imagined tying him up when he was asleep and then kicking him and hitting him with the poker until he cried, but she wouldn't stop

20

until he realised how unfair he was and apologised to her mother.

Kit knew it was silly of her really, because her mother didn't like her at all and would never have thanked her even if she did manage to save her, and Kit cried about that, but always in her room away from everybody. She had learned to guard herself and it was very important to her never to cry in front of anyone. When Tamsin cried, which was often, she was soft, with a dipped head and big tears, and it was natural for arms to go around her and for her to be soothed. Kit's crying was hard and tight and lonely; she didn't want or imagine arms around her when she cried.

She lay under the Christmas tree and listened some more for noises from the library, but couldn't hear anything else. She was aware of her heart thumping and the hot feeling of it in her chest. She stared up into the tree again and worked hard at imagining the snowflakes falling on her, but they had gone away. Then she heard the library door open and the footsteps of her mother. Kit held her breath. Claire stopped by the bottom of the stairs and looked at Kit's feet sticking out.

'Why don't you get up? You'll spoil your frock.'

Kit slithered out and Claire turned away and went upstairs before Kit could see her face, just the back of her straight wool skirt and cardigan, and her heels tapping up the polished stairs.

'I'm sick and tired of you, Kit, you do nothing but make a mess and spoil things. If that dress is ruined you'll just have to change. Do you hear?'

*   *   *

The people started to arrive promptly at one. Kit's dress had been spoiled, so she'd changed into another one her body was too narrow for, and the sash made creases in the skirt where it was pulled tight to disguise the wrong shape of her. She stood in the shadow of the stairs and watched the people arriving and taking off their coats and hats. The long hall table piled up with overcoats and minks, fox furs and white scarves and men's hats, and Kit wanted to jump onto it and climb underneath and wriggle about, and had to hold her hands behind her back to stop herself.

Outside the house Preston helped to direct all the cars that arrived. A couple of the cars had drivers who went into the kitchen to wait. Elizabeth would have liked to save the petrol and walk through the woods to the party, but Gilbert wouldn't hear of it—'Walk there in mud and home in the dark? Are you mad?'—so they drove, with Lewis bouncing on the back seat and shoving the door with his shoulder and being told off.

'This is our third Christmas since Daddy came home,' he said. He counted lots of things like that; he thought that was to be the main event of his childhood, and he underscored the memory of life with and without his father in his mind.

Gilbert stopped the car by the steps and they got out, and he gave the keys to Preston, and thanked him. It wasn't a cold winter, there hadn't even been a hard frost yet, but it was dark and wet, and inside the house was all brightness.

*　　　*　　　*

In the afternoon, during the party, Elizabeth stood

22

on her own with her back to the bare window and Gilbert fought his way through his neighbours and friends to get to her.

'You can say one thing for Dicky and Claire, they always have enough to drink,' she said.

'Lizzie, you promised to try to behave properly about this.'

'Darling, I love parties.'

'You hate them. You hate people.'

'Nonsense. People are adorable. I wonder what the children are doing. Rolling around in cake, I should think.'

'Dicky wanted me to talk to him in the study. Or the library.'

'The study or the library or the gun room or the blue room or the pink standing-up room—'

'Elizabeth—'

'What royal line was it he came from again? Oh, silly me! It was the Northern Line, wasn't it? Straight out from Camden Town.'

'Ssh! Lizzie, can you manage until I come back?'

'Of course I can. I'll find Tommy Mulhall and flirt with him.'

'You do that. And eat something or you'll drown.'

'Ha-ha. See you later, darling.'

He went, and Elizabeth stood and waited with the black windows behind her.

*   *   *

Gilbert found Dicky in the library, standing by the fire and smoking a large cigar with his legs spread out as if he were practising to be Winston Churchill. Gilbert thought of Lizzie and smiled.

23

'Dicky. Lovely party. As always.'

'Another year over.'

'Wonder if the next one will be any better.'

'Human modus operandi seems to be making a mess of things and killing each other. Don't see what can be done about it. Brandy?'

Dicky had asked Gilbert to talk to him because he was going to promote him and they both knew it.

'There's a certain amount of entertaining amongst the executives at Carmichael's. Terribly important. Oh—you do have that flat in Chelsea, don't you?'

'Cadogan Square.'

'Of course, we've been there, haven't we? Elizabeth isn't too keen on all that, I gather. Boring old business dinners, and so forth.'

'Nonsense.'

'Well, we'll see. Claire's always been marvellous at that kind of thing.'

'Claire's a charming hostess.'

'Well, her family, you know ...' He let their joint knowledge of Claire's superior family hang silently in the air for a while. 'But also Elizabeth isn't—'

'I was away for a long time.'

'So much of business is about one's social—'

'I understand.'

'Claire says she doesn't see much of Elizabeth. What do they get up to, our wives, I wonder? Actually I know what Claire gets up to, spending my money,' he laughed. 'Elizabeth isn't much of a one for the shops, is she? Not all that interested in the high life? Enjoys a party though, by all accounts.'

'She's very sensible.'

'I'm sure. I'm sure. Terribly important to be one of the gang though, isn't it?'

Gilbert was too angry to speak. He smiled and nodded.

'Anyway. All that taken into account, I'd like you to take over the reins from old man Roberts. From April. If you're interested.'

He teased out the conversation some more and wouldn't go into detail about money, and Gilbert didn't like him or the way he spoke or the way he stood there, but he took it, and he told himself how pleased he was, and gradually became pleased as the meeting drew to a close. It was a good deal and he was happy about it. He just didn't want to have to look at Dicky's face any more and he wanted to take Lizzie home where she belonged and love her there. She was too good for any of them. She had her own way of looking at things. She was his and she was clever and lovely and he didn't know what she saw in him, but he was grateful.

'Cheers then,' said Dicky. 'To the new year; hard times over, good ones on the way, whatever anyone says. 1948.'

'1948.'

*   *   *

The two men drank brandy to seal their deal and the air downstairs was hot and thick, while upstairs, in a linen cupboard, Lewis lay on warm wooden slats squashed against Tom Greene's back. A child called Norman, whom nobody knew very well, was on the lower shelf. Lewis was hurting from being bent round. He shifted.

'Ow! Stop it!'

'Sh! There's somebody there.'

They held their breath. They could hear someone on the landing. The boards were creaking.

'Have a look.' Tom was barely whispering.

Slowly, Lewis pushed the door open with his finger. There wasn't much light, just what came from one of the bedrooms. He could see a winter moon through the leaded window and a tiny figure tiptoeing past.

'It's Kit.'

'Who?'

Tom was panicking and Lewis thought how silly he was being; the worst that could happen was four sardines instead of three.

'Let's let her in,' whispered Norman in a strange hoarse voice that made Lewis want to laugh.

Tom, scandalised, 'Why?'

'We'll be here for ever otherwise,' said Norman, who was plainly not having the best time. He didn't wait, but pushed the cupboard door a little.

'No!' said Tom, but Lewis hissed at Kit to make her turn.

Kit had been wondering if she was the only seeker left, if the others had gone downstairs for Welsh rarebit and she'd be laughed at later. She'd really stopped looking. She turned at Lewis's hiss and managed not to scream.

'Who is it?'

'Lewis. And Tom. Here. Get in.'

Kit went. She was on the bottom shelf of the linen cupboard with Norman and squashed against the hot pipes in two seconds flat.

'Hello.'

'Hello.'

26

Giggling.

'Where are the others?' said Tom.

'I don't know. I saw Tamsin, but I don't think she's playing.'

'Did you see Ed?'

'I haven't seen anyone for ages.'

Kit didn't tell them her fears of being last and hopeless; she had been invited into the boys' hiding place with Lewis Aldridge and she wasn't going to spoil it. It was the best thing that could have happened.

Kit couldn't remember all that far back, but as far back as she could, she had wanted to be Lewis. He looked just right to her. He looked how people should look. She remembered seeing him in the summer holidays when she was trying to join in with the boys who were climbing trees in the woods behind her house. She was five then and couldn't manage. Lewis was there and he, at nine, was so grown-up—grown-up first and then heroic—because he had stopped a boy teasing Kit and taken her to the edge of the woods so that she could find her way home. He hadn't talked to her or anything; it was that he was kind. She wanted to be him, and knowing that he was coming to the party had been a good thing that came into her mind sometimes and made her smile and feel nervous in case he wouldn't be as nice as she'd thought.

'Maybe they're outside.' This was Tom, worrying.

'We weren't including outside,' said Lewis.

'But maybe they are.'

'They might be in the attics.'

'There's mice there. Rats,' said Kit, who heard

27

the mice above her room at night. She tried not to lisp like a baby, but it was hard with no front teeth.

'There are mice in here,' Tom said, staring down through the slats at her, and doing a creepy voice.

'No, there aren't,' said Kit, wanting to look round and hunching up her shoulders. Norman sniggered.

'And spiders,' said Tom, realising he was onto something.

Lewis looked at Tom, 'I can see a spider on your head,' he said.

Tom jumped and banged his head on the ceiling. All four momentarily exploded into hysteria. Footsteps. They froze. There was light around the edges of the cupboard door and an adult voice, one of the nannies.

'Boys and girls! Come along! It's time to go. I want Lewis Aldridge, Joanna Napper and Ed Rawlins. Right now, please!'

The children exchanged looks of resignation.

'You can keep on playing,' said Lewis to Tom.

'It's no fun now,' said Tom, and all four allowed themselves to fall out of the cupboard. Kit tried to stop smiling at Lewis—not that he was looking at her—he'd gone already.

'Bye,' he said over his shoulder to anyone who was there, and started down the stairs.

*   *   *

'Aren't you glad we drove?' said Gilbert, pulling away from the house. He peered through the glass, wiping the inside with a gloved hand.

'Terribly,' answered Elizabeth, resting her head against the cold glass and imagining running

28

through the dark woods. It was dead of night now and winter rain fell onto the windscreen.

Gilbert felt a sudden rush of joy. He decided he couldn't wait to tell Lizzie about the job. He'd planned to get home, and have the boy safely in bed and tell her properly, but now seemed the only time. He took a hand off the wheel a second and put it over hers in her lap, looking across.

'Lizzie, Dicky's given me Roberts's job. You know he's retiring.'

'No! Gilbert! Lewis, did you hear? Gilbert, that's wonderful.'

The car swung out of the drive and into the road.

'Steady!'

'But Gilbert! That's superbly and fantastically lovely news.' The headlights barely made an impression on the darkness and the rain that was falling. 'We'll be so very rich.'

'Well, not exactly.' He laughed, pleased she thought so. Lewis leaned forward between the seats to be included in the excitement, and Gilbert steered the car around the big bend towards home. 'Can't see a bloody thing!'

'Maybe it will freeze later; be awfully pretty tomorrow.'

Their own drive appeared through the blackness before there was any more talking and Gilbert turned the car into it. He saw his house shining white ahead of him.

CHAPTER THREE

Lewis was ten on the twenty-ninth of December and thought it a particularly important age. Elizabeth always decorated their places for birthday breakfasts; holly and small white snowdrops for Lewis in December and narcissi for Gilbert in the spring. In November, for Elizabeth's birthday, Gilbert would send Lewis out into the wet garden early to look for flowers, and then together they would dry them and put them around her place, enjoying that they were men and not good at it. If it had been very mild, there were sometimes still roses in the garden for her birthday table and Lewis would cut them and carry them back to the house with the petals dropping onto the grass. Whatever else happened on birthdays, whatever treats there were, or presents, nothing came close to that feeling of seeing the decorated table, the unusualness of the garden come to the house.

Gilbert made a speech for Lewis's being ten and he got a bicycle and a penknife, and the bicycle was pleasingly too big for him and the knife was sharp enough to cut quite big bits of wood if you sawed at it, and Lewis was very happy with them.

It was a good year and they felt they had habits now and didn't have to learn everything fresh again. There was still a strange blank feeling of the war being over and no sense of return, just rebuilding, but work and school and ritual had begun to fill the gaps with normality and the foundations felt strong, and valuable for being hard-won.

The boys at Lewis's prep school played rugby in deep snow in the spring term and the snow and mud mixed together. In the summer they played cricket on dry pitches, with short green grass that was rolled and cared for. Lewis captained the cricket team. His games master told him it wasn't because he was the best, but to teach him team spirit; he had a tendency to daydream and wasn't much concerned with beating the other boys at things. He was the sort of boy who was popular because he was easy to be around and not demanding particularly. You often had a sense with Lewis that the real business of his life was elsewhere and that was attractive to people, they didn't feel the responsibility of his presence too much. Where he was, actually, was in his head, and in that he was like Elizabeth. He wrote long stories and poems about sea battles in classical settings or doomed cavalry charges—not to show to people— just because they were fun to do and he could travel in his mind when he wrote them, and make the world just.

When he came home for the summer he'd grown so tall Elizabeth had to take him up to London for new clothes. They went to Simpson's of Piccadilly and then to a Corner House for tea. Lewis thought no day could be more appalling than a day spent shopping, but it was nice to see all the buses and cars.

There were building sites everywhere, or strange gaps in the streets that were about to be building sites, and Lewis wondered which of them were going to be built by Carmichael's. He liked to think of it; his father's mark on the city.

Before coming home, Elizabeth said that as there were twenty minutes before the train left they should stop at the hotel by the station and she would have a drink.

She had a Martini and Lewis got the olive. He hadn't had an olive before and the taste of it, salty and drenched in gin, stayed with him. They nearly missed the train and kept dropping their bags and shoeboxes, and Lewis jumped on first, helping his mother up after him and taking the packages from her. He felt grown-up to be helping a lady onto a train, and proud of his mother, who was so pretty.

At home his school report had arrived and that evening there was the usual ritual of his father reading it and discussing it with him, and Lewis was summoned into the drawing room for what his father called debriefing.

Gilbert was always surprised to see Lewis in the holidays and had to get used to him all over again. He knew that Elizabeth was happier when he was at home and that she got very bored all on her own. She was the first to admit her painting wasn't very good and although she loved doing it, it's hard to stick at a thing if you're aware you've an unshakeable mediocrity. Often when Gilbert came home in the holidays, the house would be empty, and he'd walk in and see three places for dinner and wonder who on earth she had invited and then realise it was the holidays and Lewis was home.

On week nights Gilbert would come home a little after half-past six. The train got in just before twenty past; once he'd come down from the platform, got into his car and driven home it was half-past. If the weather was bad, Elizabeth and Lewis would be in the house; Lewis usually upstairs reading and Elizabeth either in the drawing room with a book and a drink or in the kitchen talking to Jane. Jane left at seven and supper was at eight. In winter this meant it was rewarmed and not very nice, but in summer it was luncheon meat or, if they were lucky, ham, and Jane found it hard to spoil those.

It was a warm, muggy summer, and towards August the white skies and stickiness irritated the grown-ups. The children didn't care about the mugginess, so long as it wasn't raining and they could go out on their bikes. It didn't rain. It didn't rain for weeks, but nor was it hot. It was like waiting weather: blank skies, flat warmth and dry grass, and every day the sense of waiting grew greater, as it does in a drought or when there is no wind, and Elizabeth missed Gilbert.

When Lewis was out playing she often walked from room to room or out into the garden and then back again, just lost in her thoughts. She tried to have strict rules about her drinking, but the wait for her sherry at half-past twelve made the morning seem very long. She absolutely wasn't allowed a drink after her coffee at lunch, so that meant fitting it all in and knowing she then had to wait till half-past six for her cocktail. She knew it shouldn't mean so much and it was important to stay in control, but she often found it hard to remember why, when it seemed a perfectly good idea to carry on drinking and Lewis was fidgeting at the lunch table and wanting to go and play with his friends.

She loved it when they all knocked on the door, all those sweet faces, hands resting on their handlebars: Tom Greene and Ed Rawlins, Tamsin

33

Carmichael, Joanna Napper, the Johnson boys and little Kit trailing behind.

'Good afternoon, Mrs Aldridge, is Lewis there?'

'He's in the garden. I'll call him.'

She would stand at the French doors in the drawing room and call. Lewis would be in the garden reading or on the cracked tennis court hitting a ball against the wall and he'd call back, 'Coming!'

Most days were good days and she found she could paint or read and live in her mind happily, but some days were bad and then it was the event of her day, the children coming round and her calling Lewis in from the garden. She would watch him cycle off with them, the bikes swerving and crossing each other under the blank white sky. Then she would go inside and read or listen to the wireless or have long and involved conversations with Jane.

She and Jane had two topics. One was food— never the cooking of it, but rather the rationing of it; what she or Jane could get their hands on or where they'd heard about a supply of something, and arrangements for obtaining it. Their other topic was the various members of each other's families and what part of the country they lived in. They would take one or both of these conversations as far as they could, and Elizabeth would listen to Jane talk, and picture Lewis and his friends and wonder how far they were going, and if they were having fun.

Lewis had got used to his bike and it was a better size every day. In the group of children, he and Ed and Tom were usually in front, Tamsin somewhere in the middle with whoever else was there that day, and little Kit always slogging along behind. She fell off all the time, she couldn't manage the corners very well and one or other of them would have to stop and help her, which made her proud and angry. Lewis felt sorry for Kit, she was so quiet and intense and never seemed happy to be with them but just constantly striving. He thought it would be horrible to have a sister like Tamsin who was pretty and always seemed to be having such fun. She had the boys helping her carry her bike over ditches and unhooking her hem from wire from the age of ten, and there was never any doubt she was the best and most loved even amongst a group of children. Today was very still and there were flies so that the children had to go quickly to escape them.

'Keep your mouth shut!' shouted Ed, 'I just swallowed one!'

There were tiny black beetles that stuck to their clothes, which they called thunderbugs. You could crush them between your nails if you wanted and they didn't have any blood.

There was still no wind at all. They were going to the top of New Hill, which was a haul, but once you were up you could freewheel really fast down the other side and then buy toffees in Turville. The bikes wobbled from side to side up the hill. Their breath came in puffs and shunts like small steam trains. Lewis was counting in his head to get to the top and thinking about campfires. There was a metallic snapping sound and the familiar scrabbling scuffle of Kit falling off. They stopped in a ragged group and leaned on one foot or twisted round to look back.

'Typical,' said Tamsin, whose favourite word this

35

was.

'What is it, Kit?' called Joanna, but she was stalling for time; it was plain Kit's chain had broken and Kit herself was bleeding—if not dramatically, then at least quite noticeably from her elbow.

'Are you all right?' shouted Tamsin, and Kit, in some pain, nodded.

'She'll have to go back,' said Ed. 'You'll have to go back!'

'She can't go back on her own,' said Joanna, 'It's miles.'

They all stared at Kit who glared back, guilty and defiant. She bent down as if to mend the chain and picked up its dangling end.

'Well, don't do that, that's just stupid, you'll get covered and it can't be helped.' Tamsin wished just once she could go and have fun without Kit being everywhere all the time.

Kit's throat burned. Her eyes were stinging, partly with sweat and partly with tears. She wished they'd all stop looking at her. She bit the side of her tongue to keep from crying properly, but her throat hurt. She stood on one leg and scratched the back of her calf with her sandal.

'You'll have to go back,' said Tamsin.

'Go back!' said Ed, shooing her, like a dog.

Kit didn't move. She stood and stared at them all. They were on a higher part of the road and their various poses of disapproval and boredom were silhouetted against the white sky like a tableau of judgement.

'Go back!' said Tamsin, 'Go on, Kit!'

Kit thought she could trust her voice. 'What shall I do with my bike?' she asked.

'You'll have to carry it,' said Ed, but they all knew this was ridiculous.

'Kit, you're ruining everything!' said Tamsin, her patience at an end.

Lewis saw Kit's chin start to go; he hadn't seen her cry before and he didn't want to.

'It's all right,' he said to them. 'Put your bike in the hedge, we'll get it on the way back. You can go on my crossbar.'

Nobody questioned this; so long as Kit wasn't their problem they didn't care. One by one they started up the hill again. With no momentum, it took an effort to get going. Lewis laid his bike down and went over to Kit, picking up hers.

'That looks pretty nearly bust up,' he said.

He shoved it into the hedge. Kit wiped her face with dirty hands, and her eyes, and Lewis pretended not to notice.

'Come on, we'll have to walk up to the top.'

They started to walk, and to begin with they weren't slower than the wobbling bicycles. Kit twisted her arm around to look at her bleeding elbow and then wiped it on her shorts. At the top Lewis got on his bike. They looked down, letting the others get away from them with screams and yells. They could see the country spread out and the hill dropped away sharply. It was steep enough to be frightening, but not so steep you'd actually fall on your face, if you were careful. Tamsin and Ed had gone away immediately, followed by the others, and the shouts got quieter very quickly as they speeded up.

'Sure you'll manage?' said Lewis, and Kit nodded. She was terrified of the hill. She'd been terrified of it all the way up, even on her own bike,

37

and now the prospect of sitting sideways on Lewis Aldridge's crossbar was the most horrible thing she could think of. She knew she would at least break her neck, but there was no way out of it at all.

'Come on then,' he said.

He seemed to be thinking about something else, so she just clambered on. Lewis was wondering how he'd explain to Mrs Carmichael that her younger daughter had died going a hundred miles an hour down New Hill on his bike. He had to hold the handlebars awkwardly with her in front of him.

'You've got to balance and sit in the middle or we'll both come off, all right?'

She nodded. Her mouth was so dry she couldn't have spoken. Ahead of them the others were nearly at the bottom.

Oh hell, Lewis thought, they'll all watch.

He pushed off, and the first few feet they almost fell sideways, first one side, then the other and again the first way; the steering wasn't doing what it should and Lewis's legs kept kicking into Kit. She fell backwards and sideways and then the bike was going fast enough to balance and seemed steadier. The steepness of the hill took them by surprise and they both went forward.

'Lean back!' he yelled.

They both leaned and they were going quite quickly now. Her plaits were knocking against his arm and he couldn't be sure they were going straight. The wind made him close his eyes half-up. There was terror and excitement and, just in the middle, a moment of speed and balance where nothing else mattered at all. They weren't going to fall and it was fast and perfect. Then the bottom came up too fast and stupid Tom Greene was in the way, and Lewis practically burned his feet off trying to slow down and they ended up on the verge and falling on their backs. Kit's head bashed against Lewis's lip and he had blood on the inside of his mouth. They got up. Kit was quivering all over like a little animal. Lewis put the back of his hand to his mouth and saw the blood. Joanna was inspecting a bee sting she'd sustained the day before. Tamsin stepped onto her bike again. No-one spoke for a bit.

'Let's go back the short way, over the fields. We can push the bikes and look in the river,' said Ed and, after buying their sweets, they did.

When Kit got home she told her mother about the broken chain and where she had left her bike. Her mother said if she was careless enough to leave it there, she didn't deserve a bicycle and she certainly wasn't going to ask Preston to go and collect it. The bike had been Tamsin's originally, but Kit loved it and didn't have another, so she spent the next day walking out to New Hill and pushing it back. It was heavy and banged against her legs all the way. She asked Preston to mend it for her, but by the time he got round to it, it was almost time to go back to school.

*   *   *

Every few days Elizabeth kept Lewis at home and they took a picnic into the woods and down to the river. He liked being around her and they would read and swim. Sometimes she would fall asleep in the afternoon and, after watching her for a little, he would climb trees or swim on his own, but never too far away in case she woke and didn't know

39

where he was.

There was a buzzing of flies and bees and a whirring of crickets in the ferns and grass, and Lewis carried the blanket and towels for swimming. It was the woollen blanket from the car and it was itchy and crumbs got stuck in it. Elizabeth carried the basket with bread and a bottle of wine and some pork pies, which weren't proper pork pies at all, but mostly salt and lard. They had strawberries from the garden for afterwards which were very sweet so it didn't matter about no cream or sugar. The woods were dim around them and seemed to be sweating; the leaves were dark and still. There was the sound of a distant plane and Elizabeth thought immediately of the war and how much she hated the sound.

'Mind out for the nettles,' she said.

It was the time of year when the nettles are coarse and big and dark and don't sting you too badly, but they had grown out over the path so Elizabeth and Lewis had to go in single file. One brushed Lewis's leg, but it just itched a bit so he didn't say anything.

'Do you want to go further along, where it's deeper?' she asked him.

'Yes, let's go by where there's that boat,' he said.

It was nice of her to ask because it was quite a walk and they knew they'd be hot and sick of carrying the things when they got there, but it was the best part of the river to go to because of it being wide and deep there and more like an adventure.

'I hate this weather,' said Elizabeth and Lewis was surprised; it was summer and you could be out and he didn't know what she meant.

The clearing by the wide part of the river was sandy with short grass in patches. The cow parsley and all the prettier things were over, but Lewis liked the longer grass now it had seeded itself. It was like pictures he'd seen of Africa and he thought if he'd been younger he would have played that there were lions. Sometimes he played that there were lions anyway, or at least imagined they were there, watching.

Elizabeth spread out the blanket and they flopped onto it. She was wearing a blue and white patterned dress; the blue was dark, and it had square shoulders and short sleeves and a straightish wrapover skirt. She had used to wear it for going out with smart shoes, but now she wore it just any time because it was old, but it still looked nice. They looked at the pork pies, which had gone shiny and soaked through the paper they were wrapped in, and she opened the bottle of wine. She had brought mugs for their drinks, because of not breaking glasses, and they laughed about her pouring her wine into one.

'Taste?' she offered and he sipped the wine and made a face.

The only nice thing about it was its connection with her. He ate the pork pies and she just drank, thinking perhaps they'd look better after more wine. Her dress was sticking to her, she could feel the sweat trickling down inside it, but she didn't want to swim yet—she knew once she did she would be cold and she put it off.

'I'm going to swim. Are you coming in?'

'You go ahead, I'll watch.'

Lewis went behind a tree to change, which Elizabeth thought very funny and teased him

41

about. He ran out quickly and did a running jump into the water with curled-up legs. The river hadn't noticed it was summer, and had been for ages, and he swam up and down shouting until he got warmer and then floated and swam around the bend and back.

He inspected the wreck, which was a wooden boat about seven feet under the water, and tried to pull the rudder off.

'I can't get it,' he said, coming up. He went down again and tried again and surfaced, breathing hard.

'Come and have strawberries before I finish them. You'll freeze,' called Elizabeth and went back to her book. She'd nearly finished the wine and the pork pies didn't look any better. He came out and rubbed himself dry on the towel and then sat down by her.

'Cold?'

'Not too bad.'

'Did you get it?'

'What?'

'The rudder.'

'No, I said I didn't. It's all dug into the bottom.'

She poured the last of the wine. He lay back and stared up at the white sky. She drank and then stood and walked towards the river and spread out her arms.

'Oh, I do love it here.' He didn't look up, he was used to her loving things. 'We must make Daddy come here. He never has. He never does. Why are you laughing?'

'Daddy swimming.'

'Your father is an excellent swimmer. Ooh—' she stumbled and steadied herself with one hand on the ground. 'I can stand on one leg,' she said.

'Mummy, everyone can stand on one leg.'

'But look, I do it beautifully.'

He looked.

'Right then!' she said.

'Right then?'

'This dashed rudder. I'm going to get it.'

'You can't get it. You're only a girl.'

'I say I can get it and I'll wager fifty pounds.'

'Two hundred and fifty says you can't.'

'I bloody bloody can, Lewis Aldridge.'

She was excited and laughing, and pulled off her dress. She had her slip under it and walked straight into the water. She screamed a bit, but didn't really feel the cold at all, it just seemed so lovely and strange to have the water creep up her body. She held her arms out and walked deeper and deeper, and forgot to swim until she had to and then the swimming felt very light and easy. She remembered the rudder and turned around in the water, fluttering her hands from side to side. She saw a dragonfly.

'Where's this wreck then?'

'You know where it is. There. There.'

He stood up and pointed and she swam over to the place and tried to look down through the water, but put her face in it by mistake.

'You won't get it,' he said and laughed at her with her wet hair.

'You just watch me,' she said and dived.

He saw the see-through cream silk of her back and the bottom of her slip and her white feet flick up into the air and then ripples. He could see her white shape under the water, but he couldn't see what she was doing. He thought that it felt like he was alone when she was under the water even

43

though she was so near. He looked around at the wood and the white sky. The wood was very quiet; it felt very quiet. He saw the dragonfly. Then she was up and shaking hair out of her eyes.

'You're right. It's silted up,' she said and she was quite determined.

She went down again. Lewis waited, smiling, but his smile going. He was hot. He felt something on his arm and he looked down. It was a splash of water. The brown skin was browner where the water was. It was rain. He looked up. The sky was still pale and very thick and you couldn't tell how high it was. He looked back to the water for his mother. An internal clock told him she should come back up now. She hadn't, but he could see the water moving. He wondered how long had gone by since he had thought it was time she should come up. He wondered if he had thought that she should come up at the time she should come up, or just after. He wondered if maybe he had been thinking about the rain longer than he thought. He walked forward into the water a little way. He thought perhaps the time wasn't as long as it felt. Or perhaps it was longer. Two more fat raindrops fell on his arm and he heard thunder.

'Mummy,' he said and didn't know he was going to say it.

He could still see her white shape and her legs moving, but only very vaguely; the water was brown and shining, and deeper in it was churned up and he couldn't see anything very clearly. He walked in further. He thought, she's not coming up, and knew he had to get her. He started towards the place and seemed to be going very slowly. He forgot to swim at first because he was just thinking

44

about getting to her and then he swam the short distance very quickly. He thought she was about to come up and she'd laugh at him—but that was the last thought he had before fear came over him.

He couldn't feel his body and his breath was very quick, but he didn't know that it was. He dived down, without thinking and without taking a proper breath, and he couldn't see anything because of the bubbles and had to come up again. He took a big breath this time, but his heart was going so fast it didn't last like it normally did and he had no idea what to do, so he just swam down and stared through the water and he saw her. Her head was sideways and she opened her mouth and he thought she was trying to say something, but he didn't know why she would do that. He couldn't see properly because of the bottom being churned up. He had sand in his eyes. He looked again and it looked like she was lying there on her side like a mermaid relaxing and he couldn't understand what he was seeing. His breath ran out and he surfaced. He should have waited, but he took another breath and went down again.

The water was dirtier and he couldn't see and he just pulled at her, he didn't know where, at her slip or her arm, and made no impression at all. Then he knew what it was, and why she was lying sideways like a mermaid—her leg was stuck under the boat. He started to shove against the boat, but that was hopeless and he'd run out of breath again. He came up and his head felt very light and strange. He had a moment of clarity and of strength and purpose. He thought, I have to get down there and hold her around the middle and push my legs against the boat. He dived down straight for her this time, not looking, but going for her so that his head hit the side of the boat. He didn't feel his head hit the boat and he got both arms around her. He pulled and she moved, and he felt a jolt of joy and pushed off from the bottom, but then she moved suddenly too, writhing very violently; she grabbed onto him and they both stayed down. The water felt heavy on top of them and she wasn't really free and they were struggling together and he didn't know what they were struggling for, except that he didn't have any breath at all and there was a bad pain in his chest. He started to choke. Her fingers were gripping him and he was held down by her. He was swallowing water and felt terror and pushed off from the bottom again, wrenching her hands away, and got free and when he surfaced he could only get his face out of the water, he couldn't seem to come out of the water properly. Why doesn't she come, he thought, why doesn't she come up? He tried to get up in the water and get his breath, and he was so angry with her, and then he went down again, half on purpose and half because he couldn't help it. Her hair was floating over her face and in the way of them, and the sand and mud were all around them. He tried to pull her again, but she was much heavier somehow and even though she didn't grab him, he couldn't do anything with her; he got her hand and tried to swim, but he was tired and had no strength. He tried to swim pulling her hand—as if he were tugging along the road, to show her something—but he kept letting go. He came up again. He felt weak and he couldn't seem to think what to do. His mind felt weak and his body wouldn't connect with it and he heard a

46

sound coming out of himself, but couldn't feel himself making it.

He tried to go down again, but found he couldn't. He tried to peer down through the water, but his breath and panic made it move too much to see anything, and anyway it was muddy and he didn't know where she was now. He felt himself cramp up; he felt his legs, or his breath, or whatever it was that made him a swimmer stop working and he knew that he was going to drown. He knew that he wasn't going be able to get out of the water. Then he thought, in a normal way: this hasn't taken very long, I can run and get help. It was as if all of it, however long it had taken, had never happened. He'd heard of lots of people nearly drowning, lots of people didn't breathe for ages and then they were saved.

He was very near the side of the river, not the bank with the picnic, but the other one, and he made for it. He almost didn't get to it and, when he did, he fell. After trying to get up a few times and being angry with his body, he started to run to the trees, trying to remember what house was nearest, but he couldn't. He couldn't remember any of the houses, or any of the villages, or where the path went; there was just the wood and no picture of anything past it. He started back to the water, but it seemed hopeless and he was so frightened, so he ran back towards the trees again. He imagined someone walking in the woods just near him with their dog and he thought they'd be bound to help him. He shouted, 'Help!'—thinking the person with the dog would hear, and then he remembered there wasn't a person with a dog and his mother was under the water and he didn't have time to

47

find the person with the dog, and he ran back to the river and stopped.

The water was still again and he could see her; he could see her paleness and then a dark shadow where her head was, but not her face. He saw that she was under the water, but not if she was moving. She seemed to be moving, but the water was moving. He was going to go back in. He pictured very clearly going into the water and diving down to save her and what she would feel like when he got hold of her, but then he was on the ground. His mind made a lot of pictures, pictures of him in the water, of his pulling her out, of the person with the dog coming and seeing him, but he was just lying on the ground next to the river. His mother was under the water. She was about ten feet away from him and lying still under the water.

*   *   *

The drops of rain were sluggish at first, then colder. He stayed where he was. He thought he'd go back in and get her out when he could move. He didn't know when that would be. The rain was harder for a while, but never like a real rain and then it stopped, and the whiteness came back and the wood was just the same.

*   *   *

Lewis lay by the water. His eyes were half open and he had stopped shivering. He had been sick and had moved away from it and closer to the water. It was darker now, but he kept his eyes on the other bank where he could still see the basket

48

on the blanket and the towels and his mother's book. He could see the empty wine bottle on its side and his shoes on the ground nearby. The time went by him and he had no sense of it, but he kept his eyes on the bank opposite with the picnic things on it.

*   *   *

In the morning there was a mist and the sun coming up made it very bright and pearl-coloured. Gilbert and the policeman came out of the woods into the bright light and saw Lewis, and the remains of the picnic on the ground on the other side of the river. He didn't answer any of their questions, or seem to see them. Gilbert picked him up to carry him home and Lewis's head was pressed against his father's chest. Gilbert was talking about what could have happened, saying all the terrible possibilities, and the policeman was walking next to him and answering him and then Gilbert stopped. He put Lewis down, onto the ground, and went to the bank. He looked down into the water and then went down on his knees, still looking. Wilson ran over to him and the two men stared down into the water and Lewis, lying on the ground, didn't move.

CHAPTER FOUR

Elizabeth's elder sister, Kate, travelled up from Dorset on the Monday before the funeral. On the train she thought about what should be done with

Lewis, if he should live with her and her husband and boys. She had to change trains and the journey was long and she brought sandwiches with her, which she shared with a little girl who was travelling alone and whose mother had asked Kate to keep an eye on. She and the little girl played beg-o'-my-neighbour, resting the cards on the seat between, and Kate felt absolutely calm and cool about travelling to see Gilbert and Lewis, with her sister dead. She placed the cards carefully on the sloping seat and planned the funeral and imagined taking Lewis back on the train with her.

*　　　*　　　*

Gilbert met her at Waterford station. The house felt strange and cold and Kate tried to be efficient, while Lewis and Gilbert were almost silent and kept apart from one another, and from her.

*　　　*　　　*

On Tuesday morning the coroner, doctor, two policemen and a stenographer came to the house to talk to Lewis about his mother dying. The rest of the inquest was to be in Guildford the next day. Kate led Lewis into the drawing room and sat him in the straight-backed chair brought in from the hall.

'Now, Lewis, how are you feeling?' This was Dr Straechen.

'Fine, thank you.'

Gilbert sat on the arm of the flowered armchair next to Lewis, and looked down at his hands on his knees.

'Let me introduce you to all of these scary people,' said the doctor and Lewis looked around the faces.

'Of course you know me—and I've known you since you were born, haven't I? That gentleman there is called Mr Liley, he's what we call a coroner, which is a sort of official who finds out about things, often sad things, like deaths. You know Constable Wilson don't you? And Detective-Sergeant White. Your daddy's going to sit by you and all you have to do is answer the questions we put to you, calmly and sensibly, and tell the absolute truth. Do you understand?'

Lewis nodded.

'I'm afraid you need to say "yes" or "no" because that lady there is called a stenographer and she's going to take down everything we all say on that clever machine, so that Mr Liley can look at it all later, and she can't put down nods and head shakes. All right?'

'Yes.'

'Let's start with an easy one. What's your name?'

'Lewis Robert Aldridge.'

Kate, watching him, glimpsed the boy he had been in the way that he said it.

'How old are you, Lewis?'

'Ten.'

'Good. Well done. Now, do you remember what happened on Thursday? Do you remember what happened on that very bad day?'

'Yes.'

'You went for a picnic with your mother, didn't you?'

'Yes.'

51

'Where did you go to?'

'To the river.'

'It was quite far away, wasn't it? Near what's called the Deer Park, by Overhill House, wasn't it?'

Kate felt removed and quiet. She wondered if she really should take him back to Dorset with her, if she should offer to Gilbert to take him away. That's what many people would do. That might be the best thing, four boys instead of three; Gilbert would help with money.

'Did you have a nice picnic? . . . Did you swim?'

'Yes.'

'Did your mummy go swimming too?'

'Yes.'

'Were you swimming together?'

'No. I went first.'

'Then her?'

'Yes.'

'I know this is very difficult for you, Lewis, we're all very sorry indeed for you. Do you think you could tell us, in your own words, what happened to your mummy?'

Everybody waited.

Nobody knows but this child, thought Kate; she looked at Gilbert, wondering what he could possibly be thinking, waiting to hear this. Then she looked back at Lewis and found she couldn't look away from his face. She didn't ever want to know. She had to know.

'Can you tell us what happened to your mummy?' said the doctor again. Lewis looked back at Dr Straechen. 'Lewis? Tell us what happened.'

'Does he understand?' Gilbert, perched on the arm of the chair, leaned forward.

'Everyone needs to know, Lewis.'

'Lewis? Would you speak to us, please?'

'I went swimming and I was trying to get the rudder off the wreck that's there.'

His father was still leaning forward and hungry-looking, and staring at him. Lewis started again, his eyes on his father's face.

'I couldn't get it off. My mu— My m— She— My—'

This was terrible. They were all waiting and he couldn't speak. How can you not be able to speak? There was a boy at school who had a terrible stammer and he thought he sounded just like him. His mind felt very small and he couldn't make himself speak at all.

'It's all right. Try again.' This was the doctor.

Lewis tried very hard to think of words, but then, after a moment, he bowed his head in defeat. Kate saw his head go down and it was unbearable. She couldn't understand why Gilbert didn't hold his hand, or stop them, and she wanted to get up and shout at him. She thought of her own boys, her house and the world she had made over years and she knew, clearly and shamefully, that she wasn't going to take him. She didn't want Lewis in her house. She imagined the upheaval of having to love him and sort out the jealousies and the rows that would be inevitable, and of seeing Elizabeth in him all the time. It was beyond her; she didn't want this motherless thing in her home. She looked at the top of his head, dipped down like that, and he could have been one of her boys. Her boys were vulnerable, too. She had no pride, she knew she wasn't going to help him. She got up quickly and went out to the garden. The door stuck slightly and made a loud noise and everybody except Lewis looked up. Kate walked quickly away from them up the garden and only knew she was crying because she couldn't see. She hadn't cried yet. Oh God, she thought, here it comes, here it comes.

The people in the room focused their attention on Lewis again.

'Lewis?' said the doctor, 'Lewis?'

Lewis looked up.

'Try again, Lewis,' said the doctor, very gently.

'I w— I w— I w—' He took a breath. 'I wanted to get the rudder up. Off the boat that's there.'

'Well done. Good boy. You asked her to help you?'

'No, she said she would do it.'

'Did you help her?'

'No, I was watching.' He knew how that sounded.

'Was there anyone else there, Lewis, or was it just you two?'

'We were on our own.'

'Just you two, you're absolutely sure?'

'We were on our own. Please, sir, I'm sorry.'

'There's no need to be sorry, Lewis, it's all right. Did you run for help?'

It was no good, his mind had shut down.

'When did you see she was in trouble in the water?' This was another voice, from the other side of the room.

'Did you see what went wrong?'

'Did you try to help her?'

He felt water closing over his head.

'Did you go in with her?'

He could hear water in his head and he couldn't breathe. Gilbert took his hand suddenly and it

54

shocked him.

'Tell me how it happened! Tell me! Lewis, tell me.'

'She sh— sh—'

'Lewis, you need to try to explain to us what happened to your mother.'

'It's no good. Look at him.'

'I don't think he can understand.'

'I'll take him upstairs. We should have left it another day. Gilbert, are you all right?'

Dr Straechen took Lewis upstairs and sedated him. He had spent two days sedated before, and he went back into nothingness and the numb feeling inside his head with something like gratitude.

*   *   *

The day before Lewis went back to school Gilbert took him to the Nappers' for tea. When Mary Napper greeted them at the door she hugged Lewis. Since his mother died, people kept touching him. They were either shaking his hand or rubbing his head or patting him on the back, as if now that he didn't belong to his mother he belonged to everybody. At the funeral a lady bent down and did up his shoelace without saying anything to him at all and he wanted to snatch his foot away; he didn't even know whose mother she was.

'Gilbert, I'm so glad you came. Lewis, everyone's outside, why don't you run and find them?'

Lewis left the house and walked down towards the sound of playing. The badminton was set up some way from the house and the grass wasn't smooth and flat like at the Carmichaels', but sloped down from the red house in bumps with a paddock and a ruined well.

He saw Tamsin and Ed playing badminton. The other children, Joanna and the Johnson twins, Robert and Fred, and others, were watching, or climbing an old apple tree nearby. There were a few apples, but they were mostly sour and wasps hovered over the ground for the rotten ones. Kit, in a good position up in the tree, saw Lewis come towards them. He stopped to watch with his hands in his pockets.

Tamsin and Ed stopped playing and looked at him. The other children stopped too.

'Hello, Lewis!' said Tamsin, and Kit thought she sounded just like their mother. 'Do you want to play?'

'No, s'all right,' said Lewis, standing still.

Everyone stood about and seemed to have forgotten whatever it was they were doing. Lewis leaned against the tree and watched and later, to be polite, played against Ed, who beat him and then kept apologising for it.

When Gilbert came down to collect him, his black suit showed up hard in the September light and the children stared as Lewis went to him. His mother dying was embarrassing and disgusting to them. They should have liked to turn their backs on him. They all said goodbye politely and carried on playing.

Kit watched him go away across the grass next to his father. He didn't seem like Lewis to her any more. She laid her cheek against the bark of the apple tree and tried to picture his mother. She couldn't. She wondered if Lewis could.

Gilbert took Lewis to school in the car the next day and spoke to his headmaster before leaving him. Lewis stood outside in the corridor and waited. He could hear the other boys arriving in the dorms downstairs. Gilbert and his headmaster came out and Gilbert put his hand on Lewis's head, quite gently, before he left him.

Gilbert drove straight up to the flat. He left the curtains closed in the drawing room and sat down in a chair with his hands on his knees. It was three o'clock in the afternoon.

'Lizzie died ten days ago,' he said.

He could hear the traffic, muffled by the windows and the thick curtains. Daylight blurred around the edges of the curtains.

'Lizzie died,' he said. 'Lizzie died ten days ago. My wife is dead. My wife died recently.'

The next day he went into the office and his work went well.

When he got home that night he went about the flat and found all Elizabeth's things. She had evening dresses hanging in the cupboard that were just for London and he pulled them off the hangers and put them in a heap on the floor in the drawing room. He added to the pile her scent, shoes, books and some things of Lewis's; jumpers and a board game and some souvenirs of trips to museums that he had kept in a biscuit tin.

He went carefully about and made sure there was nothing left. The pile of things on the floor didn't remind him of her at all. They looked like second-hand things, just a mess, a pile of nothing, but the things that had belonged to Lewis were cluttering up the place, so he took them out and threw them away separately in the kitchen. He went down to the porter and asked him to please organise the removal of the pile while he was at work the next day. He tipped him five pounds, ashamed of his extravagance, and was irritated that the man would probably make money out of Lizzie's belongings, which were good-quality. He went upstairs again and made himself a drink and sat down with the bottle next to him, looking at the pile on the floor. At the bottom was a photograph frame with a picture of him and Lewis in it that she had kept by her side of the bed. He could only see the corner of it sticking out, but he knew the picture very well, it had been taken the first Christmas after the war, Gilbert standing in the garden holding Lewis's hand. They were both smiling, and crooked, because she had been laughing at them and held the camera crooked and Lewis's coat was buttoned up wrong. Gilbert sat in his chair and looked at the corner of the picture frame. He almost took it out and held it in his hands, but he didn't, he just stayed in his chair, looking.

When he returned from work the following evening the porter had taken the things away and the floor was empty.

He stayed in the flat that night, and every night after that, and didn't think of going back to

Waterford. After a week or two he began to be invited out. He accepted every invitation. There were cocktails and dinners and Gilbert was very much in demand. He was hardly alone at all. He went from one occasion to another and felt that he had entered a new world.

CHAPTER FIVE

One Thursday afternoon, towards the middle of December, Jane telephoned Gilbert in the office to remind him that Lewis would be breaking up for Christmas the next day. He didn't need reminding; the boys had to write home every Sunday night and Lewis had said he was looking forward to the holidays in his last letter. Gilbert left the office early on Friday and went to Victoria to meet the school train.

He hadn't met the train before and he felt ridiculous waiting by the barrier with all the women, so he went into the station café and had a cup of tea. He waited until the mothers and their sons had all gone and Lewis was the last child on the platform, and then he left the café to collect him.

Lewis was standing by his trunk with a porter and a man Gilbert thought might have been one of his teachers, and when he saw his father coming towards him he ran into his arms and clung on to him with small strong hands. Gilbert felt the tension of his body and the heat of it through his coat, holding him. He took Lewis's hands firmly, and took them off him and pushed him away.

'None of that,' he said, not looking at him, 'time to go.'

*   *   *

It took an hour and a half to make the journey to Waterford in the car and Lewis fell asleep, with his cheek leaning on the passenger door. Gilbert steered the car through the blue-cold evening.

They stopped in front of the house and Gilbert turned the engine off. He took Lewis's hand.

'Come on, little chap, wake up,' he said, and Lewis woke up.

He looked at his father, mistily, and then at the house above them and Gilbert saw him gradually come back into himself. He saw the moment between the not knowing and the knowing, as he woke, and he recognised it, because it was how he felt on waking too. He wanted to obliterate it. He wanted to take his son's head in his hands and crush the feeling from it. He wanted to hold him hard and kiss him and make Lizzie come back to them through loving him badly enough. He wanted to hide his face and never think of it again.

'We're home,' he said. 'Out you get, Jane will have supper for us.'

*   *   *

Through the Christmas holidays Gilbert took the train to the office as he had used to and spent most nights at home so that things would seem more normal. He never mentioned Elizabeth, and Lewis, responding by instinct, never mentioned her either. The silence around her memory became brittle

60

and dangerous and neither dared break it. It had been both a good thing and a very lonely one that at school, too, almost no one ever mentioned his mother. Working and doing normal things was all right, and he developed a technique for going to sleep, which worked even if his nightmare woke him up. He would imagine he was in her wardrobe, in her bedroom where he'd often played. It was very easy when he was tired to put himself there, on top of the shoes, with the smell of lavender and wood, and the material of her clothes very soft in his mind. Then the water that filled his head sometimes would drain away, and he'd be asleep very quickly. The first night home from school, alone upstairs and getting ready for bed, he went to the door of his parents' room, not to go in, but to look, but the wardrobe wasn't there, just the empty wall where it had been.

*   *   *

After his mother's death Lewis instinctively cast around for other attachments. It was a blind instinct, like the way an animal, if the parent is taken away, will hook onto anything for survival, so Lewis attached himself to Jane and his father. He spent the Christmas holidays following Jane around, trying to help in the kitchen or just sitting and watching her, then, at half-past six, he would wait at the end of the drive for his father. Gilbert would come around the big bend and see Lewis hovering at the gate. He'd stop the car and say, 'Jump in', and Lewis would drive the short distance to the house with him. Gilbert began to dread seeing him there and it got so that as he pulled

61

away from the station, he would begin to feel anxiety at the thought of the small figure waiting for him. If it was a wet day, or cold, like today, he'd hope Lewis wouldn't wait, but there he was, kicking the gravel and then looking up with his intense gaze.

Gilbert stopped the car, but he didn't lean over and open the door, he gestured impatiently for Lewis to walk. Lewis peered at him through the glass, muddled and waiting for the door to open. Gilbert wound down the window.

'For God's sake, you haven't even got a coat! Go up to the house.'

As he opened the front door, Lewis reached him, running to catch up. Gilbert wouldn't look at him.

'Go on in then.'

Lewis went into the hall, waited to see which room his father would go into and then followed him. Gilbert hadn't wanted to be angry with him today, he wanted to be kind. He had bought his Christmas presents in London and they were hidden in the boot of the car.

Lewis hovered about in the doorway and watched Gilbert make himself a whisky and water.

'Lewis, would you sit down? There's something I want to talk to you about.'

Lewis sat opposite his father, like on school report day, and waited.

'Lewis, I've some very good news for you. You're to have a new mother—you know, a stepmother. I met a lovely young lady some weeks ago, who I think you'll like very much, and in the spring we plan to be married.'

Lewis's grey eyes looked at him without

blinking.

'She's called Alice. Alice Fanshawe. I thought you could meet her on your birthday, we'll have a special lunch in town, would that be nice? Lewis?'

'Yes, sir.'

'I don't want you to be difficult about it. You'll see it's the right thing. Now run along, there's a good boy.'

*   *   *

Gilbert finished his drink and went up to change for dinner at Dicky and Claire's. The door to Lewis's room was closed. Gilbert still dressed in the spare room, as he had when Elizabeth was there, and he had trained himself not to notice the silence from the bedroom, no smell of scent, no brush being placed on the glass-topped dressing table.

He was combing his hair when he heard a crash—and the sound of glass breaking—and then the reverberation of something heavy going over, which made the floor shake. He dropped his comb and ran out onto the landing. Jane was at the bottom of the stairs, looking up.

He opened Lewis's door and a cold wind blew through the room. The window was broken, with the frame smashed. The room felt empty and he ran to the window.

There was glass on the icy ground below and a drawer upside down with the clothes spilled out of it. Then Lewis started to cry, and Gilbert turned and saw him huddled behind the door.

He had to walk on broken glass to get to him. Lewis's mouth was open and ugly as if he couldn't

63

close it and he was staring at his father as he cried. Gilbert went right to him and grabbed his arms, and Lewis began to fight, kicking out at him, kicking his legs and trying to hit his head against him. He was surprisingly strong. His face was wet with tears.

'Stop that!' shouted Gilbert. 'Stop crying. Be quiet. Be quiet. Quiet!'

Gilbert forced Lewis's arms down and used his weight to pin him into the corner, and then he stopped crying and tried to cover his head with his arms, but Gilbert grabbed his wrists and forced them away from his face.

Gilbert was panting. He looked around the room—the chest of drawers was on its side, with the rest of the drawers torn out of it; it was the mirror from the top of it that had smashed and covered the carpet with glass.

'Jane!' he shouted, and Lewis began to shake in his hands, but he didn't make any more noise. 'Jane!'

They both waited, out of breath, with Gilbert holding Lewis against the wall and Lewis rigid and shaking as if he couldn't control himself.

Gilbert heard Jane come upstairs and then she stood in the doorway.

'God—' she said, 'Lewis—'

'Get him out of here. I'll clean this up.'

'No. You get him out. Let's stick to our proper jobs, shall we?'

Gilbert was shocked she spoke to him like that and then realised how extreme the situation was, and how undignified, and at the same time he realised that she didn't like him. He pulled Lewis to his feet and dragged him out of the room and across the landing, with Jane watching and Lewis pulling away, silently using all his strength to resist. Gilbert kicked the door shut behind them, hating her seeing it.

He stood in his bedroom gripping his son's wrists hard. There was silence and Gilbert thought Lewis must realise it was pointless to fight. He seemed small suddenly.

He began to worry about Lewis's wrists being hurt and his arms, and he relaxed his grip. Lewis was still quiet, so Gilbert took him to the bed and made him sit.

He stood over him, not sure if he dared to sit next to him, and then he did, and there was silence. Lewis's face was blank. He seemed to have disappeared.

'Are you feeling better?' Gilbert asked, and he made his voice gentle, so as to reach him, but Lewis didn't move. 'A lot of fathers would thrash you for a thing like this. You are my little boy and I want you to make me proud of you, not ashamed. Are you a bad person, to do a bad thing like this? Is that what you want to be? I want you to listen to me very, very carefully.'

He saw Lewis's eyes flicker and then he turned his head and met his father's gaze.

'You'd better not make your mother's death an excuse. That would be a terrible thing to do, and like hurting her again.'

Gilbert waited. His son didn't speak, but kept his eyes on his face. Then Gilbert got up and went to the door. He opened it, wide, and stood back.

'Now why don't you help Jane clean up that mess you've made? I'm out to dinner tonight. I'll see you in the morning. There'll be no more of

65

this.'

Lewis got up and went past him.

'Look at me, Lewis.'

Lewis stopped and looked up.

'Do you have something to say?'

He waited and saw Lewis frown with trying to think what it was he ought to say.

'I'm sorry, sir. Thank you.'

'Go now, please.'

He closed the door behind him.

*   *   *

Jane gave Lewis supper in the kitchen and while he ate she cleared the rest of the glass from the floor of his room. She put a wooden tray over the broken window and stuffed eiderdowns around it. She would have liked to have comforted him, but he wasn't crying.

*   *   *

Gilbert drank too much at the Carmichaels' to drive home. It had happened before. It seemed Elizabeth's death allowed him to do all sorts of things that would have been otherwise unacceptable and still carry on with people's opinions of him unchanged. In later years it was forgotten that he used to fall asleep on the Carmichaels' sofa after dinner, or that once he had left the table before the main course and been brought in from the garden much later by Claire. If one didn't mention a thing afterwards, it was as if it hadn't happened.

Kit was up at six, before anybody, and she got

66

dressed and crept down to let herself out into the garden. She sneaked into the drawing room to take a box of matches and saw Gilbert's feet sticking up over the side of the sofa. He was sleeping in his clothes, head sideways, tie undone. There was an ashtray and a whisky bottle next to him. Kit looked around, half expecting to see Lewis. She watched Gilbert sleeping for a bit and thought how old and ugly grown-ups were and wondered why everybody always said Mr Aldridge was 'so attractive' and if he was staying for breakfast. It would be nice if Lewis came too and she could show him her camp, but she hadn't seen him all holidays; he hadn't come round, and when she was with the bigger children they never went calling for him like they had in the summer. She collected the matches from the coal bucket by the fire and tiptoed out.

Kit let herself out of the side door by the kitchen. Frozen grass snapped under her feet as she ran up to the woods; she would light a fire and get warm and pretend to be a gypsy until it was time to go in.

CHAPTER SIX

You couldn't see daylight from the inside of the shop at all, so there was no knowing what time it was and the air was dry and hot. Kit and Lewis could see Tamsin and her mother's legs and the legs of the sales assistant if they put their faces on the linoleum and looked out from under the rack of mackintoshes. Kit had three marbles in her pocket and Lewis had seven and a piece of chalk, and if they sat opposite each other with their legs apart and their feet touching they could play and not lose them across the vast floor. They were both hungry and the morning had gone on for ever. Lewis was to meet his father and Alice Fanshawe at her mother's flat in Knightsbridge and they were going on for a special birthday lunch at the Ritz. He wasn't thinking about it, just playing marbles with little Kit and being dragged round having clothes bought by Mrs Carmichael, who'd taken Gilbert's stack of accumulated clothes coupons and included Lewis in her shopping for the girls.

'You're going to look very smart,' she kept saying and buying things so big he thought he'd never have to wear anything else again, which was an appalling prospect from one point of view—that you could wear the same thing for ever and never like it to begin with—and an encouraging one from another, that you would never have to enter another shop and get measured and breathed on by ladies whose breath smelled like the inside of their noses.

'That gives me sixteen,' said Kit, lisping intently, and Lewis noticed the way she had to talk sideways out of her mouth to accommodate the gaps in her teeth and wondered if she'd always talk sideways and what that would look like. Not pretty, he concluded.

For his birthday that morning, his father had Jane decorate the table with twigs and winter berries from the garden. When Lewis came down and saw the table, and the presents, he had a sick feeling in his stomach, as if someone was playing a trick on him. He stood in the doorway of the dining room and looked at the table and his decorated place. Gilbert was in his seat already and he stood when Lewis came into the room.

'Happy birthday, Lewis.'

Lewis felt tight and foolish and oddly ashamed.

'Thank you, sir,' he said, and sat down.

It felt silly to have holly branches in front of him getting in the way of breakfast. He unwrapped his presents and they ate, not looking at one another, but when Gilbert left for work he stood in the doorway for a moment and lifted his hand to Lewis's head and stroked his hair.

'Well done,' he said. 'Good boy.'

Gilbert left and Lewis sat on the stairs until Claire Carmichael arrived in the car with Kit and Tamsin to take him up to London, and now he was standing on the steps outside the mansion flats in his new oversized jumper and shorts and duffel coat and surrounded by boxes and bags. He thought he looked like an evacuee, but up to London instead of away. He rang the bell and Claire, Tamsin and Kit stared at him from the pavement. It was a very cold day, but he was hot in all his layers. The door was opened by a uniformed porter who looked at Claire Carmichael as if she were a burglar.

'Good afternoon, madam.'

'I'd better take him up. Come and wait in the lobby,' said Claire, sounding very tired indeed at having to follow Lewis.

She came up the steps and held his elbow and they both went in and there was a lot of discussion with the doorman about leaving the packages and girls downstairs, and which flat and which floor and whether to take the lift. Lewis thought he'd boil in his coat and wished Mrs Carmichael would

69

let go of his arm. She had a faded sort of coldness and was always just one colour, a kind of beige fawn from top to bottom. They toiled up the red carpeted stair to the first floor and rang the bell of number two. Lewis wasn't nervous, he wasn't going to be nervous for Alice Fanshawe, he didn't care if she liked him.

*　　　*　　　*

'He doesn't like me.'

'It's not for him to like or dislike you.'

'That's easy to say. I'd like him to like me.'

'I like you.'

The waiter cleared away their plates and Alice leaned closer to Gilbert. Her hair was very soft and light brown, like child's hair. He wondered if she put it up whether she'd look older, and if he wanted her to look older or if he liked her ingénue quality. Perhaps at twenty-six she was too old to be an ingénue anyway, but she was one to him, she seemed terribly young and she smelled of violets, not like Parma violets but fresh ones, and he couldn't think how she did it.

'Can I give him his present when he comes back?'

'Of course.'

'Will he like it?'

'All children like sweets.'

'Gilbert, am I all right, do you think?'

'You're lovely.'

'All right for him?'

'All right for anybody.'

Lewis came back into the dining room. The room was very big and mirrored, and the walls and ceiling and curtains were pink and gold and the tall windows to the park were shaded in pink, so that you felt conspicuous in the room for not being the right colour. He saw his father and Alice at their corner table from far across the room. They were leaning together, whispering. He had seen his father look like that all his life, with just that expression and just that pose, except he had been with his mother. He simply looked exactly the same but with the wrong woman, and the familiarity and welcome feeling it gave him to see his father as he remembered him was corrupted.

Lewis glanced to his right and saw the waiters standing like sentries at the door to the restaurant. Past them was the long entrance, with sofas and chaises with ladies in hats, drinking tea, and potted palms, and then there was the street, and the light looked blue and bright compared to the pinky warm light in the hotel. Lewis turned towards the daylight and made for it. His father and Alice hadn't looked up and he wasn't conscious of trying to avoid them until he passed the waiters and thought they'd stop him and then he realised he was escaping.

He walked down the very long carpet towards the blue daylight and the doorman at the end of it. His back felt vulnerable and strange and his new shoes rubbed his heels. When he reached the door, the doorman opened it and Lewis stepped out onto the pavement under the grey colonnades. There were a lot of cars and people hurrying and he didn't immediately know what to do, but he knew he could be seen from inside the hotel, so he walked a little way to his left before he stopped.

He didn't have his coat. He'd never been out on

his own in London before and it was an odd, nothing feeling to be on the street with people walking past and not speaking to him.

It was very cold, with the deadness about the cold that you get just before snow. People kept going in and out of the hotel and every time they did he thought they were going to be Gilbert, but they weren't. It wasn't as if he had any feelings, he wasn't upset and he didn't want to make a scene. He would go back inside to the table and be perfectly normal.

He tried to act normally and seem interested in the buses and things, but he knew he looked like a lost child. He wasn't lost; he was waiting. He was waiting for it to be easier to carry on.

'Lewis?'

He turned at his name and saw Alice.

She hadn't got her coat on either and hugged herself with her arms to keep warm. The people in their dark coats and hats walked past them and Alice was all pale colours and nothing covering her skirt or dress, or whatever it was that was light and not thick at all. Behind her, the doorman glanced at them curiously and then away again.

'Would you like to come back inside now?' She said it very gently and kindly, and smiled at him.

Lewis saw that she had softness. He hadn't seen that in anybody, anybody that was for him, for what seemed like for ever. It was everything he wanted. She looked cold and he wanted her to be warm and he didn't want her to look so worried. He was going to cry. He had become used to not having any feeling at all and now he was going to cry. He stared at her, terrified, willing himself not to.

'Why don't you come back inside?' she smiled.

He wished she'd stop it, there was no need to be so sweet.

'Come back in, I've got a present for you. Wouldn't you like your present?'

She said it temptingly, with a little smile, as if there was no more to any of it than giving him a present and winning him over. After that it was easy. He didn't feel sad any more, it just went away and he felt hard as anything, hard as diamond. She shivered and hugged herself some more, but he didn't care and he didn't feel cold, he didn't feel anything.

'Lewis? Do come back in. Please.'

What could he do? He went.

*   *   *

The sugared almonds were in a box and wrapped in cellophane and tissue paper and had three different coloured ribbons tied around them in a bow. Lewis had never seen anything like it in his life.

'Happy   birthday,'   said   Alice,   then, conspiratorially, 'It's sweets.'

The only sweets he'd seen were in paper bags and smeary jars. There were no boxes, there was no having fun about them. This box was shiny and joyful. It was like a thing from another planet. The cellophane alone was extraordinary.

'My mother got them in New York. I asked her to get them just for you.'

'What do you think about that, Lewis? All the way from America!'

'Isn't it lovely? I hadn't seen anything like that for years.'

73

'Aren't you going to open them?'

'Don't you think it's the prettiest box you ever saw?'

'Say thank you. He doesn't know what's inside,' said Gilbert.

'Well, he should open it.'

'Come on.'

'They're almonds. I think you'll like them. They're covered in sugar. In lovely colours. It looks too pretty to touch, doesn't it?'

Lewis looked up at her doll-like eyes. He waited. He stared at her and he took pleasure in it.

'It's a girl's present,' he said.

She blinked. She didn't look very clever. That was what was wrong with her face, he thought, she wasn't very clever, so none of it added up to anything. She could be soft, she could be a woman if she wanted, it didn't make any difference to him; she wasn't clever and she wasn't a mother.

'Lewis, that's rude,' said Gilbert, 'Apologise.'

Lewis thought about it. He decided not to.

'Apologise to Alice.'

'Gilbert, it's all right,' said Alice. Coward, thought Lewis.

'I want you to say sorry, and thank you, or you're to give them back. Then you won't have any sweets.'

Lewis stared at her and didn't blink and pushed the box across the table in front of her. She looked down at the box. She straightened the bow on it.

'I'll get the bill.' Gilbert turned to the room.

Lewis looked at Alice fiddling with the ribbons on the box. He hated himself, but he was used to that, and anyway there was nothing he could do about it now.

74

CHAPTER SEVEN

Gilbert married Alice in March and took her to Scotland for two weeks' honeymoon afterwards. Alice was keen to get back to Waterford. She was very eager to fit in and be liked, and Gilbert's friends and neighbours talked behind his back about rebound marriages and Alice's naïvety and invited them to dinners and parties as a matter of course.

Alice loved playing house. She dismissed Jane and hired a woman called Mary as housekeeper. Mary lived in Turville and had grown-up children and hadn't known Elizabeth or anyone connected with her. Mary was more in charge of Alice than the other way around, and Alice liked it that Mary was motherly and knew something about the running of houses, which Alice didn't and was the first to admit. Alice felt as if she were dressing up in her mother's clothes and pretending to be a wife. She waited to get pregnant. She paid calls. When Gilbert came home, Alice was there, with cocktails, every night. At first it was just a game to be there with a drink and say, 'How was your day?'—but then it became normal. She was always there, at half-past six, in the drawing room, freshly made up and dressed for dinner, with a jug of Pimm's or Martinis or something new she'd read about somewhere; and Gilbert, who at first found it delightful and funny, very soon came to take it for granted.

Alice spent days in London, shopping for clothes and lunching with friends, but in the school holidays she decided to be home all the time. She had given herself a pep talk. She was going to be a proper stepmother to Lewis and not so frightened by him. She envisaged his gradual softening, and his surrender to her. She reminded herself Elizabeth had not been dead five months when Lewis was introduced to her the first time, but it was a difficult thing to bear in mind because Gilbert's life before her seemed shadowy and far away.

The first time she went to Victoria to meet the school train was in April, for the Easter holidays. She saw the boys all dressed alike and she was terrified she wouldn't recognise him and would be shown up, the stepmother. She joined the other women at the barrier and searched the crowd. Far from all looking alike as she'd feared, a lot of the boys were odd or funny in some way: buck teeth, clumsy, or not grown into themselves. Lewis wasn't like that, he looked all right in his clothes, and in his body, and careless of them both. He got off the train a little behind three or four others who were pushing and joking with each other as they looked around for trunks and parents; they were obviously the set to know and she was reassured that he was included and felt proud of him.

She didn't know the form for greeting one's child off the train so she looked around at the other mothers, who all seemed at least forty and absolutely frightening with very set hair and determined expressions. The woman next to her was trying to make her son stop running towards her and go back to the others, but he kept running up and laughing. He had wet lips and knock knees and Alice didn't like the look of him at all. She wanted to say, 'Look, that one's mine, the tall, good-looking one over there!' but, tiresomely, it looked as if the thing to do was not look too pleased to see your offspring, so Alice just raised a careless hand to wave at Lewis, hoping he'd see her and just come over. It was extraordinary to her that he might; he barely knew her, but then, he had no choice.

Lewis wasn't looking down the platform to the barrier like the other boys and he didn't see her wave. He collected his trunk in the scrum by the luggage compartment and waited. She started towards him and managed to get a porter on the way. What should she say? What did the other mothers say? Hello, darling? Hello, Lewis? Hello! She reached him. She was right next to him, he still hadn't seen her.

'Hello, Lewis.'

He looked at her vaguely.

'Hello.'

There was no surprise to it, no warmth, nothing at all. He stood by while she organised the porter with the trunk and they got to the platform for their train back to Waterford.

She faced the front and he sat opposite, looking out at the track going away from him. Getting off the train with the others he'd had vitality and she'd warmed to the sight of him, but now he looked more as she remembered; resigned.

'It'll be lovely to be home,' she said brightly and he nodded.

At home, he went to his room and after a while she decided she was being feeble and went up. She knocked on his door. She didn't know if you were meant to do that with children, but it seemed

77

polite. She imagined saying something about jigsaws, and went in. He was sitting on the windowsill with his knees up and looking out of the window. The windowsill wasn't big and he had his arms wrapped around his knees to be on it, squashed in, as if it was something he had used to do and was growing out of. She wanted to go and put her arms around him and thought of Gilbert.

The first time she had seen Gilbert had been at a party given by some people in London. He had been standing in the middle of the room, talking to a woman who had her back towards Alice. He had been listening and smiling and Alice thought he was the saddest man she'd ever seen. She'd had this same feeling, of just wanting to go over to him and put her arms around him. She'd found out who he was and had herself introduced to him and they'd talked oddly and immediately about loss and death and Elizabeth. They had left the party and gone out for supper, and got quite drunk together, and he'd cried at the table, putting his hand between him and the rest of the room, surprised at himself. She adored his grief, was honoured to witness it. It was as if they'd known each other for ages. There was no initial suspicion or curiosity, no finding topics and interests in common; from the beginning it was her need to love him and his pain drawing her.

This child, though—he had sadness too—but he didn't seem to want or need her. His sadness came at her across the room and she recognised it, and stopped, and didn't know what to do with it.

'What are you up to?' she said.

'Nothing.'

Alice was overwhelmed by acute social

embarrassment.

'Daddy will be home soon,' she said and went out, closing the door.

She went to her room and sat on the coral-cushioned stool at the dressing table. The stool was new, because she had felt strange sitting where Elizabeth had sat, and the mirror was new too because she hadn't wanted to look in a drowned woman's glass. She had made do with putting her make-up in the drawers of Elizabeth's dressing table, though. She put on some lipstick. Gilbert would be home soon. She smiled at herself in the mirror. She wasn't going to be put off. She was going to make Lewis better. She would think of something. She needed to make the drinks for Gilbert, there wouldn't be time for her to have her taster before he arrived if she didn't hurry. She went downstairs.

* * *

'So, Lewis, what shall we get up to today?'

'I don't know.' He fiddled with his spoon, longing to get down.

'It's a bit cold for playing outside. I know! As a special treat we could go up to London and visit a museum. We could catch the train, there's one at about half-past nine, I think, and we'll be in Victoria by half-past ten. Would you like that?'

'All right.'

'Come on, Lewis, what had you planned to do today? Had you thought about it at all?'

He looked down and shook his head.

'Well, why don't we go to a museum then? It'll be fun.'

Alice was relieved to have something to do and to be going up to town. They spent the morning at the Natural History Museum, had sandwiches for lunch and then went for a walk in Kensington Gardens. Alice felt more herself in London and having things to look at made it much easier to be with Lewis. It was a bitter cold spring day and there weren't many people in the park. They walked to the Round Pond. He ran on ahead of her to the water and Alice tucked her face into her fur collar against the wind.

There was a sailing boat on the pond that Lewis was running towards. It was impressive: about two feet long and varnished, with a light blue sail. The boy sailing it was Lewis's age and Alice observed the way Lewis played out the social rituals of childhood; he stood and watched with his hands in his pockets, then he got a bit nearer and watched some more. Then he started glancing towards the boy who owned the sailing boat, who had noticed him by then and was playing with it more showily and demonstrating his pride in it. Alice found a bench and sat down as the boys moved around each other and eventually made contact, with words coming last.

'D'you want to try?'

'All right.'

It was a good day for sailing boats and the ripples ran evenly in one direction so that when they let the boat go on one side of the pond, it sailed pretty briskly to the other side, without ever getting stuck in the middle. The other boy's mother was on another bench watching and there was no-one else but them. Observing their own rituals, the two women looked across at each other and smiled a few times before meeting on the bench between the two.

'Jolly cold.'

'Awful.'

'Nice boat.'

'It's his pride and joy. How old is your boy?'

'He's eleven.'

'He's tall for his age, isn't he? Paul's twelve, we're hoping he'll shoot up.'

Alice felt an absolute fraud. She kept wanting to say, 'I'm not his mother', and felt sure the other woman would start asking her searching questions about measles or something that she wouldn't be able to answer. She always felt this way, as if she were pretending Lewis was hers and trying to fool people.

Lewis glanced over and smiled at Alice, he smiled at her quite naturally because he was enjoying himself, and she smiled back and felt suddenly very happy. He went back to tying on the sail or whatever it was he was doing and Alice, in her joy, said, 'Don't they look happy?'

The other woman looked surprised.

'Well, it's the holidays. Nanny's gone to visit her ill mother and we haven't found a replacement. I'm absolutely desperate, frankly, but my three seem to be getting along fine.'

Alice laughed. 'We don't have a nanny.'

She suddenly thought it looked as if she couldn't afford one, or that she was the sort of hopeless young woman with messy hair who spent all the time in the park with her son, so she said in a rush,

'Lewis never had one before and he's away at school . . . I mean, I'm not his mother, I'm his stepmother. His mother never had a nanny, she was—' She didn't want to say 'eccentric' about Elizabeth, but it did strike her as odd.

'Is she dead?'

'Yes, she died last year.'

'She died? How ghastly. How did she die?'

Alice felt the curiosity and glee, but she didn't mind. It was a relief to tell her.

'She drowned.'

'No?'

'Yes, in the river near their—our—house.'

With a meaning look, 'And when did you . . . ?'

'I met his father last November.'

'And she died . . . ?'

'In the summer.'

'Well, men can't manage alone, can they? What's his name, your boy?'

'Lewis.'

Alice was beginning to regret saying anything. She'd wanted to tell her and now she was wondering how to get out of it. She didn't want to stop Lewis playing and take him home.

'And his father? Does he mention the wife much?'

'No. He used to. We don't talk all that much about it.'

'I should think not. Well. One's used to fathers dying of course, but a mother!'

'Yes.'

'And whereabouts do you live?'

'Surrey. Waterford.'

'I know it. We used to know some people near there.'

'Really?' Alice was relieved, this was safer territory.

'The country can be so hard to get along in. Even Surrey. Do you find you're fitting in all right?'

'Yes, everyone's very nice.' Alice began to dislike her.

There was a shout and Lewis came running over. He had put the whole of one leg into the water and the drenched wool sock was hanging down. His shoe was spilling out water and he was laughing. He stopped in front of her, like a puppy about to bark, and stuck his wet shoe and leg out towards her.

'Look!'

'It doesn't matter,' said Alice and laughed and felt very fond of him; she liked him for laughing and for thinking she would think it was funny too.

'Lewis, isn't it? I'm Marjorie Dunford-Wood.'

Lewis was out of breath, smiling—'How d'you do—'

'I was so sorry to hear about your mother.'

It was like watching an accident and not being able to stop it. Alice could see Lewis was making an enormous effort to do something.

'Thanks, that's all right,' he said.

'Were you having fun with the boat?' said Alice, in a rush, 'I think we should probably be off, don't you?'

The other woman mouthed an exaggerated apology to Alice that Lewis couldn't fail to see. Alice didn't return her look, but got up and took Lewis's hand.

'Goodbye,' she said and turned away.

The boy with the boat stood up from the water

and waved and grinned.

'Bye!' he shouted then, thinking he hadn't been heard, 'Bye then!'

*   *   *

They walked back towards Kensington Gore and all the way across the park Alice tried to make up for it, but he didn't speak to her. The cold was vicious and worse for being in the spring. Lewis's shoe was squelching water and it should have been a funny sound and the sort of thing children liked laughing at, and Alice wanted to make him laugh about it, but couldn't think of anything to say. They walked on through the empty park with her heels and the wet shoe the only sounds.

'You can see your breath,' she said.

They walked on.

'We'll be there soon.'

She wanted to cry and she nearly did just to make him feel sorry for her, but she thought maybe that wasn't a fair thing to do to a child. In the taxi to Victoria she watched him look out of the window at a troop of Horse Guards go by and he looked like a normal child, leaning on his arms with his face against the glass and looking at the shiny swords and plumes. Just like any other child. She felt terribly lonely and rather desperate, and decided to wait for Gilbert at Victoria.

It was nearly five o'clock and dark by then, so they waited in the hotel there. Alice had tea and then found herself ordering a cocktail, and then, quite soon after, another. She took out the olives and put them in the ashtray, which was full.

'Lewis! Stop it! Don't you know it's rude to

84

stare?'

'I wasn't.'

'Yes, you were! You were staring at me.'

'I was looking at the things. The olives.'

'What on earth for? Haven't you seen an olive before?'

'Of course I have.'

'Tell me one thing, will you? Will you just tell me one thing? Tell me how it is you can look at horses and boats and have a perfectly fine time when you feel like it? How's that?'

He had no idea what she was talking about, what horses?

'And how is it, you just save all of this,' she emphasised the word, gesturing at him, 'all of This for Me? How is that, Lewis?'

He wanted to think about something else.

'Come on!' her eyes were fixed on him. 'Why don't you make an effort? Everybody else bloody does.'

Lewis looked at the green olives in the ashtray. They were shiny and wet, but resting in the cigarette ash and covered with it on one side.

She asked for the bill and spilled some money from her purse in paying, and then they went down to the platform and walked along the train looking for Gilbert.

'Come on. Keep up for God's sake! I've had enough.'

Gilbert was surprised and pleased to see them and it was a huge relief, just as she'd imagined. Lewis saw her put her pretty face on when she saw him. They got in, but there was nowhere to sit and they had to find an empty compartment in third class.

'Lewis, you're looking very messy. Where are your gloves and why is your sock in that terrible state?'

'I got it in water.'

Alice hadn't thought to bring him gloves and she hadn't noticed his cold hands. She felt the tears starting again and decided to let them.

'What on earth?'

After that there was no stopping the way it went. By the time they got to Waterford it was difficult to get off the train with everybody they knew and pretend things were all right. Lewis had gone inside himself, it was impossible to do anything with him, and Gilbert had to remind Alice to pull herself together and her being drunk and crying was Lewis's fault.

The embarrassment and the publicness made Gilbert helplessly angry and at home he shut Lewis in his room. Alice had a bath and made herself pretty for him again and after supper everything was in its proper place; Lewis was impossible, Alice had done her best and Gilbert forgave them both. He forgave Alice in bed, but Lewis never knew about the forgiveness part. He had supper in his room, slept in his clothes and at breakfast nobody mentioned the day before.

Alice watched Lewis, and she came to think of him as broken. She tried not to, and she never told anyone, least of all Gilbert, who so needed to think he'd grow out of it, but she felt that he was broken and that there was nothing to be done about it. She hoped he would mend, but she lost sight of the idea that she could help. He was like a damaged bird. And they always die, she thought.

CHAPTER EIGHT

It was windy up on the terrace and the pages of the musicians' sheet music fluttered and blew up, and the striped awnings over the balconies of the rooms snapped and quivered. The hotel looked like an ocean liner and even more so when the sky was moving above it and it seemed to head out to sea. Bright sunshine glanced off the brass instruments so that it hurt to look at them, and the couples crossing the terrace had to hold their skirts down or pin their hair back with their hands.

Down on the beach, near the rocks, it wasn't so windy and the July sun had baked the sand to scorching. Lewis was playing a game. He stepped off a rock and stood on the sand with his bare feet and waited. At first there was nothing and then it would hurt and he would wait some more. The hurting didn't feel like anything at first, it was far away, but the more it hurt, the more he felt connected to it, and then it would become unbearable and he'd have to move and, standing back up on the rock, he could feel it better, hard and rough and pressing into his burned feet; and then he would feel released, as if he was back in the world again.

To begin with, his feet would only hurt at the time he was doing it and just after, but then it got so that the pain would go on, and he'd feel the burning later, even hours later; and it reminded him of how he'd felt himself present and connected with the place, and not just numb and in his head, like he was most of the time.

When he hadn't spoken for a long time he felt very far away from people. His French was not very good, but apart from Alice and his father, most of the people he spoke to were French and if he wanted anything, or to talk to anybody at all, he had to speak it. He'd make a sentence and practise it in his mind in preparation, but then not be able to forget it. 'Un verre d'eau, s'il vous plaît', the words went round and round his head and even though he knew they were simple, he worried about saying them or that the waiter might say something back to him that he didn't understand. He was frightened he'd get it wrong, or stutter, although that had never happened. He didn't know why he had such a clear and frightening image of stuttering, but he often had the fear he wouldn't get his words out, or he'd stumble over them and get caught helplessly between the beginning of a word and the end, like time stopping and being trapped, while everybody else's time just went on as usual.

'Come on, Lewis, French please, speak up.'

'Un verre d'eau, s'il vous plaît.'

'Good. And we'll have a bottle of the Sancerre. Chilled, all right? Really cold.'

Alice looked at him from under the wide brim of her very white hat, which she held on with one hand, and Lewis felt the soles of his feet burning inside his sandals and prickling in fascinating discomfort.

'Have you made any nice friends, Lewis? There are lots of English people here—and I saw the Trehernes!'

'In this hotel?' asked Gilbert, and they started talking about the Trehernes and if they were related to some other Trehernes, and Lewis was left in his mind again.

Usually once he'd said the stupid sentence about the glass of water or whatever it was, it went out of his mind again, but today it stayed there going round and round, so that it irritated him and he wanted to shake his head to get it out, and had to stop himself. Un verre d'eau, un verre d'eau . . .

'Don't scrape the knife against the table, there's a good boy, try not to fidget.'

He tried. He tried to sit still and the lunch went on for ever and Alice and his father behaved like children whispering together and giggling. Gilbert had never been like this with Elizabeth; they had been close, they had looked at each other like that, and touched and everything, but it was different. Elizabeth and Gilbert had fought. It had been lovely to watch. Lewis had seen the fighting was a ritual between them, a playful struggle re-establishing their fascination with one another. Alice and Gilbert were boring and horrible to watch; everything about them seemed to be concerned with flattery and approval, and was pretty disgusting when all it involved was hand holding and looks and no gentle fighting at all. Lewis craved their company so as not to be alone all the time, and then craved being alone just to be away from them.

He watched the English children playing, and had no idea how to go about joining in. Joining in wasn't something he'd ever learned, it had just happened and now it had just stopped happening. The others in the swimming pool played diving games and bombing games and their shouts and splashing weren't anything he wanted. He was

89

sitting near Alice, who was on a lounger by the water looking at a magazine. She had a hat and sunglasses and a tall drink and she was utterly absorbed in looking at the pictures of clothes. Lewis thought the hotel could have crumbled into the sea around her and she would be unmoved. His father was just sleeping. In the middle of the day. Not having even been to work. Lewis got up and went over to the edge of the water. He looked down into it and watched the ripples and sparkles bounce off. He looked up at the enormous dark blue sea that shrank away and expanded in one swelling wave that came to meet him and went away in rhythm.

The concrete was warm under his feet, but the sounds of people were getting far away again. He wondered if he was visible or invisible. He put one hand down to the edge and slipped into the water and felt it close over his head. It tasted of salt and not like a river at all. He wondered how long he could stay under without any breath. He let all the air go out of him and went slowly down until he got to the bottom. It was much quieter underwater. It felt much more like him. He lay down on the bottom and spread his arms out.

It didn't take long at all, with no air, to need to come up, and the first breath was something that had to be done, not something he decided to do, and that felt good. He played that for an hour. Having no air and being deep underwater made you feel very alive when you came up, but apart from that it was just something to do.

PART TWO

PART TWO

CHAPTER ONE

JULY 1952

The sun was shining down onto Tamsin's hair as she walked, not all the time, but when it could find its way through the leaves and, when it did, it made her glow. All of her skin seemed to be golden, as if being blonde had burnished her all over. The colours of her went together now. She had a primrose coloured dress, and her waist was very narrow and the skirt of the dress went wider to the knee and stopped just on it, so that her calves were perfect below the skirt. Her arms were bare and her neck seemed particularly bare coming out of the dress and Lewis hadn't known why that was; everybody else had bare arms and neck, but they didn't seem so bare. Her cheek, looking at the side of her and just from behind, as he had, was curved and then he could see her mouth, smiling. It was her hair, though, the paleness of it, the way it was so soft and held back with a white ribbon—or hairband, or hairband covered in ribbon, held back with something—that shone, and then went into a heavy curl at the bottom of her neck and it seemed like he could feel it.

Everyone else was just walking along. Nobody else seemed to notice at all, except bloody Ed Rawlins, who had always got to be the same age as her, and would always be. Tamsin and he were walking together and being sixteen together, and just lending their presence, with the understanding that they didn't really have to be there.

Last holidays she hadn't been sixteen and she hadn't been blonde. Her birthday was in May and Claire had finally taken her up to town to get her hair done, and Tamsin looked at herself in the mirror of Henri's on Walton Street and knew that she was about to emerge. She felt as if she was returning to something she had always been inside. Being a blonde child, and then losing blondeness, made her feel cheated. She knew she was really blonde, and she would one day show that she was again, but it had been awful having to wait with brown hair and not have people know. She was blonde until she was six and when it darkened down she never did accept that it had, and every summer when the sun made it lighter she would think: there, that's my blonde hair trying to come out again. So sitting in Henri's, with Henri himself taking off the bleaching lotion and putting in her rollers and checking the tone and the texture, and all the assistants and her mother and even other customers looking at her in what could only be described as wonder—well—it was nothing less than a restoration to a throne. She was herself again. Now Ed was plainly in love with her and she thought Lewis Aldridge was too, except he was so quiet. Fred and Robert Johnson were walking next to Lewis and she thought they were too immature to be in love with her, but she wouldn't have been surprised. Lewis seemed older than them, he was as tall as Ed and didn't have all the things wrong that fourteen-year-old boys often did, but if he wasn't awkward physically, he certainly was in every other way. He was so quiet and odd, and no-one really had anything to say to him any more.

Lewis walked with his head down and wished

the twins would shut up. Fred and Robert always seemed not quite whole people; maybe it was being twins, there wasn't enough of them to go round, as if they'd had to share materials. They were still little boys and were having conversations with no disagreements in them about *The Beano* or insects, and Lewis wasn't interested.

Away through the trees, and on her own, was Kit. Joanna Napper was away and there just wasn't anyone else of ten for her to be with. She was with a child called Annie, who was staying with the Johnson twins and being ignored by them, and who was very young indeed. She'd been following Kit around all summer and Kit had to endure being 'you little ones' until she thought she'd slay herself. Annie was trailing behind now and Kit was being nice because she knew what it was like, but was hating being nice, and she had her big frown on and was getting hot and miserable.

It had rained for the first two weeks of the holidays and Kit had read nearly all of *Of Human Bondage* while Tamsin arranged her hair and talked about frocks with her mother. They had been up and down to London buying things and even going for cocktails, and the thought of that was death to Kit and she wouldn't have gone even if she'd been old enough.

Lewis had no expectations of the summer. He and Alice avoided each other pretty much in the daytime and then it was just a matter of either rowing or not rowing with Gilbert and her through the evening. Some evenings were better than others; alcohol and the mood between the two of them were the main variables. He could have called round to Ed or Tom or the twins, but he'd got out of the habit of that years ago and now didn't think it would be an easy thing to do.

The family went to church on Sundays and Lewis endured that all right, being used to chapel every day at school. Standing out in the pouring rain, he had seen the Carmichaels getting out of their car at the gate. Tamsin and Claire each had an umbrella and Tamsin was wearing a silk scarf over her hair. He hadn't seen her all holidays, she'd been up in town with her mother the first couple of weeks and now, when she ran under the porch of the church, laughing and pulling off her scarf, dressed like a woman—and what's more, looking like one—he'd just stared at her. The only woman he'd seen since he'd wanted to see one was matron and, however hard you tried, she just didn't count. Tamsin ran towards him and he'd had to move out into the rain again to make room for her. As she pulled off her scarf she saw him and said, 'Oh, hello, Lewis' over her shoulder.

He'd spent the whole service looking over at her and pretending not to.

She knew he was looking, she knew everyone was looking, and knowing it made her happy and not at all embarrassed. The rain beat so loudly on the roof you could hardly hear the vicar, even if you were listening, and it was cold enough that steam was coming off the wet coats. After the service the families had gone home to their respective Sunday lunches.

Lewis had thought about Tamsin sometimes and when, a few days later, he had seen her and Ed and the others walk past his gate on their way up to the woods he'd followed and joined them. He wasn't soft over her, he just wanted to see her and check if she really looked that good. She did. The twins were the same and so was Kit, except taller and with teeth. She'd been happy to see him at least, but the others, when he'd called to them, had turned around and looked at him as if they'd all never met. Still, here they all were, walking in the woods and towards the river and Lewis was wondering which way they'd go and hoping they'd change direction soon. Being with them was all right, and looking at Tamsin was good, but the woods were oppressive and he wanted to get out of them.

Kit looked at Lewis and tried to remember what he had been like when he wasn't like this.

'We could walk into Turville,' said Ed.

'Too far,' said Fred.

'Too hot,' said Robert.

'Be rather nice to swim,' said Ed, smiling at Tamsin.

'I don't have a bathing suit. None of us do,' said Tamsin, knowing Ed was wondering what she'd look like with and without one, and smiling back at him.

'Let's go back and get our things and swim,' said Ed.

Tamsin looked over at Lewis, who hadn't spoken for ages. He was still looking down and he looked as he always did, closed and not really there. She decided she felt awfully sorry for him. He obviously didn't want to go to the river and it was tactless of Ed to keep going on about it; after all, it must be in all their minds what had happened to his mother. The last time she'd seen him (and she supposed anyone had seen him) was at Easter when it had been very warm and Ed had his birthday outside. He'd invited Lewis because it seemed rude not to and everyone had such a jolly time, except that Lewis hadn't spoken. He hadn't spoken at all. There had been no reason for it. It wasn't surprising he didn't get on with people; often she thought he didn't try. She wondered what he was like at Harrow; the boys she knew there were in higher years. He felt her watching him and looked over—and she felt it, the look—and she looked away. She thought, gosh, he's only fourteen, I must pull myself together, it's not as if he's anyone one would consider, and he's a baby! Ed was saying something about swimming, why did he keep going on about it?

'I don't want to swim,' said Tamsin. 'Lewis, you don't want to, do you?'

'No, I don't want to.'

'Well, Lewis wouldn't,' said Ed.

'And nor would I,' said Tamsin quickly, 'and if we must go to the river, I'd rather go to it in Woldham where we can have tea or ices.'

It took a moment for them to realise that Lewis had stopped walking and they only realised because Kit said, 'What?'

They all stopped and looked back. Lewis was standing and looking at Ed.

Kit had been watching all of them. She was to one side and looking at him. He hadn't spoken much, but he'd seemed all right so far. They were all still now, and Lewis carried on staring at Ed, who finally got fed up with it.

'What?'

'Why wouldn't I?'

'What do you mean?'

'Why wouldn't I want to go to the river?'

There was silence. Nobody said anything. Lewis had a look about him that was immediately dangerous, not just the promise of danger, but danger right there, and Kit felt frightened, but Ed seemed oblivious to it and enjoying the confrontation.

'Why wouldn't I want to go to the river?'

'Come on, Lewis, everybody knows why.'

'Say it.'

Tamsin touched Ed's arm, 'Ed—'

'Because of your mother,' he said it mockingly, sing-song, 'Because of your mother dying there.'

Then Lewis started towards Ed, he walked up to him quite fast and Tamsin backed off quickly and Ed stood his ground, but didn't step towards him. They all stared, they were all waiting.

'So what? So what about it?'

'Nothing about it. You're being ridiculous.'

'Don't laugh.'

'I'm not laughing,' said Ed, laughing, 'I'm just saying you're being ridiculous.'

'Take that look off your face.'

'What look?' Ed laughed again and looked around at everybody. 'I must say you're behaving in an extraordinary way.'

'Take that fucking look off your face.'

Kit had never heard anyone of their age say that word before. She'd heard her father use it, in another room, and she'd heard it in the street, but this was different.

'How dare you speak that way in front of the girls,' said Ed and it would have been funny, but somehow wasn't, and Kit thought how awful he was and that she'd never liked him.

Lewis went towards Ed again. Ed managed to

move away and make it look as if he was taking up the pose of the philosopher, the commentator, but he was ready and his face looked very sharp.

'It seems to me you're being rather over-sensitive. If you will come walking in woods with rivers in them, on hot days, you can't be entirely surprised if the subject of swimming comes up. We're all very sorry your poor drunken mama had the—'

He didn't finish his sentence because Lewis punched him in the face. Ed had known Lewis would hit him and he'd thought he'd be ready for it—he was looking forward to hitting him back and beating him—but he hadn't expected Lewis's punch to be so hard or so fast and he went down. His nose was broken and the pain was terrible and he didn't get up, but lay there shouting, with blood pouring through his fingers. At school it was never like this; in a fight you never went for a chap's face and even if you were really angry, it was more show than actual damage, with a lot of clothes-grabbing and wrestling.

Ed was lying there bleeding and Tamsin turned on Lewis, who looked as if he might kick him or get down to hit him again.

'Oh my God! Oh my God!'

Annie burst into tears and the twins looked thrilled and amazed and got closer to Ed and further from Lewis. This wasn't what normally happened, this wasn't the way things were; it had a surreal quality, all the rules had gone, and Kit suddenly wondered if that might be normal for Lewis, not having anything to go by. She knew the feeling. Her father hitting her mother had always given her that vertiginous feeling of there being no

100

rules.

Ed wasn't getting up and Lewis turned and walked away, not on the path, but through the trees. Kit watched him go and envied him his violence, and pitied him for it. She wanted to go after him, but only watched him and then turned back to the clearing where Tamsin was having a lovely time helping Ed walk, and the others were following in a group like medieval villagers, scandalised.

'Appalling, just appalling,' Tamsin was saying.

'—deserves whatever he gets!' said Robert.

They had all seemed to turn into their parents, Kit thought, and hated them.

*   *   *

They went back to the road and trooped towards the village. Ed's nose bled for ages, but eventually stopped. He kept his hand up to it. Tamsin and Kit's house was nearest, after the Aldridge house, and Tamsin said Ed should come to them. She sent little Annie home with the twins.

Tamsin took Ed into the kitchen where he washed his face—this was drama enough, as Tamsin hadn't been in the kitchen for about two years.

'I'm going to call Dr Straechen.'

Ed uncovered his face, 'Does it look bad?'

'Awful. Wait here, I'll phone. If it's broken he can set it for you. Can you set noses?'

She went off through the baize door and Ed waited at the table. Kit sat opposite with her feet up on her chair. She had a scab on her knee. She wondered if she'd ever grow out of scabs on her

101

knee; her mother seemed to think it was her defining feature.

'You were horrible to Lewis,' she said.

Ed couldn't speak very well for the blood sitting between his nose and mouth and the swelling, but he managed outrage.

'He hit me!'

'You asked for it. You know you did.'

'He wanted a fight,' he said, thickly, 'you saw him, I couldn't back down!'

She couldn't go on sitting there with him. She got up and went into the hall. Dicky was standing by Tamsin who'd just come off the telephone.

'Is it broken?'

'I don't know, Daddy. It looks it. It's gone awfully big.'

'Where is he?'

'In the kitchen. I didn't want him to bleed on things.'

'What about Lewis? Where did he go?'

'He ran off into the woods.'

'No, he didn't,' said Kit, 'he walked.'

'Shut up, Kit,' said Tamsin.

'What was he thinking, doing a thing like that?' said Dicky, and Kit remembered the time he'd broken her mother's arm against the fireplace in the drawing room and she'd had to tell everyone she'd fallen off a ladder picking apples, which was absurd in the first place as she'd never been up a ladder in her life and almost didn't know where the orchard was.

Kit thought of Ed's voice in the woods, 'your poor drunken mama . . .'

'Daddy,' she said, 'Lewis hit Ed because Ed said something about his mother.'

102

Neither Tamsin nor Dicky seemed to have heard.

'Ring Harry Rawlins, Tamsin. Where's Claire? He should have some ice put on it.'

Kit saw it wasn't going to go well for Lewis.

Dicky went off to look for Claire, and Tamsin started through the telephone book on the table.

'Tamsin! Ed was awful. He said a really awful thing.'

'R . . . R. Rawlins . . . I know, Kit, but it's no excuse. You saw the way he was, how he looked. He was horrid. You just don't do things like that.'

'Well, I'd have hit him if—'

'Sh! Go away.' She picked up the telephone. 'Guildford 131 please.'

*   *   *

Lewis had just wanted to get out of the woods. If he hadn't wanted to look at Tamsin, he wouldn't have been there in the first place. His hand hurt from hitting Ed, and the feeling of Ed's head going back and the contact of skin and the bone beneath it had stayed in his hand. The day was hotter than it had been and ahead he could see unbroken sunshine and a field. He went for the edge of the wood and soon came out of it.

He wasn't sure exactly where he was, somewhere on Pitt's property probably; there was a barn in the distance and the field was bright with stubble. He stopped. The landscape was wide and still and he felt uncomfortable in it. He didn't want to panic, but he could feel it starting. If he'd had someone there to talk to he could break the silent feeling, but he couldn't think of anybody.

103

He started to walk around the field with the vague idea of making a big circle home. He guessed he should apologise to Ed, but the thought of his face and what he'd said made him feel sick and he wanted to go and find him and make sure he had broken his nose and then break his legs for him, too. He let his mind play pictures of violence; it was better than feeling sick and the weakness and panic at any rate.

He had ended up walking all the way around the wood so as not to go back into it and that took ages. He hid himself and didn't go into the house until after supper.

He'd thought when he got home he could explain to his father about what Ed had said— anyone would see how bad it had been—but when he got there he couldn't make himself think of it, let alone use it to get himself out of trouble. He and his father sat opposite one another by the fire and Alice sat at the card table by the window with a drink and watched them. Lewis wished she'd go and find something else to do.

'Why would you do a thing like that?'

'I don't know.'

'You seem pleased to have done it.'

'No, sir.'

'Well, tell me then! I'd like to know what possessed you—'

'Nothing, sir.'

'Nothing? You broke a boy's nose—you hit the son of good friends for no reason? You punched him in the face—'

'I had a reason.'

'What was your reason?'

'He— It was— I was trying to stop him.'

'Trying to stop him what?' Silence. 'Stop him what, Lewis? You were trying to stop him? What was he doing?'

'. . . Nothing.'

'Lewis! This is absurd—you have done a violent, horrible thing and you have taken pleasure in it. And you have no explanation? What's wrong with you?'

There was always that, the thing that was wrong with him; he didn't know what it was, either, but he knew there was something.

'Why can't you get on with people? Do you see how hard it is to look after you?'

Lewis kept quiet and his quietness made his father worse, he seemed determined to break him in some way, but Lewis didn't know what he wanted from him. He sat and listened and couldn't think clearly enough to find a way to please him.

When he was finally sent upstairs he hadn't been able to stop walking up and down the room. He couldn't remember what had happened, or why he'd done what he'd done, only that his father hated him and he thought he was right to.

He kept walking back and forth in his room, from door to window, and he couldn't stop; the door came towards him, then the window and then the door, and he kept walking the little distance again and again.

He heard his father and Alice come upstairs and go to their room and the house was quiet, except for his head. He stopped, listening. He was numb. He thought if he could feel something it would be better. He had been scraping his nails up and down his forearm trying to feel pain—sometimes that worked if he did it hard enough—but the

105

scratching wasn't doing anything, even though his arm was raw. Then he remembered what Ed had said about his mother. It wouldn't leave his head. He couldn't breathe. He left his room and went downstairs, thinking he might get out of the house.

The stairs were dark and it felt strange being out of his room when Gilbert and Alice were asleep. He saw the drawing room door open and the drinks table. He went in and shut the door, so that if they came to the top of the stairs they wouldn't see him, and looked at the bottles and wondered what could be in them all. He couldn't remember ever tasting alcohol before, sips of grown-ups' drinks maybe, at parties as a child.

The whisky looked dark and he'd never liked the smell of it on his father. He chose the gin, and when he drank it—from the bottle—it nearly took the back of his throat off, but the taste of it, bitter and sugary, was familiar; it was like a taste he'd always known and it was very normal to him. He drank some more and looked at the wall in front of him and waited for something to happen.

The drink felt hot in his empty stomach. He felt his throat burning drily and the strength of the gin in his mouth, and after a few moments the hit of it in his blood and his heart felt it too. The hit went through him and it was dangerous and comforting. And then it slowed his head down. His thoughts were slowed down, and the repetitive, loathing rush of them eased.

He lifted the bottle and drank some more, and even smiled. He knew he'd found something then. He knew he'd found something that worked.

CHAPTER TWO

DECEMBER 1952

After everybody had left and while the servants were clearing up and Dicky and Claire and Tamsin were picking over the party, Kit went from room to room and found little things people had left. She found Alice Aldridge's red silk evening bag with her lipstick and cigarettes in it. She found a stiletto shoe under the dining table. She found three lighters, two of them gold, but only one engraved. She went quietly around, sorting through the mess for treasures, and thinking about the party.

It had been mid-afternoon when she had got up the courage to speak to Lewis.

'What are you doing?' she had said, leaning against the wall in the hall and propping her foot up behind her.

'Nothing.'

She'd spent the whole party wanting to talk to him, and it wasn't as if anyone else was.

'Happy Christmas.'

'You too.'

'How is it?'

'It's all right, thank you.'

He didn't seem to mind being spoken to.

'Where's your father?'

'In there with Alice and everyone. Where's yours?'

'Shouting at the servants. He'll come out through there in a minute.'

They were in the hall, where it turned the corner

behind the stairs, and they had a good view of both party rooms, the baize door, the stairs and the front door. It was quite dark, so nobody walking by paid any attention.

'I'm eleven,' she said, and felt an absolute fool and wanted to die.

'Congratulations.'

She decided not to talk any more, it only made her look ridiculous. She would keep quiet.

'When's your birthday?' she said, 'You'll be fifteen, won't you?'

Why couldn't she shut up?

'Thursday.'

'Oh, happy—'

She had run out of words at last, but at the wrong time.

Lewis looked at Kit, standing there on one leg, and took pity.

'Do you remember that time we went down New Hill on my bike?' he said, and was rewarded by her smile, which was transforming.

'I was six! I was terrified!'

'So was I.'

'Were you?'

It had never crossed her mind that Lewis would be frightened.

To begin with, when she was very little, he had been a hero to her and not distinguishable from the ones in books; she used to muddle him up with them, pointing him out to her nanny, 'There's Lewis!' 'No, dear, that's the boy in the story . . .' Then, through her childhood, when she'd seen him in the holidays she'd been too small and a girl, and couldn't be his friend exactly, but he'd always been kind. He either hadn't noticed her, or he'd been

108

kind. Now she was eleven she knew she was in love with him. He was her secret. He was her imagining. She didn't long or yearn, or other things she had read about being in love, but she had him in her heart. Sometimes she felt surprised that he didn't know it.

'You're never out with everybody any more,' she said.

'No. I'm at home mostly. Reading and things.'

'I read too!'

He stopped himself from making a crack about successful schooling or medals, she looked so earnest and it was a relief to talk to someone; he was beginning to forget what his voice sounded like.

'What are you reading?' he asked her.

'*Anna Karenina.*'

'Getting through it all right?'

'Yes, thanks.'

'I liked the bits with Levin. On the farm.'

'Me too. I don't like Anna, she's a drip.'

'What else?'

'Dickens?'

'Soppy.'

'Yes!'

'Hardy?'

'Not yet. I liked Somerset Maugham, but Mummy stopped me.'

Dicky came out through the baize door then, and they watched him march off into the drawing room. Lewis turned back to her, seeing her face as she watched her father go, and how it changed.

'Are you one of those child prodigies?' he asked.

'I don't think so, why?'

'You seem pretty brainy.'

'Well, I'm not thick.'

'Glad to hear it.'

He smiled at her, and Kit forgot to speak.

Ed Rawlins crossed the hall and passed them, going into the drawing room, and Kit started to laugh. Ed ignored them and Lewis started to laugh too, and they stood laughing at him until he'd gone.

'Isn't he noble-looking?' said Kit, and they were laughing and leaning against the wall, not looking at each other.

*　　*　　*

Ed went into the party and didn't acknowledge either of them, but he heard their laughing after he'd passed. They were giggling and bloody babyishly laughing at him. He stood in the door of the long drawing room and looked for Tamsin and his face was red with rage and embarrassment. Laughed at by Lewis Aldridge and Tamsin's kid sister; it was so uncivilised—first that awful violence in the summer and now this—if he wanted he could knock all Lewis's teeth out. Ed stepped aside for some people to leave the room and saw Tamsin by the fire with her father. He leaned against the door and waited. He didn't want to go and talk to her while his face was still red and he was terrified of Mr Carmichael. Tamsin had her hand resting on Dicky's shoulder while they talked to someone. She looked up at him as he spoke, and Ed imagined her looking up at his face admiringly like that.

'Look at Ed Rawlins!' laughed Alice, pointing, 'he simply drools over Tamsin Carmichael! He's

110

not the only one.'

Gilbert wanted her to keep her voice down. She was drunk. It wasn't funny drunk, or sweet, it was just dull, coarser-than-usual drunk and he hated to see it.

'I'm going to talk to Mackereth. Duty chatting. See you later.'

Alice looked around at everyone and smiled. She took another drink from a tray; she wasn't sure what it was, a champagne cocktail, possibly. She wanted to adjust her roll-on, which was digging into her hips, but she couldn't do it while people could see. She smoothed it down at the back, hoping it wasn't spoiling the line of her dress. The dress was new and she'd had it made for the party. It was dark-red shot silk and extremely glamorous. Alice had taken two hours to get ready and they'd been late. She had hated arriving. She looked around the room knowing she looked prettier than most of the women there, and that at thirty she was younger than most of them too, but she felt terribly self-conscious. She smiled at Bridget Cargill and tried to remember when she and Gilbert had last made love. She'd just had her period and it certainly wasn't since then. She tried to remember when her last period had been . . . before Lewis broke up, when they had the Johnsons to lunch; she didn't think they'd made love more than once since then, either.

'Alice, Gilbert run off has he?'

Claire Carmichael was in front of her.

'Yes, but only with that accounts man.'

Claire made small talk while Alice drank. Across the room, Ed fought bravely through the crowd to Tamsin, who was lovely but on her way somewhere else and he had to endure being interviewed about school by Dicky. Gilbert found Mackereth in the drawing room and they talked numbers for an hour, while in the hall—after little Kit Carmichael had reluctantly left him for nursery duty—Lewis was alone. He thought he'd see what he could find to drink. He went into Dicky's study.

The study was empty, with a fire burning and one lamp lit on Dicky's desk. The rest of the room was dark. There were drinks laid out on a tray and Lewis took the gin bottle, went over to the window, opened it and stepped out onto the grass. The grass was frozen hard and brittle to walk on and the cold was a relief. He opened his bottle and wandered off towards the garages. He could hear the talking from the party, and the music, and he still felt hot from being inside, and the gin was very good and he drank slowly. He had to hold the bottle down when he passed a couple of drivers, who were looking at Dicky's cars and talking about them, but they hardly looked up. He walked on down to the tennis court. The night was black, with a small, silver moon high up in a blank empty sky.

*   *   *

Kit held her collection of things in a napkin and cast her eye around the room for more. Her eyes were hot with tiredness and she felt restless. She found a handkerchief, quite clean, with the initials T.M. on it and tried to work out whose it was. The fire was a smouldering heap of ashes and cigarette ends, almost more cigarette ends than logs. She opened the window and the cold air came straight in and moved the hanging smoke around the room.

She went into the hall. Her father was there.

'Hello, Daddy. Look.'

'What's that?'

She tipped her spoils onto the hall table. 'Things people left.'

'Why aren't you in bed? It's past ten.'

'Mummy said I needn't.'

'You should have gone to bed when the children were taken home. You weren't meant to stay up.'

'Sorry.'

'Go now.'

She hated the way he spoke. She felt cross and irritated by it all. He was the main one. Of all the people she hated for their smugness and bullying and picking on Lewis and talking like they were better than everybody, of everybody she hated, he was the main one. She bent to pick up the stiletto shoe, which had fallen, and didn't look at him.

'All right.'

'Did you hear me? Go now and don't speak to me in that tone.'

'I said all right!'

She straightened up and he smacked her, with a hard open hand across the face.

They both stood there waiting.

He had never smacked her before; he'd never touched her at all that she could remember. Claire came out into the hall; she stood away from them, watching from the door and not saying anything.

Kit's face burned, but she didn't touch it and she didn't look away from Dicky, she kept her eyes on his face. She saw excitement.

He raised his hand again, quickly, and she flinched, and hated herself for flinching, but he didn't hit her; he smiled at her, and they both knew

113

this was the beginning.

'Go up to bed,' he said.

'Good night, Daddy,' said Kit, 'good night, Mummy.'

She went upstairs and Dicky turned to Claire.

'Why don't you get on with what you were doing?' he said.

*   *   *

Kit went up the stairs and along the landing to her room, which was past Tamsin's and on the other side of the house from Dicky and Claire's rooms. She sat on her bed.

She felt she was meeting an inevitable fate. Part of her wanted to run away and cry and find somebody to save her, anybody at all, but most of her felt strong, like a soldier. She thought of being brave and coping. She thought, I'll have to be very strong to manage this, and I won't let him see how frightened I am. She got up and went down the corridor to the bathroom.

The bathroom was freezing, she could see her breath and there was cold air like a knife coming between the window and the sill. She undressed, shivering, and wishing she had brought her dressing gown. She pulled off her hated party dress and stepped on it for warmth while she took off her underwear. She saw in her knickers that she was bleeding. For a silly moment she thought it was because of her father hitting her and then she realised it was her first period. She thought of Tamsin and Claire and their resigned and conspiratorial conversations about the curse, and she felt tired and at the beginning of something she

114

had no interest in. She held her dress up over herself and ran barefoot down the corridor to Tamsin's room, with the gloomy portraits of other people's ancestors staring down at her as she ran. She looked in the dressing table and found all the clumsy, quasi-medical equipment she knew you had to use and, holding it, ran back to the bathroom again.

She dealt with it and put on her nightdress and did her teeth. She wrapped the knickers in lavatory paper and hid them at the bottom of the wastepaper basket. She could hear her mother and Tamsin talking over one another and laughing as they came up the stairs. Looking into the bathroom mirror she saw that she still had the red mark on her face from Dicky's hand hitting her. It wasn't a complete print because his hand was much bigger than her cheek and hadn't fitted on.

CHAPTER THREE

1953

At the beginning of the Easter holidays Alice met Lewis at Waterford station. She stood at the end of the platform wrapped in her coat with her fur hat pulled down. Lewis thought she looked like Anna Karenina and wished she'd jump under the train. Anna Karenina made him remember little Kit Carmichael for a moment; he wondered if she'd ever finished it. Alice didn't throw herself under the train; she waved in that awful false way she had and started towards him.

'Hello, Lewis! Jolly cold. I've got the car. Come on.'

*   *   *

When Gilbert came home that evening he paid the taxi and stood on the gravel as it drove away. He had to make himself go inside. Alice paused brightly in her drink-making and greeted him. Lewis began to smile. Gilbert looked at his son's face. He saw Elizabeth and Lewis's own increasing presence. It was unsettling. He saw Lewis, observed, stop smiling. The three of them stood, forming a triangle—schoolboy, father and wife—speechless, facing three weeks together.

*   *   *

On Saturday, they had breakfast as usual. Alice had all her make-up on except her lipstick, because she knew it was common to wear lipstick at breakfast, but couldn't have a bare face. Mary brought in the tea and toast and a warm dish of sausages and tomatoes because it was the weekend. Gilbert wore his old jacket instead of his suit. Lewis sat with his back to the window where he always sat. Gilbert's paper was folded on his side plate. He picked it up.

Alice ate with quick looks around the room, a constant performance of finding something interesting to look at that she kept up through all of every meal. Sometimes she remarked on what she saw, 'We must get the hedge cut', 'Those flowers need changing'; today she said, 'It's a shame the weather turned colder for the weekend.'

116

Lewis ate fast and looked at his plate and tried to ignore the silence and tried not to feel each dead moment touch him.

He was reading *Crime and Punishment,* which he chose because it was long with tiny print and he thought it would be boring enough to pass the time with and not go too crazy, but now he was getting lost in the claustrophobia of it and wished he'd never started it, but couldn't stop. He couldn't read at mealtimes, and there was nothing to distract from the fact they were all together and how bad that was. Very often Gilbert and Alice were fairly drunk by supper anyway, so it wasn't as bad as lunch and breakfast, but sometimes the being drunk was worse—you could see what was underneath.

After breakfast he went upstairs and lay on his bed. He stared at the crack in the ceiling that he'd always stared at when he was little, that had been a river and a coastline and a cliff edge. It wasn't any of those things; it was a crack in the ceiling and he wanted it to split apart and the house to fall into rubble.

He picked up his watch. It wasn't yet ten o'clock. His room was cold and dim and he could hear rooks in the woods and a car drove by the house. He had two and a half hours until lunchtime and the afternoon after that and the endless night and breakfast and church and school and just empty waiting for something better that never happened.

He stood up. He took his coat and his birthday money and he left the house and walked to the station in the dead cold weather and bought a ticket to London.

He was very cold and frightened his father

would come in the car to take him back, but he didn't come, and the train arrived and Lewis got onto it.

He watched Waterford station getting smaller as the train got faster, until he couldn't see the station any more and was on his own and away from them. The suffocating feeling left him and he felt bright and fast and full of something good.

*   *   *

It started to snow, wetly, as he got off the train and he left the station and walked down towards the river and then along it. There were high buildings around him and the pavements shone with rain and melting snowflakes. It was almost dark now, and bitter cold and his hair got wet with the snow and he felt connected and alive. There were people walking by and talking to each other and nobody paid him any attention. Black cars passed him; their tyres spattered the dirt and slush.

On one side of him was the water and all the boats on it, moving slowly with coal on them and covered loads and men standing at the front of them with lights. On his other side was the street and the buildings. He was surprised when he saw the Houses of Parliament and Westminster Bridge, and it seemed amazing to him that all of these things and places he recognised were just there in front of him, laid out for him to look at.

He walked along Whitehall and into Trafalgar Square and the city was vast and battered and mysterious. There were cars and people, but also a feeling of giant brokenness that was romantic.

He walked to the National Gallery and stood in

front of it. It was unlit, and he pictured all the paintings on the walls in the dark inside and it was a nice thought. He saw big dark rooms with Caravaggios and Constables and huge canvases, crowded with angels. He carried on walking, past the gallery and up Charing Cross Road and saw the theatres ahead of him. There were more people around him now; people in evening dress outside the theatres and others in coats and hats pushing past. There were women wrapped in furs and the sound of metal tipped heels on stone as they climbed out of taxis, and the noise of conversation. He thought the plays must be about to start because the pavements and the steps to the theatres were crowded. He kept his head down, suddenly thinking he might see some friend of his father and have to explain himself. He turned off the main road into a street that was much narrower and dark.

The small dark street felt completely different. Behind were lights and taxis and people you might know and ahead it was just strange to him. There were people and pubs, but they looked different and even the sound of them was different.

He looked at the people drinking and standing in the street talking, and just the way they talked was incredible to him; he couldn't understand them half the time. It was like another country—or a mess of other countries—and he passed coffee bars with dirty windows you could hardly see through, that were full of people. He looked at all the women walking around without men and it took him ages to realise they were prostitutes. He'd heard about prostitutes, he knew there *were* prostitutes—and he even knew some of the things they did for you—but he just didn't expect to see them walking about on the same streets. He was shocked and then delighted with it. This was real life and he could just get on a train and be in it and nobody knew him here.

He walked up and down the streets; Lisle Street, Old Compton Street, Frith Street, Greek Street, and he tried to remember where he was, but really only knew that it was the roughest thing he'd ever seen and that he loved it. He stopped at the end of a street, not knowing which way to go, and saw a black unmarked doorway on the corner opposite. Some people stopped by it and a panel slid aside for the unseen doorman to check who was there, then the door opened, letting them in, and closed quickly behind them and Lewis forgot about going anywhere else and stayed, watching.

The rain was dripping down the back of his neck and he was very cold and shaking with it. He didn't want to go home. Some more people knocked and the panel slid back again and when the door opened Lewis heard music—jazz trumpet and drums—and he crossed the road, quickly, towards the sound. He tried to get close enough to the people so that he'd look as if he was with them, but the door closed in his face and he felt desperation.

He had been too long on the wet streets in the dark. He didn't know where he was, he didn't know what to do next and home was drawing him and mocking him in his child's attempt at escape. He should have had a stick with a handkerchief on the end, he should have had boiled sweets in a paper bag in his pocket.

Then the panel in the black door scraped open. Lewis looked for eyes, but saw only darkness.

'Come on then,' said a reluctant voice.

The door opened. Lewis stepped inside. The noise and warm smoke-filled air touched him and he looked for the person behind the door, but glimpsed only a white shirt and crooked bow tie. He smelled whisky and was transported, briefly, to his father's chair at home. Then he started down the stairs, forgetting.

The walls were painted black, and peeling. Lewis could see the end of a bar at the bottom of the stairs and people's legs and a woman's green dress, glittering, as she climbed onto a bar stool. The noise made it easier—nobody was watching him—and when he got to the bottom of the stairs he stopped. There was a band playing, and a crowd at the bar, but it was still early and there were empty tables and a damp chill in the air.

Lewis tried to get to the bar, hunching deeper into his coat and feeling in his pocket for his birthday money. He had to turn sideways and put his back to the woman in the green dress to do it, looking down, trying to get served and be invisible at the same time.

'Do you mind,' said the green-dress woman and Lewis saw he'd pushed her arm and was going to apologise when the barman saw him.

'How old are you?'

The barman was black and spoke with an accent and Lewis stared at him blankly a moment before remembering to speak.

'Eighteen.'

'You want to get me into trouble? When's your birthday?'

'December.'

The green-dress woman laughed and the

barman smiled a big smile and looked at her.

'All right, Miss Jeanie?'

'All right, Jack,' said the woman.

'What'll it be?'

'Gin.'

'Gin and?'

'Gin. Please.'

Jack poured the gin into a short glass and pushed it across the bar.

'Thank you.'

Lewis handed him money and hoped it was enough. Jack put his change down on the bar and turned away to serve somebody else. Lewis looked down at his drink. He wasn't used to glasses. He drank half of it straight down. His fingers still hurt with coldness and he looked around at the band and at the other people and waited for the gin to reach him.

The band was a five-piece jazz band, playing songs Lewis knew from his childhood, but almost unrecognisable. It was like *Alice in Wonderland,* things were the same but different. The drummer was sweating and lit by a white light, and Lewis had never seen anyone that age sweating like that, like they'd been cross-country running, and never seen a white light filled with dust and smoke, and never seen a saxophone or people dance the way the couple by the stage were dancing.

He finished his drink. His hand was shaking, but not with cold or fear, just trembling with all the new things, and he had to concentrate hard to keep from smiling and to keep from betraying himself. He felt braver now and turned back to the bar. It was much more crowded since Lewis had come in; Jack was busy, putting drinks onto a tray the waitress was holding. Lewis waited and looked at the bottles behind the bar and the mirror behind them and the people reflected.

He saw the woman in the green dress. She was next to him. They looked as if they were together. She was looking down, getting cigarettes from her bag, which was green like her dress. Her skin was very pale and she had dark copper hair, piled up, with a diamond clip. Seeing her in the mirror was like watching a painting or a film and Lewis was absorbed in it and in looking at the woman. She lifted her head suddenly—turning to the boy next to her, and Lewis realised she was looking at him.

'So what's the story?' she said.

She was close to him. She had painted lips.

'A kid like you. What are you doing here?'

'I'm sorry—'

'Why?'

'You want me to leave.'

'Did I say that?'

Jack leaned across the bar to him.

'Another?'

Lewis nodded. Jack took his glass and the woman turned her eyes on Lewis again.

'My name's Jeanie Lee. What's yours?'

'Lewis.'

'Lewis what?'

'Lewis Aldridge.' Lewis had a sudden picture of it in ink, at the top of essays at school, but she didn't seem to know it was a child's name, she didn't laugh.

'You were looking at me, Lewis Aldridge. Do you always look at women like that?'

'Like what?'

'Dirty.'

123

He couldn't believe she'd said it. He tried not to look as shocked as he felt. He didn't know if he had looked at her like that or if he should apologise. She patted his cheek and he was embarrassed and didn't know how to feel about it.

'Don't worry about it, sweetie. It's not rude dirty, it's good dirty.'

She came near to him, scrutinising his face, as if she were counting the rings on a tree trunk.

'You're just a baby,' she said.

Lewis wasn't breathing. She was very close. Then she picked up her glass.

'I need to see some people. Don't go away,' she said.

She turned away from him and started talking to a short wide man who looked like he slept in his suit. After a moment they both went into the back.

Jack put the new drink down in front of Lewis and he drank it quickly. He was still reeling from her talking to him and touching his face and calling him dirty. Jack carried on serving customers, shaking hands with some and calling others 'sir' and switching back and forth easily. Lewis sat at the bar waiting for Jeanie and thinking about women.

He thought of Tamsin Carmichael, and her prettiness was familiar and he knew all about it. It was to do with her coolness and the way she looked just like the girl you imagined yourself with. He'd thought about Tamsin a lot, because of course he would, but there was something obvious about wanting her, and he'd always been able to want her when he felt like it and forget her the rest of the time. He knew this made no sense because in real life she'd never have anything to do with him, but in his mind her prettiness was something he could walk away from. He thought of one of the master's wives at school who had been a bit of a pin-up for the older boys until she got pregnant. Lewis had never seen what it was about her. He thought about actresses and people's mothers, and how with people's mothers they weren't usually like women, but sometimes were; and it was unsettling and much easier if they weren't.

So Tamsin Carmichael was definitely a girl, and Mr Stevens's wife was definitely a woman, but this woman, this green-dress Jeanie Lee, she was nothing like either of them. She wasn't like people's mothers, she wasn't young or old, but she was beautiful. She'd asked him not to go away. He got another drink and waited for her, like she'd asked, and missed his train home and didn't care. Home seemed entirely distant and unreal and the music was very loud and the crowd thick and moving around him.

Finally Jeanie came out. He couldn't stop looking at her. He didn't try. She crossed the room to a table which had been empty all night. Her table, Lewis thought. She sat down. She looked up and met his eye as if she'd been waiting to do it, and gestured him over.

'Here—take this,' Jack handed him a soda water in a tall glass and Lewis took it to her, feeling conspicuous and strange.

'Well, sit,' she said, and he did.

The band was playing Cole Porter tunes and Lewis gripped the remains of his gin in his hand and tried not to stare at her. He knew he should say something. You were supposed to say things to girls. He didn't know what.

125

Her eyes were restless, looking past him at somebody, and he tried to think of conversation and failed. It didn't matter though, because she got up almost immediately and spoke to some people and when she sat down again she scanned the crowd like before, and Lewis might as well not have been there. She said a few things to him, not paying much attention, and when people stopped at the table and interrupted her she seemed happy to be, and never carried on talking to him or apologised.

It got late. She was the one who had wanted him to wait for her. She was the one who'd wanted him to sit with her and spoken to him so nicely like that, acting as if she liked him . . . He was hungry and he'd drunk too much and missed his train, and he didn't know what he was doing here anyway.

'What's up, baby boy?'

'Nothing. I have to go.'

'Where to?'

'It's late.'

'So where's home?'

'It doesn't matter.'

'Yes, it does.'

'It doesn't matter. I'm going.'

'Don't get up. You're angry.'

Looking down, 'No, I'm not.'

He knew it was crazy, how could he be angry? She didn't owe him anything, he didn't even know her and he wasn't anyone.

'Yes, you are. You're jealous.' She laughed and leaned in towards him and was gentle. 'Don't be jealous. I have to talk to people. It's Teddy's place, my brother, it's sort of my place. Baby . . . It's my job, all right?'

126

She was talking him round. She was bothering to make him feel better. He tried not to smile.

'What?'

'Nothing.'

'What?'

He looked at her bare arms and her mouth and her dress, gleaming. He lifted his hand from the table, thinking about whether he had the nerve, and how it would feel, to touch her. Jeanie watched him. Slowly, he put his hand on her and didn't hold her, but moved his hand down her arm, feeling the skin and the rest of her under the skin. She looked at him and she went very still. His instinct told him he had her somehow. He thought he might kiss her, but he didn't dare. He carried on looking at her and he saw in her look that the hand on her arm was enough, she wasn't thinking about anything else at all, she was just thinking about him. Somebody came up to the table, a man and woman, a rich-looking couple, slumming.

'Hello, Miss Lee, it's so nice to see you.'

It wasn't like before, now she didn't look up immediately. She exchanged a look with him and took her eyes away slowly and with regret, and while she talked to the people it was as if she was ignoring him, but she wasn't, they were still together. The couple went away and Jeanie looked back at him.

'Do that again,' she said.

He put his hand on her arm again, with his thumb on the inside of it, where the skin was very white and softer, and frowned with thinking how it must feel to her.

'Yes, like that,' she said, 'baby.'

They weren't doing anything, they weren't doing

anything you shouldn't do in front of people, but it was as if they were. It was everything. He could see she felt like he did, that every part of her could feel him. The crowd was thinning out and they carried on sitting and not talking about all that much. She took his hand and looked at it and they compared hands, and he looked at her rings and she told him about the different ones.

'I've got nowhere to go,' he said.

'That's a good one.'

'No. I really haven't. I missed my last train.'

'Does your mum know you're here?'

He was jolted.

'No.'

'Does she just let you run all over town?'

'No.'

'Do you know how old I am?'

He shook his head.

'Well, I'm not telling you.'

'All right.'

'You can sleep on the settee in the office if you like.'

*　　　*　　　*

Jeanie went at two and Lewis walked her up the stairs and they stood in the dark doorway for a bit. It was the same doorway he had watched from the other side of the road at the beginning of the night, locked out from everything, unknowing.

'Nice, aren't you?' she said.

It was very cold and she got inside his coat with him. She was looking up at him, close like before.

He kissed her. He kissed her and they kissed for a long time, while her taxi waited. Jeanie pressed herself hard against him and Lewis felt lost in her and in the wanting her and he could have pulled her apart and had to make himself be gentle. He held her and there was the wanting her, but also gratitude and feeling lucky, and he almost didn't dare touch her at all, she seemed so precious.

'This is like being a kid,' she said and she put her face into his neck by his collar and he could feel her smiling, and he couldn't remember anything so sweet ever happening to him.

He couldn't remember ever having been touched, not touched and held, like this, or in any way at all, and it made him hurt inside it felt so sweet to him.

When she left, nothing else seemed surprising or strange. He went back down inside and Jack showed him the office and where he could sleep and it wasn't an adventure, like it would have been the day before, it was just the thing that happened after Jeanie left.

CHAPTER FOUR

The next day Lewis let himself out of the club into the street, which was full of bright white sunshine and very cold. He walked to Victoria. It was a Sunday and he nearly missed the only train and had to run along the deserted platform and jump on as it eased away from him. It felt as if he was the only person on the train. It felt like a different train going faster through the sunny morning.

*   *   *

The road from the station was quiet and bright. It was colder than in London and the frost hadn't gone completely from the verges and was still in patches under the trees where the sun hadn't melted it. It was all still, with the sharp sun and the sky high and blue like it hadn't been for a long time. Lewis took deep breaths of cold air and felt everything in him alive to it and smiling.

*   *   *

Kit thought that the cold in churches was the cold of death. It wasn't like cold outside or anywhere else; the air was flat and smelled of stone that was like graves. There were paraffin heaters on wheels at the front, facing the pews, that made no difference at all, but hissed. She tucked her hands under her arms. The more people came in, the better it was, and the smell of scent stopped the air being so deathlike. The organist started playing something shapeless, just for the people to come in to. The Nappers came, and talked to Dicky and Claire, and sat behind them.

'Deadly,' whispered Joanna.

'Slay me now,' said Kit.

The doors closed and the vicar walked down the aisle and turned to them. Joanna started to giggle behind her and Kit hid her face to stop from snorting.

'No Gilbert and Alice,' said Claire and Kit looked up.

It was true, first Sunday of the Easter holidays and no Lewis.

130

Lewis came off the road at the big bend, climbed the fence, and cut through the edge of the woods and across the garden to let himself into the back of the house.

It was late morning. He thought Alice and his father would still be at church. He didn't know what he was going to say to them and he didn't care—he wanted to eat something and he wanted to sleep, and needing those things was simple.

He came down the lawn and stopped. He could see through the window that his father and Alice and a uniformed policeman were in the drawing room.

He didn't move for a minute, but they'd seen him coming across the garden and there was nothing to do but go in. He went up to the house and opened the French doors and stepped into the room. The room was hot after the cold outside, with sun glaring through the glass. His father stood up.

'Lewis.'

'Sir?'

The policeman—it was Wilson—was by the fireplace.

'You're all right then?'

Lewis nodded, but Wilson hadn't said it to him, he'd said it to his father.

Alice got up and took Wilson into the hall. Gilbert and Lewis stood in the drawing room and looked at each other, and they heard her close the front door and the three of them were alone in the house again with all the houses near them, empty, and all the other people in the church.

131

'You're not at church,' said Lewis as Alice came back into the room.

Gilbert's voice was low.

'You didn't come home and we've been very worried. We didn't know what might have happened to you.'

'Nothing happened to me.'

'Just—be quiet, Lewis, please.'

Lewis was quiet. He wanted to be unaffected, he wanted to just think about Jeanie and not feel he was really there, but he couldn't.

'You were gone all night.'

'Yes, sir. I'm sorry.'

'If you run away again we'll have to think about sending you away to a special school. Do you know what that means?'

Gilbert came closer, addressing his blank face, angrier now and loud.

'Do you hear? There are places to send boys, places where you are taught to behave and where you can be controlled. You wouldn't come home for holidays like you do now. Your life would be very different, do you understand? The way you have behaved recently, the way you've been to me and to your stepmother, and now this running away . . . It's unacceptable, do you understand?'

Lewis was staring at his father's face so hard that the side of his vision was going dark.

'If you are in my house you will follow my rules, and if you can't do that you will be sent away, do you hear? We will send you away.'

Lewis nodded, it was an effort. He thought of saying, 'Please don't, please—' He looked at Alice, but she looked down at her hands in her lap.

'Now go upstairs and think about what I've said

and when you come down—if you come down—for lunch, I want to see a change in you. Go!'

*   *   *

The small white bedroom was his childhood room, and the room where his mother had sat on his bed and where he had lain awake and thought his thoughts all his life. His school trunk was open on the floor with things half out of it and waiting to be washed. There were his books on the shelves, some of them children's ones that he'd grown out of. He would be sent away. There was a place for people like him. He couldn't seem to make the things in the room stay still like they should. He stood in the middle of the breaking, moving room.

*   *   *

Downstairs Gilbert and Alice sat opposite one another by the hot fire, with one side of them warmed by it and the other arm and cheek chilled in the cold air of the room.

'Do you think he listened?' said Gilbert. 'Do you think it will make any difference?'

'You frightened him, I think.'

'I want to frighten him. I don't think he even heard. I don't think it made any difference at all.'

Alice looked into the fire and Gilbert turned his face to the cold garden.

*   *   *

Lewis went to the window. The glass was close to him; hard and thin. He had a sudden memory of

Jeanie holding him, and the sweetness of the feeling, and had shame about it.

He put his hand onto the cold glass pane. He felt far away from himself. He imagined putting his fist through it and the jagged hole in the pane and the points of glass still attached to the wood. He imagined dragging his wrist and his arm against them so they would cut into him. He didn't think he would feel it. He pictured putting his face through the glass and wondered if he would feel all the pieces cut him.

He closed his eyes to stop imagining it, but it was the same, picturing the glass going into him, needing to do it. His heart started going quickly, pushing the cold blood around. He turned from the window. He realised he'd been scraping his arm with his other hand and stopped doing it.

There was a sudden stillness like the gap between ticks on a clock, but the next tick never coming.

He couldn't hear talking downstairs, they must have been sitting silently. He thought of them sitting opposite one another, staring, not moving.

He went into the bathroom and shut the door and locked it. He stood at the mirror, and looked, and the need to damage himself took him over. All he could think of was hurting himself and how to do it. He picked up his father's razor. It was an old-fashioned one, the kind you open. He opened the razor and looked at the blade. He knew he wouldn't feel it if he were to stick it right into himself—but the sight of the blade stopped him for a second. It had a power about it, the strength of the forbidden, and it was fascinating. It was beautiful.

134

His hand rested on the basin, holding the razor, and he waited. He felt cool and curious, like he could do anything and it didn't matter. He held out his left arm and pushed up the sleeve with the hand holding the razor. He pressed the blade against his skin and immediately, just at the feel of the sharp blade on the skin, his heart went quicker and blood came back into him. He was breathless with wanting to do it. He could taste the need to hurt himself in his mouth and, when he did, he cried with the relief of it. He made a long cut down his forearm and the red line filled with bright blood very quickly and started to run. He was frightened of the blood and trying not to cut too deep, hurting himself just enough—and it did hurt, and he held his arm over the basin and rested his forehead on the edge of the basin, and the sadness and hurting were comforting to him because he could feel them.

He waited, with his head bowed, till the arm wasn't running blood any more and rinsed it off in cold water and went back to his room to try and find something to put on it.

He felt pathetic and small and stupid now. What a stupid crazy sick thing to do, he told himself; if they know about this they will put you in a special school, they'll put you in a hospital . . .

He found a school shirt that had ink on the sleeve and tore it into pieces and bound himself with it. It was tricky to do it up and he had to use his teeth to help with the knot, but once he was bandaged it was better, the cotton felt tight and steady on his arm, and he put his sleeve down and did it up. He lay on his bed and let his thoughts rest.

He wasn't used to being up late and he hadn't eaten since breakfast the day before. His mind felt still. His arm began to sting and ache under the cotton of the torn-up shirt. He concentrated on that and waited for Alice to call for lunch, but she didn't call; she knocked on the door and came in before he had a chance to sit up, but then he did sit up, against the headboard, and looked at her.

'Are you all right?' she asked.

Lewis thought that in no sense could he consider himself all right. He nodded. She looked very nervous, and wanting to please, and it made it difficult. She hovered in the doorway.

'Lewis . . . Is it something I've done?'

He considered this, and thought what a silly question it was.

'Have I hurt your feelings? You know I want what's best for you.'

She was doing what she always did. He was supposed to feel sorry for her and tell her it wasn't her fault. She wanted him guilty and herself absolved. He could ignore her most of the time, but when she got that face there was nothing he could do; even knowing she was making him feel it, he couldn't help feeling sorry for her. He tried to think of the best way to shut her up: give her what she wanted without having to go into anything.

'I'm hungry,' he said.

She smiled at him. She was so relieved she gave him a big smile.

'It's lunchtime,' she said.

136

CHAPTER FIVE

Taking his father's razor like that, and cutting his arm with it, had scared him. He promised himself he wouldn't do it again. It worried him that the cutting felt so good; it was extreme and much worse than anything he'd done before, but it was the way it worked, the release he'd felt, and the rush of it, that scared him most. How do you not do a thing that you know will help? How do you stop yourself doing a bad thing if it only hurts you?

He had decided never to cut himself again, but he had cut himself again. The second time he did it was about a month later, when the arm had healed, and then again just a few days after that. Then he stopped counting. He didn't think about it at school; it waited for him at home—the razor, neatly folded in the white bathroom, drawing him. After he'd cut himself he had to clean up and be organised and make sure nobody knew, and there was ritual in that. The basin had to have no blood left in it, the razor had to be put back where it was. Each time he did it the release was more powerful and the shame afterwards was greater. It became a habit, and normal, and the rush of it and the ritual and the shame became normal, too.

*   *   *

He hadn't been able to get up to London until the next holidays and the fear of his father almost stopped him, but Lewis had been holding the memory of Jeanie close to him all through the long

137

spring term. He had been at school and a child again, but he knew he had held Jeanie and kissed her and not felt like a child then. He pinned all his desire and all his hope onto her, and even his father couldn't keep him from that.

* * *

He slipped out of the house on the last Saturday of the holidays. He got to the club long before it opened and went to a pub to wait. He got a drink and sat in the corner with it. The pub smelled of beer and the windows were dirty. There were stains on the red seats and two old men near him talking about dogs.

He had got drunk in the pub, but not felt quieter like he normally did, just agitated and frightened about seeing Jeanie and angry with himself for getting that way. He had drunk some more and then gone back to the club and knocked again, but there was nobody there and he was angry, and when he hit the door he couldn't feel it.

'Hey, man. Hey, Lewis, isn't it? Remember me?'

Lewis turned around. It was the barman, Jack. He was standing just near him and Lewis hadn't seen him and it took him a while to look at him properly now.

'. . . Jack.'

'Right. Jack. Come with me, man.'

* * *

Jack took him to a café and bought him a pie and some tea, and smoked roll-ups and chatted to the waitress about the police and licensing and raids

138

on places they'd both heard about. The pie had thick brown gravy that shone, and the tea was brown too, and very strong. Lewis put sugar in it and drank it while it was hot enough to burn. When he'd finished, Jack pushed his tobacco tin over the table and Lewis shook his head.

'You came for Jeanie?'

Lewis nodded. Jack picked up his hat and examined the sweat band inside it minutely.

'Where's home, Lewis?'

Lewis had a feeling there was going to be a lecture. Jack had a look teachers sometimes got. Lewis was grateful to him, but he didn't want to talk about anything.

'Where's home for you?' he asked.

Jack nodded, accepting. 'I have a flat I share with another fella just up the road,' he said, and then, 'Jamaica.'

Lewis had a vague picture of his school atlas and little islands in paper blue sea.

'Lewis . . . you look to me like a boy in trouble.'

There was no arguing with that, but nothing to say about it, either.

'What time will she come?'

Jack smiled at him. 'Jeanie pleases herself. Come back with me, I have to take a delivery. You can help me.'

Jack stayed up on the pavement and handed boxes to Lewis down in the cellar, who took them and stacked them. He got hot and took his shirt off to work because he didn't have another one for the evening. Jack peered down at him. It had started to rain and he was wet from taking the boxes off the lorry. He laughed.

'Forty-proof sweat, man!'

139

Afterwards Jack showed him where he could wash and Lewis put his shirt back on and they sat in the office for a while 'resting', and later on Jack counted out the float in the bar while an old man swept the floor.

The club opened and filled up, slowly, and Lewis sat at the bar and waited for Jeanie. He kept his eyes on the stairs and waited for her. Jack told him about the trumpet player who was going to play and how they'd booked him, and Lewis was interested and happy to hear about it, but he felt he'd been waiting for a long time. It was very busy that night and the people and the dark and the smoke seemed to press against him. Jeanie would never come and the whole pitiful day had been leading to this—then he saw her coming down the stairs. First he saw her shoes, and then her legs. She wasn't in green this time, she was wearing black. He saw black shoes, fishnets, and the bottom of her fur coat, wrapped around her with nothing showing underneath it, and then her gloved hand on the rail. She had a big beaded bracelet over her gloves that was pearl coloured and shone. She paused and her eyes scanned the room and she saw him and wasn't surprised. She walked past the people standing at the bar and came over. Lewis wanted to get up, but didn't move.

'Hey, Jack,' she said, keeping her eyes on Lewis.

'Miss Jeanie,' said Jack, not turning.

'Waifs and strays.'

'I couldn't leave him in the street.'

Jeanie smiled at Lewis.

'Don't you look sweet,' she said, and kissed him on the cheek.

Lewis couldn't think of anything to say that

140

didn't sound stupid, so he kept quiet.

'Where've you been then?'

'Nowhere,' he said.

'I know what you mean,' she said. 'Jack looking after you?'

Lewis didn't know what to say. He needed her and he didn't know her and he was helpless. She moved up close to him and he put his head down into her neck, forgetting the people around them, and held her wrist, very carefully between his thumb and forefinger, looking at it.

'Hey,' she said, but she said it gently.

'I've been waiting.'

'And you wait so well,' she said and laughed. 'Come with me.'

Whatever he'd imagined—and his imagination had been vague—it wasn't this. She had taken him into the office at the back, where he'd slept before. There were no windows and a bright bulb hanging from the ceiling. He hadn't imagined, in his blurry schoolboy plan, that she would be so businesslike, or that he would have had her on a sofa, or that when he did have her it would feel like it did.

At first there was the need for her, needing to touch her and get to her and not knowing how, and then, when he was inside her, it was exquisite, and overwhelming. He shut his eyes and going into her was like going into the blackness inside his own head, and he had cried when he came and wanted to keep on crying like a child and had to stop himself.

When it was over she had laughed. The sound of it was shocking to him. He didn't know how he felt, but he couldn't have laughed. Then she stopped laughing and clambered out from under him. She

141

became very practical, fixing her face and her clothes and wiping herself, and Lewis watched her and felt lonely, but it was nice to watch her.

'Don't worry,' she said, 'I can't have children.'

He looked at the back of her; he couldn't see her face, except for her mouth in the mirror as she painted it.

'Why not?'

'None of your business.'

'Do you mind if I use the telephone?' he said.

'No, I don't mind if you use the telephone.'

She was laughing at him. He stood up and went to it. She seemed to realise he didn't want to be overheard, or else she didn't want to know.

'You've got lipstick on your face. I'll see you out there,' she said and unlocked the door, and left him.

He went over to the mirror and got the lipstick off. He looked around the room. The bottom half of the wall was painted dark green with white above. The sofa had a rip in it. He picked up the phone.

'Guildford 645,' he said to the operator and after a while he heard Alice's voice and got through.

'It's Lewis.'

'Lewis! Where are you?'

'I'll go to Euston for the school train. Will you be there, with my trunk?' His heart was beating very hard.

'What? Are you all right?'

'Will you be there? I need my trunk for school.'

'Yes. Of course. Your father—'

He put the phone down. Jeanie took him home with her that time.

*   *   *

Lewis had nearly missed the train in the morning and when he got to school he was put into detention for not being in proper uniform. It made him smile to have a child's punishment for sleeping with a woman and not being a child any more. He had to translate some passages from *The Odyssey*, and he wrote about Odysseus trying to sail home to Ithaca and remembered he had used to write stories about heroes. He sat in the detention room with his writing drying on the lines and tried to remember what his stories had been about and what the heroes had fought for, but he couldn't remember, and the light faded from the room as he sat there. After a while the master waiting with him stood up and collected his pages and put them in the rubbish bin in the corner and let him go up to his room.

*   *   *

When he was a little boy Lewis had seen his life in sections; before and after his father had come home and then, later, with and without his mother. The section of life he felt himself to be in now had a more common, universally recognised watershed. It was before and after Jeanie. The before had the sweetness he felt kissing her, and her being close to him that first time, and the after had the familiar coldness he felt when he had slept with her and ever since.

It was an odd affair, even to Lewis. He saw Jeanie just a few times each holidays—when he could get away from home, and bear the prospect of the consequences—and she hardly asked him where he'd been. He didn't even know if she knew he'd been at school until one day she'd said, 'It's been ages', and Lewis, feeling a small delight that she'd noticed, confessed, 'I've been at school.' Jeanie had laughed again, opening her mouth wide, while he waited, nervous, and then she said, 'I suppose posh boys don't leave so young, do they?'

At first he had tried to hide his cut up arm from her, but she had seen it, and never said anything. Mostly she was sweet to him, but he never knew quite what she would be like. Sometimes he'd have to wait in the club all evening before she noticed him and he got used to waiting and would talk to Jack and the waitresses, and the evenings without Jeanie were often easier and lighter than the evenings with, except for the need for her tugging at him. It made Lewis feel free to be a different person when he was in London and when he was with Jeanie, but it made him feel like nothing too, just invisible and that he deserved to be. A part of him was still a child, with a child's need to be watched over and comforted, and Jeanie didn't see him; even when he was in her bed with his arms around her, he felt entirely alone.

Before and after Jeanie, before and after the club, before and after jazz, and Soho, and knowing somebody who was black, and gin out of glasses, and learning to drive and smoking . . . Jeanie had taught him both of those last, and he would have loved her just for that. When he started smoking he couldn't believe it—he hadn't had any idea they made you feel like that; grown-ups smoked and

144

didn't give any indication that the tops of their heads were coming off, or that they couldn't think straight. He supposed you must get used to it. He didn't know how anyone could smoke a pipe; his father did and it was horrible and he couldn't imagine how you'd start. Cigarettes were bad enough to begin with—although the hit of them was almost as good as drinking when you did—but a pipe, a pipe was just ugly and complicated and for old people. He'd never do that.

At home he was careful to hide himself; he never uncovered his arms, he barely looked Alice in the eye. Even when she tried to be kind he turned away from her, but all the time he hoped, shamefully, in his child's heart, that she would notice him, and hold him, and help. The bad things he did had been useful at first, but now they were stronger than he was. He knew he needed her help, or somebody's. He scared himself.

CHAPTER SIX

Alice had her new dress laid out on the bed and the different shoes she might put it with arranged nearby. She could hear Gilbert dressing next door and the familiar sounds of the wardrobe door opening and his footsteps.

'Gilbert?'

'Alice.'

She put on her stockings and sat at her dressing table and looked into her own eyes and tried to see deep into herself.

'What is it?' He was in the doorway. 'Aren't you

dressed? They'll be here in less than an hour.'

'Gilbert?'

'What?'

'My period is late.'

There was a pause.

'How late?'

'A week.'

'It's been late before . . . Well. We'll see.'

'Gilbert . . .'

'Don't get your hopes up.'

'I'm not. A whole week, though.' He sat on the bed. She shouldn't have told him. 'Wouldn't you be happy?' she said.

'You know I would be. It's been a very long time for you. Waiting. I know that.'

'Then we'd be a proper family.'

'I know.'

She got up and went over and knelt in front of him.

'I shouldn't be excited.'

He stroked her face.

'You're looking very pretty,' he said. 'Let's just wait and see. Try not to think about it.'

'No. I'm not.'

'It never helps.'

'I know!'

'Get ready now. They'll be here soon.'

'I'm getting ready.'

*   *   *

Dicky Carmichael stood in the hall and tapped his watch and waited. The big house was all around him and he knew where each of the servants were and his wife and his younger daughter and the

146

state of each room; how tidy or how warm and whether empty or being used for something; and he felt his control and he was satisfied with it. Except that he missed Tamsin so much. The house without her felt wrong; almost under his hand and yet not quite under his hand. When she went to London it was practically intolerable not knowing where she was. He pictured her at parties, he imagined her being flirted with and he knew all of her dresses and wondered which one she was in and if she was warm enough and how late she was staying up and who with. Sometimes he pictured faceless boys taking her out onto terraces, or into strange bedrooms, and what they might do to her—what he had done to girls at that age—and he pictured their hands on her and had to control himself, and try to forget.

'Claire! Katherine! Will you come down now!'

Kit was sitting on her window seat, reading. She didn't want to go down one minute before she had to. She'd spent the morning in the woods trying to light campfires with damp sticks and getting scorched and watery-eyed from smoke, and Claire had shouted at her and made her change. She chewed the end of her plait and turned the page.

'Katherine! NOW!'

That was the tone that said, if you don't come now I'll save it up for later and if you displease me I'll belt you. Kit wasn't going to be bullied. She read another paragraph, just to show him, and then got up slowly.

She came down the stairs and watched her father and mother as they put on their gloves, not speaking to each other.

Lewis was lying on his bed. He wasn't drunk enough for lunch with the Carmichaels. He didn't think you could be drunk enough for lunch with the Carmichaels. He heard Alice laugh. He called it her 'love me, love me' laugh. He lay back and shut his eyes and heard the car arrive and thought about getting up.

'Lewis! They're here.'

He had a bottle of gin under the bed and he stood up to see if he should have some more of it now or save it for later, when Dicky and Claire and Alice and Gilbert were in full flow. Later, he decided.

He washed his face in the bathroom and made sure his sleeve was down and done up. It was, but there was dried blood on it. He went back to his room and put on a clean shirt and went downstairs.

. *   *   *

Claire and Alice stood by the door to the garden looking up at the bare winter border. Kit was in a chair by the fire, biting her thumb nail. Dicky and Gilbert stood in front of the fire with drinks.

Lewis sat at the card table by the window and went invisible.

'And alchemilla is so pretty,' said Claire, looking at the bare earth.

'Well, it is, but the slugs always eat it.'

'Hostas.'

'Oh hostas, sorry, not alchemilla. Alchemilla . . . pretty when it rains.'

'What about some campanula in there? That

might cheer it up.'

'Yes . . .'

'It is rather cottagey, but it's not a large bed, is it?'

'Campanula is pretty,' said Alice.

Lewis stared straight ahead. Come on Alice, he thought, tell her you don't know what they are, stick up for yourself.

'I thought a rose would be nice,' offered Alice.

'Don't you think you have enough roses?'

Kit looked at Lewis, and he saw her looking and she looked away again. She should stop chewing that plait and biting her nails, it bordered on self-cannibalism. He watched his father and Dicky at the fireplace and marvelled at Gilbert's ability to laugh so very jovially at Dicky's stories. Gilbert rocked slightly on his heels, which made him look like a dog waiting to have a ball thrown for him.

Gilbert's threats of special school hadn't materialised. Somehow the very bad consequences of Lewis's behaviour never did seem to happen. If Lewis was careful, he could keep it all under control, and still get by at school, just about. He just had to balance it right. He just had to keep control.

'Of course, it looked all right in the summer,' said Alice, and Lewis agreed with her, everything had looked all right in the summer.

The summer had been long and lazy and there had been ecstasy in it, even in the solitude. There had been London, a few times, and just the beauty of being alive and hoping. In winter it was harder to feel like that.

Kit stole another glance at him and wondered what was going on in his head. How could he just

149

sit like that? So still? He was staring at the wall and everybody else was pretending he wasn't there, or that it was normal to have someone sit like that and look so separate and—she thought about it— to look so wrong.

'I think it's time for lunch,' said Alice, and they went into the dining room.

There was something in aspic to start with. They ate with small mouthfuls and talked about the golf club and possible changes in the rules of membership. Lewis's arm was hurting him and itching; he rubbed it against his leg and felt the cuts move and thought maybe they'd opened up. He excused himself and went upstairs. In his room, he rolled up his sleeve and saw the cuts were bleeding—if he didn't stop them, he'd bleed on through his shirt. He felt sick and tired and didn't want to go back down. He took a hit of gin from the bottle under his bed and then went to the bathroom and bandaged it up. He was a little drunk and it was always tricky with one hand. One of the cuts was too deep and went too far into the flesh, that was why it had opened up the way it had and it was hurting.

'Lewis, what's going on?'

Alice was in the doorway and he hadn't even heard her come up. She could see everything. His arm was a mess, he'd cut it recently on top of cuts that hadn't healed. She stared at him and looked very pale.

'What's that? What have you done?'

All of his coldness, all of his safe numbness, began to melt away under her look. She looked so upset, so emotional, he couldn't remember feeling like that for weeks. He supposed it was upsetting

150

to see the arm, it looked pretty bad.

'Lewis? For God's sake, what have you done?'

He felt shame, sickening and, somewhere, relief, and the relief grew.

'I hurt myself. I'm sorry.'

She looked over her shoulder, panicking, thinking about the people in the dining room.

'You're bleeding. Wait, wait. Wait here.' She almost pushed him out of the bathroom and went in and closed the door and leaned against it and felt faint.

She tried to make sense of what she'd just seen. She came up to go to the bathroom because she was frightened she had started her period and hadn't wanted to be anywhere near the dining room. She remembered that now, and lifted her skirt and pressed her finger into herself. She wiped it on some lavatory paper. It was pink, just faintly pink and the small, nagging pain in her abdomen started again. She felt as if all the colour had drained out of the world. She opened the bathroom cupboard and found pads and belt. No baby. Not this time. She closed the lavatory and sat down. She sat very straight and opened her eyes wide so they wouldn't get filled with tears. She remembered Lewis and what she had just seen and her mind seemed to shift, jolt against the shock of it.

She stood up and opened the door, but he wasn't on the landing any more. She could hear Dicky laughing downstairs. She saw the door to Lewis's room was closed. He couldn't leave the lunch table, neither of them could—what would Dicky and Claire think? She wanted to cry. She went to Lewis's door and opened it. He was trying

151

to bandage his arm again.

'Here. Let me do it. We have to go downstairs.'

She went over to him and took the bandage from him. She felt him watch her doing it and she could smell alcohol on him, and she realised he'd been drinking. She wanted a drink too now, she wanted one very badly.

'Did you do this?' she asked and he looked at the floor and didn't speak and she felt his weakness. She didn't have time for him. She didn't have time for any of it.

'Why would you do this?' she said. She fumbled with the bandage. 'God, Lewis, this is—'

It was so horrible, this blood, these wounds—what was he thinking? It was appalling. And then she remembered no baby, no baby again, and she'd been counting on it this time, and she'd been waiting so long.

'This is a disgusting thing to do. It's *disgusting.*'

'I know.'

'Everybody's downstairs.'

'Yes. I'm sorry.'

'There. It's done. We'll talk about it later.'

He looked at her then, and he looked just like he had when he was ten.

'Don't tell Dad. Please.'

'Lewis—'

'Please?'

'I won't. I promise. Let's go down.'

They went.

'You go in first.'

She shoved him in the back and waited on the bottom step for a moment. She made her face bright again, she thought she wouldn't look at Gilbert, he might know, and then she wouldn't be able to pretend.

Kit saw Lewis come back in and made sure she didn't stare at him. The two men didn't stop their conversation, still about golf, but now the condition of the greens, and then Alice came in and sat down. Mary cleared the first course and, after a pause, during which a different wine was opened, the beef was brought in. Claire and Alice discussed the butcher and how much trouble they both had with him.

Lewis found that he felt quite calm and as if the scene with Alice hadn't happened at all.

'So, Lewis,' said Dicky, as Gilbert carved, 'how's Harrow?'

Lewis looked at Dicky's face leaning towards him and tried to bring himself back into the room.

'Not bad, sir.'

Alice admired his blankness and thought of the bandage under his shirt, and she remembered tying the knot and the sight of the drying blood. Her throat tightened. No baby, she thought, no baby.

'Treating you all right?'

'Yes.'

'Still a keen cricketer?'

Lewis couldn't be bothered to answer him.

'Rugger this time of year, I expect.'

Gilbert looked over at him, waiting.

'Cat got your tongue?' said Dicky.

'No, sir.'

'Still getting into trouble?'

'What d'you mean?'

'Whenever your father mentions you, you seem to be in some kind of trouble.'

Lewis had had enough. The numbness had all gone and he hated this man and he could feel rage

153

starting. He looked at him and let what he thought of him show, instead of hiding it.

'Trouble?'

'Yes, boy, trouble. Always getting flogged for something, aren't you? Can't seem to get along?'

'Things aren't going too badly, are they, Lewis?' This was Gilbert, trying to help him out. He didn't want to be helped out.

'You've just been sixteen, haven't you?'

'Just after Christmas,' said his father, jolly.

'You've still got nearly three years of schooling left then?'

'So?'

'Lewis—' This was Gilbert again, warning him.

'Seems to me they might throw you out, the way you're going. Then what will you do?'

He was sick of this.

'I don't know what you mean.'

'Your father says you've been fighting, that you hit another boy. Bit of a habit, isn't it?'

This wasn't fair, it had been a fight and Holland had started it, and it was his own fault for making it impossible not to hit him; it was his housemaster who'd written to Gilbert about it, because he'd hurt him quite badly, but apart from that things were all right and his marks were all right, mostly, and just because he kept to himself—he couldn't help it if he couldn't understand how to speak to any of them any more.

Lewis was aware everyone was staring at him. He could feel Kit practically leaning over the table. Gilbert was just carving and putting the slices of meat on the plates. Lewis wanted to tear his nails down his arm and rip it to shreds, he wanted to take a knife and stick it into Dicky's neck and

154

watch the blood pour out.

'I said, bit of a habit, getting in fights.'

'I heard you.'

'Well, you should answer when you're spoken to. Understand? You know your father's worried about you, don't you?'

Gilbert finally spoke, but his voice was small.

'Dicky, it's all right. We've got it under control, haven't we?'

'Have you?' said Dicky and he laughed, loudly. 'For God's sake, Gilbert, look at him!'

Lewis got up and left the room. Nobody else moved. Claire said, 'So, Alice, have you thought what you'll do with the front at all?'

'No,' said Dicky, 'no, I'm sorry, that's very rude. You shouldn't allow him to be so rude.'

Kit felt herself go very red. 'Shut up!' she shouted and she knew her anger was ridiculous. 'Just shut up, you're horrible! Why can't you leave him alone!'

The adults looked at her mildly. Claire put her knife and fork down.

'Leave the table, please, Kit,' she said, and Kit left. Claire picked up her fork again. 'It's her age. She's terribly wilful.'

*   *   *

Kit slammed the door as hard as she could and sat on the stairs and fought her feelings. Her outrage and her fear were impossible and made her helpless. She hadn't had the words to say what she thought and had sounded like a little girl and not how she felt inside at all. She knew Dicky would hit her for it later, and she shook with the fear of him.

155

There were footsteps down the stairs and Lewis came past. He was wearing his coat. She shuffled along the step for him to get by.

'Cheer up,' he said and sounded just like he'd used to, 'it's just lunch.' And he went out of the front door.

*   *   *

When Lewis hadn't come home, and Mary had cleared and left them alone, Alice and Gilbert sat in the drawing room. She put the wireless on to break the silence. She couldn't tell him about not being pregnant. She couldn't say it. She felt she'd never be able to say it.

'Alice, come and sit with me,' he said.

She got up and sat on the floor by his chair. He stroked her light brown hair very gently.

'Not this time, then?' he said.

She, looking up, had light in her face, because he had noticed.

'No, not this time.'

That he could make her feel better about being childless was frightening to him.

'It will be all right, you'll see,' he said.

She looked down and rested her head—not on his knee, but on the edge of the arm of his chair, as if she didn't want to presume too much. He stroked her hair again.

She shut her eyes and the memory of Lewis and his hurting himself came back to her in a rush and she felt the weight of the knowledge pressing her down.

The cuts on his arm were very clear in her mind, and that she didn't know where he was. I'm his stepmother, she thought, I let him go off like that, knowing what he's been doing to himself and I didn't even get up from the table, and I've no idea where he is now, no idea at all. She felt the cold guilt of an inexcusable wrong and denied the feeling immediately. There was nothing she could have done. She was helpless, and relieved to be. She thought of his face—please don't tell Dad—and she resented being dragged into the darkness he put around himself. She wasn't prepared to be Lewis's ally in this, or anything. She would tell. She decided to tell, but then she couldn't seem to say it out loud, the appalling thing he'd been doing to himself, that she had seen he'd been doing.

They went upstairs together in the dark and she forgot about Lewis and was grateful for her marriage and her house, and tried to believe the promise she made herself that she would have a child and she would be happier and it wasn't all for nothing. In the picture she had of the future there was no Lewis, the house with a baby in it didn't have him in it. He was erased.

*   *   *

Kit couldn't decide whether to go to her room and wait for her father to come or stay downstairs and get it over with. She followed her parents into the study where the fire was lit and Claire settled with her tapestry. Kit thought she might provoke him a little to get it going; like ripping off a plaster, but she was always pretty good at that, and she felt completely cowardly about this.

He made it easier for her. He started first.

'You behaved abominably today, Katherine.'

157

Her heart started a slow dreading thud. I'm not going to apologise, she thought, I'm not.

'I'm sorry you think so,' she said.

Her mother sat by the fire and lifted her head slightly, sensing it coming. Will she leave now, wondered Kit, or will she wait till it starts? Claire had been exempt from the beatings since Kit had been big enough to take them, but Kit didn't think she particularly liked to see it, or to get in the way.

'It's not what I think; you know what you did. You know what will happen.'

Claire got up and put her tapestry on the arm of her chair and left the room and didn't look at her daughter. Dicky undid his belt.

'Kneel there.'

'No.' She was damned if she was going to kneel for it.

'I said, kneel there. You will be disciplined.'

Kit couldn't swallow and she prayed her eyes wouldn't start crying and let him see how she felt. He pulled the belt off his trousers and it made a slipping sound as it came. He held the buckle and wrapped the leather around his hand. Her fear was too physical; she could control her mind, but her body was terrified, it was shaking inside, it was shrinking. They looked at each other for a moment and she suddenly thought she might laugh. He lunged for her and it stopped being funny and he grabbed her arm at the top so hard she thought it was going to break in two, and she made a sound, but then the belt caught her around the back of her legs and the end of it whipped around. It wasn't a hard blow, the first one, but he had her now and pushed her down on the ground with one hand, easily, and held her there with his foot. She knew

158

there was no point fighting and she tried to go limp, but the fear made it impossible.

'You will learn to behave!' he said, exerting himself, working up his fury.

Now that he could thrash her with the doubled-up belt along the back of the thighs, he did it until his arm felt quite tired and then he hauled her up and smacked her twice across the face, flat-handed, and then twice again because he liked to do it.

'Get to your room.'

She went and wasn't sure she'd make it to the door because of the panic making her legs weak. Dicky stood and put his belt back on with trembling hands. It had to be done, he thought, it had to be done. He felt ashamed of how excited he felt, but pleased he hadn't really hurt her. He hadn't lost his temper.

Claire stood in the drawing room and waited. She knew Kit was never really hurt; sometimes he used his stick, but he'd never broken Kit's arm like he had hers. Children should be disciplined. Hitting one's wife was irrational and had always seemed shaming to both of them, but punishing one's daughter, even so harshly, was within the realms of proper behaviour. Perhaps Kit would be improved. She just didn't want to see it.

*　　　*　　　*

Kit lay on her front on her bed so that the backs of her legs wouldn't touch the cover. She closed her eyes and turned her mind away.

At first she couldn't make herself think of anything at all and was only distressed, but she

159

worked at it, at making pictures, and soon she could.

She made clear, pale pictures in her mind. She imagined she was travelling to the North Pole and was between camps, and had to drive the dogs hard to get to shelter before nightfall. She imagined herself wrapped in furs and the swish of the sled on the hardened snow. She imagined a vast black sky, all flooded with stars, above her.

CHAPTER SEVEN

APRIL 1955

It had started like any other Sunday. Like any other desperate, hate-filled, pointless Sunday in the stream of Sundays as long as he could remember. Everybody was out, everybody playing their parts in a play he didn't understand and didn't want any part of. There had been nothing to indicate how the day would end.

The weather had been mild and soft for days and the church was filled with spring flowers, and the dresses and the hats and the flowers made new colours out of everything.

They had sung a hymn and said a prayer and the vicar was talking and there was stillness while he spoke, except for the rustle of skirts and the scrape of shoes on the stone floor.

Lewis looked around the people he had grown up with and thought of their childish lives and of their mothers and sisters and birthdays and lunches, all pleasant, with games, manners, rules you could understand. He wanted to make everybody feel what he felt. None of these children knew anything, and they thought tiny things important and cried over test results and cricket scores. He was locked out of it. He couldn't even remember when he'd had any idea how to live like other people seemed to live. He looked at the people in the church and imagined black gaping holes in their chests where their hearts should be, big ragged holes blasted out of them. After this there was a lunch party at somebody's house, the Johnsons' he thought, and he'd promised his father he'd be there, and he was there, and he had a hangover—the hangover he called his church hangover he'd had it so many times—and this rage, and he was less and less able to freeze it out. He'd rather just be quiet, but it seemed recently it was either hurting himself or hurting somebody else and there was less and less quietness in between. But he had promised his father, and even though Gilbert didn't think that meant anything to Lewis, it did. The only reason he was here, and trying so very hard to be invisible and handle himself, was his father and not wanting to let him down; not wanting to let him down, and yet always seeming every, every time to do it.

The vicar had stopped talking. The congregation stood up to leave and Lewis stood up, too. There was the usual slow shuffle to the door when everybody wanted to push, but nobody did.

The vicar stood in the doorway and once they were past him, and outside, people began to talk. Lewis wasn't released from the church feeling yet and was looking at the ground and people's feet

161

when he heard his name. It was Dicky Carmichael who had said it, and he said it again now, louder.

'Eh, Lewis? You'll be behaving yourself at the Johnsons' house, will you?'

Other people stopped and looked too, because Dicky was talking across them. Lewis was aware of people staring at him. Dicky shoved his hands into his pockets and waited for an answer, but Lewis, pinned and examined, said nothing. He heard his father say, 'Dicky—'

'No, come on, Gilbert! David?' David Johnson turned. 'It's your party—happy to have Gilbert's boy there, are you?'

David said something, but Lewis didn't hear it, and then somebody else spoke and Dicky coughed, loudly enough for it to make silence, and said, 'Just watch yourself, Lewis, we've all got our eyes on you, boy. I was talking to the vicar earlier; he agrees. It's best out in the open how everybody feels about you.'

The vicar, spoken to earlier or not, wasn't to be seen; he was back in his church now, and safe.

Dicky kept his eyes on Lewis a moment longer and then looked at Claire.

'All right? Come along,' he said and took her arm, pushing her ahead of him, like a missile, through the people. Tamsin and Kit followed them and the other people turned away, too. There was embarrassment and some laughter before the resuming of conversation. Gilbert and Alice and Lewis didn't move.

Alice made a sort of laughing, breathy sound.

'I'm not going,' she said.

'Yes. You are.'

'No, Gilbert. Not with him. They don't want

162

him. You heard.'

Lewis wasn't sure they knew he was still there. Gilbert was very firm.

'And you heard what David said. We're all welcome. Dicky should never have done that—I don't know, I'll have to speak to him—but the worst thing we could do would be not to go. How would I face him? What would we say to David and Hilary?'

'Gilbert—'

'No! If I can manage, Alice, then you can.'

He held his hand out to her and she took it. They walked towards the road and, after a moment, Lewis followed them.

*   *   *

At home Alice did her make-up again while Gilbert and Lewis waited in the hall, and then they drove over to the Johnsons'.

*   *   *

The weather had changed and a cold wind blew huge clouds across the sun that cast dark shadows onto the earth below. It had been so mild that drinks were being had on the terrace, but now it was bitter. They all came in and crowded into the drawing room and the fire was lit.

Alice and Gilbert were standing shoulder to shoulder and Alice was shivering and Gilbert had a bland, affable stare as he looked for somewhere to go. After a while Lewis couldn't watch his father and stepmother being politely ignored because of him any more, and he went out into the hall.

163

The twins' house was an Edwardian one, with square rooms and bare walls. The hall was olive green with ugly stairs going up to a shabby landing. Behind him he heard cries of wonder and delight and, looking out of the hall window, he saw it was starting to snow. In the drawing room the people all turned in joy to the windows to see snow in April, and Lewis let himself out of the front of the house.

The day was dark now, and stormily lit, and he looked up into the sky.

Kit was pressed against the wall of the house and she saw Lewis come out. He walked a little way from the door and put his hands in his pockets and looked up. She had been looking up too. She had been waiting for the snow to fall on her. He turned and saw her.

The wind had stopped and it was still and quiet. There was nobody else.

She came and stood a few feet away from him and smiled at him. He smiled back and they both looked up at the sky again. The snowflakes were huge and there were, at first, hardly any of them. Then they began to fall quite thickly. The snow fell slowly onto their faces in single, big flakes. The sky looked deeper for having snow in it, you could see through the big flakes to the far-away ones, which were quite tiny and massed together into space. Lewis looked at Kit. She had a short-sleeved dress on and her little-girl arms were very thin and bare, but quite tanned, even after the winter.

'You must be freezing.'

'I'm all right.'

There was a perfect stillness. Then the wind started up again and first blew the snow and then lightened up the sky and then, very quickly, it was over. It was bright again and moving. They went inside. Lewis shut the door behind them and Kit glanced shyly at him and then went straight back to the party without another word.

He felt better. He felt calm, as if something had been switched off inside him. He thought he'd get through the day all right. He would not think about what Dicky had said and if he tried hard, maybe he could stop himself doing anything bad. That was how he saw the cutting; he never looked at it really because of the shame, just referred to it in his mind as doing something bad, just one of the bad things he did.

He went into the room nearest him, a room he'd played in as a child; it had been called the schoolroom and there had been toys and books in it. Now it was another drawing room and almost unfurnished, but there was still a rocking horse in the corner. He remembered fighting over it with Fred or Robert, and laughing.

'What are you doing in here?'

Lewis turned around. Tom Greene stood in the door, with Ed Rawlins behind him.

'Nothing.'

'What have you been doing?' Ed sounded like a prefect. He was nineteen now and had left school, but would probably always sound like one.

'Nothing.'

'Have you been taking things?'

'What?'

'Stealing. Have you?'

'What's going on?' This was Tamsin's voice and she appeared at Ed's shoulder and looked into the room.

165

The room was big and had bare floorboards and Lewis was by the window and the other three in the door looking at him.

Ed and Tom said something to each other, quietly, that Lewis couldn't hear.

'I think you should come out of there,' said Tom.

'I don't think Mr Johnson would like you in here particularly.'

'Come on, boys,' said Tamsin, 'this is silly. They'd like us all in the drawing room.'

Ed and Tom came into the room and Tamsin hovered by the door and looked out into the hall. She glanced at Lewis and caught his eye.

'Do come,' she said to Ed, 'please.'

There were footsteps and Ed and Tom turned around quickly, checking. It was Fred Johnson.

'You found him. What was he doing?'

'He was just there. I don't know.'

Tamsin said, 'Fred, come on, what are you all up to?'

Fred ignored her. He came into the room next to Tom and spoke to Lewis loudly.

'I want you to get out. This is my house. Nobody wants you here.'

Ed said, 'Go on Tamsin, leave this to us.'

Lewis smiled to himself, this was how it would go now, after what Dicky had said. They knew they could behave any way they wanted. Well, if they could, so could he.

'What are you grinning about?'

He couldn't be bothered with this. They wanted to fight him, but they had to get worked up about it first. They had to get their blood up and find their violence in the heat of it. Well, he felt like that all

166

the time; for him it was just a matter of letting himself. He felt invincible because it didn't matter if they hurt him and he wasn't frightened of being hurt and he knew that they were.

He went for Ed first, because he was the biggest and he hated him most, and he managed to hit him hard before the other three grabbed him. Ed punched him in the stomach and winded him, and Tom hit him in the side of his face and his head felt like it was exploding, and he loved it. Tamsin had run away to fetch help and the whole thing only lasted a minute. Fred and Tom held him down, with Tom's knee holding his head onto the boards, and there was some kicking and then Gilbert and David Johnson came in and stopped it. It wasn't much of a fight. Ed and the other boys were shaking, and Lewis's rage had got up and it took his father and David and then Ed, who was fussing about his eye, to hold him down. A lot of people came and stood in the doorway and peered into the room, and Gilbert was down on the floor and holding him tightly, with David helping him.

After the tension and the quiet of the actual fight, once Lewis was held down, there was a cocktail party buzz of conversation, and the other boys inspected themselves for injuries, which were slight and made much of. People craned past each other at the door and talked about it, and reported back what they could see of Lewis, who, after being so angry, had gone away into himself and was very quiet.

*   *   *

Kit hadn't watched any of it. She had waited in the

big drawing room by the fire. She made herself stay still and not follow them. Tamsin had been vague about the detail and not blamed anybody, but Kit knew the way it would have gone and didn't want to see Lewis held down like that, undignified and empty.

*   *   *

'Come along, everybody—let Gilbert deal with it,' said Claire and everyone regretfully went back into the drawing room, not wanting to make a fuss.

Gilbert got carefully to his feet, dusting off the knees of his trousers, and Lewis, released, didn't move.

'Alice, would you wait for us in the car, please,' said Gilbert, and Alice went, without a word, not looking at Hilary Johnson and Claire Carmichael, who were standing in the hall.

Gilbert looked down at Lewis.

'Can you get up?'

Lewis got up.

'We're going home now,' said Gilbert and started to say something else, but Lewis walked away from him and out of the house, not looking up. Hilary and Claire drew back as he passed.

Gilbert came out of the room.

'Hilary—'

'Let's not say anything about it, Gilbert,' said Hilary. 'You take Alice home.'

Gilbert took his hat from the stand by the door and left.

Hilary Johnson and Claire Carmichael would have liked to watch Gilbert's car following Lewis down the road, but there was no excuse to keep the door open.

'I didn't want him in the house,' said Hilary, closing it. 'David insisted, for Gilbert.'

'I thought it was so bad of Dicky to say that in the churchyard at the time, but perhaps it's the only way. One doesn't feel safe, and perhaps it's best we all say so. I mean, for heaven's sake! Did you see his face? There's something wrong there.'

'You know, it's Gilbert and poor Alice I feel sorry for.'

'I was there just after Elizabeth died,' said Claire. 'He was unnaturally quiet then, you know.'

'What do you mean?'

'Well, it's a dreadful thing to say, but you'd think a child losing its mother like that—in an accident—would be terribly distressed. He seemed so calm. Just strange and calm. It was very unnerving.'

'None of us saw the accident, did we? Of course it's unthinkable. But he is unnerving. He makes people uncomfortable.'

'It must be terribly hard with a stepchild.'

'Well, nobody expects one to love a stepchild, but really, imagine it, having to deal with this.'

'Mind you, Alice isn't terribly strong.'

'Sh! Did you notice her drinking today?'

'Don't! I know . . .'

They joined the others in the drawing room and the lunch party was a big success, with so much to talk about. Ed and Tom were the heroes of the afternoon and were fêted. They had faced up to evil. They had found it and cast it out.

*   *   *

169

Gilbert and Alice drove past Lewis, who was walking through the village. At their own house they stopped, and Gilbert reversed the car halfway into the driveway and turned off the engine. He could still see the road. Lewis would have to pass the house if he wanted to get to the station and Gilbert wouldn't allow him to do that.

Alice looked over at Gilbert at the wheel of the car, sitting in the driveway and not driving, or parking, or getting out of the car. It seemed a powerless thing to be doing, just waiting at the wheel like that.

After a while they saw Lewis. He was still quite far away.

Alice felt entirely cold. She felt she had come to the end of something. It was as if she and Gilbert had been fixed in time by their childlessness, and Lewis and his vile damage were binding them too. She wanted to be released. She had bandaged his arm and wiped away his blood too many times, fighting her pity and disgust, while Gilbert led his pristine office life. She was like a nurse in a war patching up soldiers so that they could go out and fight again, but it was his war, and his father's, and she didn't want to be locked into his secret.

She glanced at Lewis walking towards them. He was nearer now and had seen them, and kept walking. She decided she would tell.

Gilbert didn't believe her at first. Lewis's mutilations had become normal to Alice and she felt shame describing them as if they were her own.

'What are you telling me?' said Gilbert. 'That he does this thing to himself?'

'Yes.'

'Just to hurt himself?'

170

'Yes.'

His face moved—like a shadow passing over it—and in that moment Alice thought he would do something, some uncontrolled thing, and she felt terror; but Gilbert didn't do anything. He looked steadily at his son getting closer and closer and waited. Alice realised she was holding her breath.

Lewis reached them and Gilbert got out of the car. Alice wished she had gone into the house and didn't have to watch. Gilbert bore down on Lewis, who was trying to pass him. She couldn't hear what they were saying and didn't need to. Gilbert was shouting at Lewis, who was backing off; he made a grab for Lewis and grasped his arm, and they struggled, with Gilbert trying to force up Lewis's sleeve to look for himself. They were out of sight of the village and there was no-one to see, but Alice hid her face in shame at all of them anyway and didn't see Lewis, pulling away from his father, cast one quick look at her.

Gilbert, gripping Lewis's hand, yanked his sleeve up. Lewis's arm was bared and they were both still.

Gilbert had no way of demonstrating his feelings at seeing his son's scars, or about the day, or about the things that Lewis had done in all the years he could remember since Elizabeth's death. For just a moment, like a brightly lit photograph, he remembered the son he thought he would have. Then he let go of Lewis's marked up arm and looked into his face and Lewis saw himself reflected. Gilbert told him to cover himself and walked away. The worst had happened between them, it seemed.

171

Waterford lay in darkness. The cold wind and the warm spring air moved quietly between themselves. Kit was sleeping in her bed and dreaming and pleased with her dream. Alice and Gilbert were sleeping and holding hands, which sometimes they did without knowing they did, and never woke up like that.

The doors to the drawing room were open and swinging slowly in the moving air. Lewis was walking—or trying to walk—and drunk, and the darkness was making the being drunk like being unconnected to anything. He seemed to see the village from above and the sleeping people in their beds, and seemed to move over the ground fast sometimes and couldn't feel it when he fell, which was sort of funny and sort of not.

The village was asleep, with all the people behind the walls and through the windows and up the stairs of the little houses, blind and deaf in their beds while anything might happen. Lewis headed down the middle of the road and he kept falling and had to remember to get back on his feet.

He reached the churchyard and stood in the dark with the church even darker above him.

*   *   *

The main door wasn't locked and opened very easily when he turned the iron ring on it. The blackness in the church was like something dense and he stepped into it. He stood as well as he could with the inside air of the church touching him, and

172

then he leaned on the pew and dropped his head and went to his knees.

He stayed like that, with bowed head, and waited. He thought God might come and heal him. He waited and was ashamed for waiting, because God never came and Lewis didn't think with his black heart he'd have known him if he had. Still, he waited with his desperate hope and nothing came.

He stood up, still holding onto the back of the pew. He saw the razor in his mind, but didn't have it. He couldn't feel his arm whatever he did to it. He had to have something. He put his hand into his pocket and found matches.

The bibles were easy to light and the velvet curtain behind the choir stall was dry and old, but he couldn't find a way of lighting the wood of the pews with just matches, so he broke into a storeroom at the back and found the paraffin for the heaters that were kept there. The paraffin lit easily and there was enough of it to douse the whole place, and he poured it over everything and the floor, and watched the flames racing and meeting each other.

When the fire had really got started, when the flames were huge and nothing was going to stop them, it still wasn't enough. The wood was blistering in the heat, the varnish bubbled, and giant candles ran liquid clear over the floor. The heat was pushing him back to the door. It wasn't enough. It was nothing.

Outside, the night was calm and he drenched the unmoved graves with paraffin, and the flaming grass was smoky and green-smelling. He tried to tear the gravestones loose and to break his hands and his head against them. It wasn't enough.

173

Nothing was enough and he was at the end of it. He had lost, and there was nothing left, and he lay on his mother's grave and cried, and tried to climb into the ground, because in his stupid drunkenness he thought that was the only way to find peace.

*　　　*　　　*

The first people to see the church hadn't seen Lewis in the dark behind the bright fire. When they did see him they didn't go near him, they called the police. He was vacantly unresisting.

*　　　*　　　*

The cold and the mildness moved over the village until the cold air was stronger and it laid a hard frost over everything. The church burned very hot. The windows blew out and showered the street with glass. The frozen road was full of people watching and the sky got paler as they watched. The dim morning, and the crowd, and the church burning were strangely reminiscent of the war. People were shocked and not wearing their normal clothes or expressions, and the sight of the still-burning church, the scorched grass and the blackened gravestones was surreal and appalling. The village was as it had always been, but in the centre of it was the burning church. It was an evil sight.

*　　　*　　　*

The Carmichaels' house was some way from the church and they were amongst the last to know.

When they found out—somebody phoned at the uncivilised hour of seven—Dicky drove them all down to see what was going on and what could be done. Kit stood with everybody else and listened to the questions being asked and answered, and heard the story piece itself together and, when she knew that it was Lewis, she went to the car and sat in the back seat and covered her face and cried. She surprised herself with her tears, how freely she cried, and how sadly. She didn't know she had such simple grief in her, she didn't know she could cry like that. Other people were crying too, most were very angry; others were watching the firemen, and the men helping them. The crowd was smaller as people went to work or back to their houses, but all day, and for days after, people would stop and look, and the shock was unifying and gradually replaced by outrage and opinion.

Lewis was put into one of the two cells at the police station. The police station was small and the cell was small too, with a bed and window and a bucket in the corner.

Late in the morning they called in Dr Straechen and, because Lewis was only seventeen, Gilbert was sent for, too. Lewis was bruised from the fight with the boys and his head was battered from the gravestones. He had split his lip when they were putting him in the cell and his shirt was bloody, and when the doctor took it off, Gilbert saw more bruises and the cuts on his arm. His hands, too, were covered in grazes on both sides and one of them was burned. Gilbert handed Lewis the clean shirt he had brought for him to wear. He had to help him on with it. When he had finished, Wilson began his questions. Gilbert thought that Lewis

175

couldn't follow what was being said, but the interview established his name and the fact that he'd done it and that he'd been alone, and gave Wilson the means to make a report.

Lewis was put back in his cell. Gilbert had been scared of him and hated the sight of him and was relieved he was to stay locked up.

*   *   *

When Kit had finished her crying, she went through the village to the police station and sat on the wall opposite it and waited. She saw the doctor go in, and Gilbert, and waited there until lunchtime. She knew she wouldn't see Lewis, but she couldn't think of anywhere else to be, and the time went by her like it does on a long journey, quite softly.

*   *   *

Lewis stayed in the police station until there was a hearing, the following week, when it was decided he should remain in custody until the trial, a month later, at Guildford Crown Court.

Gilbert and Alice came to the court. They hadn't seen him since he had been locked up. With his face healed and hair damped down and with his neat tie and shirt, he looked very young, and Alice almost couldn't bear to look at him.

*   *   *

He was tried as an adult, because of what he had done, and because the judge wanted to be able to

176

send him into the army for his National Service in lieu of a custodial sentence. The army's response gave Lewis something to smile about; they didn't want him.

'We're rather choosier than that, Your Honour, when it comes to our National Security,' said the colonel summoned to discuss sentencing with the judge, and so Lewis was given a two-and-a-half-year sentence and sent to Brixton prison in June 1955.

PART THREE

CHAPTER ONE

AUGUST 1957

Kit arranged her records around the room so that they covered the skirting and made a border. There were fourteen of them now and they didn't reach all the way around, or even far along the second wall, but it was a start. They kept slipping on the wooden floor and dropping, with a slapping sound, and she would go and prop them up again. The faces seemed to look at her as she went around them, and she knew them so well she almost couldn't see them properly any more. Elvis, Gene Vincent, Fats Domino, Little Richard, Bill Haley, Julie London, Betty Carter, Sarah Vaughan . . . She had a portable record player in its own red leather carrying case and it lived on the floor next to her bed. She would sometimes hide a song from herself, in a drawer under her clothes, so she could play it again after waiting and hear it fresh. She'd done that with Julie London singing 'Funny Valentine', and Elvis's 'Mystery Train' had waited a whole month, and it had almost been like hearing it for the first time. She never heard the wireless at home because she wasn't allowed one, and the one downstairs was very big, in a wooden unit, and lived in the drawing room, but at school she did. Some of the older girls had them, and it was an illicit and thrilling pleasure to sneak into one another's rooms at night and listen to music as loudly as they dared. Kit saved up her birthday and Christmas money and every trip she'd made to a record shop was in her memory; the listening to each song, the horrible choosing. She'd had to sacrifice Little Richard's 'Long Tall Sally' for Julie London singing 'S'wonderful', and it had been worth it because 'Cry Me a River', was on the other side. It had a been a huge decision, not just because the songs were so precious to her and each one had to last so long, but because it was about who she was, jazz or rock and roll, and it had been hard to do.

She lowered the needle very carefully onto 'Cry Me a River', newly reinstated from her underwear drawer, and went to the window. She didn't put it on loudly because her parents were having drinks on the terrace below and if it disturbed them, there would be a row. The view from her window was ahead of her and the song behind, rich and bitter, and making her mind liquid and reaching. Out in the garden was normal; the evening birds singing, the lawn and the woods and the empty green and blue of nature and everyday life. The song coloured her sight and she half closed her eyes as she looked out of the window and there was an ecstasy to her frustration and her boredom.

'Daddy!'

Kit saw Tamsin come onto the terrace where her parents were, from the front of the house.

'Guess what?'

Kit looked down at them and felt pleasantly removed. They looked small and she could imagine for a moment she was nothing to do with them. Tamsin sat near Dicky, and Kit could hear her talking, but not the words. The song finished and Kit got up quickly, to take the needle off it; it was a new needle and precious.

'—not Lewis. He . . .'

Lewis. She'd said Lewis. She forgot the needle and went back to the window and leaned out to hear. Had Tamsin actually said it, or had she imagined it? Dicky got up and went into the house.

'. . . don't know what Alice will think about that,' she heard him say.

Claire got up too and they all went inside. Kit ran to her door, and out and downstairs, and the needle stayed, grinding on the spinning record.

She stood in the hall, with them in the drawing room, and waited to hear if they were going to carry on talking. She heard Tamsin.

'I told you, I was driving back from the Andersons', going to see Diana, and he was walking back from the station. I couldn't just pretend I hadn't seen him.'

'That's exactly what you should have done.'

'Well? How did he seem?'

This was Claire. Kit got closer to the door.

'Quiet. Fine. I don't know, like Lewis. I'm terribly hot, any chance of something with mint in it?'

There were noises of exasperation and sighing and walking about, and Kit looked through the hinge of the door. Tamsin was on the sofa, lying back in attitudes of languid casualness. Claire sat down as Kit watched and Dicky walked over to the drinks cabinet.

'Poor old Gilbert,' he said.

Kit couldn't understand why they weren't asking sensible questions. How long would Lewis be here? What was he going to do?

'Kit, we know you're there,' said her mother, 'you may as well come in.'

183

Kit went in.

'How long is he staying?' she asked.

'How should I know? We barely exchanged ten words. He seemed fearfully polite and rather embarrassed, if you want to know.'

'Well, he would!' said Dicky, banging bottles about.

Kit had a sudden memory of that very early morning, when Lewis was locked up, and what it had been like, and the way she had felt. She looked down. Her feelings were being made dangerous by his coming back. She thought it must be obvious how she felt. She wanted to be on her own.

The gong rang for supper soon after, and the family talked of nothing else but Lewis all through it, and Kit didn't say anything, hating them using his name and the things they said. Then, very quietly, right inside, she began to feel joy. He was back. He was there now, at home. He was there.

*   *   *

That first night, as Kit lay sleepless in her bed, Alice lay sleepless in hers, aware of Lewis across the landing and Gilbert next to her, breathing gently. She felt silly for having been frightened of Lewis when he had come into the house. He was the same. No, not quite the same, perhaps stronger. She felt hope and guilt together and reached for Gilbert's shoulder in the dark and touched him softly. Although he didn't move at all, she seemed to feel him turn away from her.

*   *   *

'Just caught me. Catching the eight-thirty?'

Dicky crossed his hall in strides.

'Thought so. I'll give you a lift, if you like.'

Gilbert stood in the doorway, very aware of Preston standing on the gravel behind him by the Rolls. Dicky shouted over his shoulder.

'Off!'

The two men left the house and Dicky slammed the door behind him.

'That's all right, Preston. Meet the five-fifteen, would you?'

They both got into Gilbert's Ford Zodiac and Gilbert pulled away from the house and towards the station.

'Lewis is back.'

'I see,' said Dicky, waiting.

'Back last night. Eager to make a fresh start.'

'Did you speak to Accounts about the review?'

'Mackereth will be there today,' he said. 'The thing is, I was wondering if you might find something for him.'

'For Lewis?'

'As I say, he's keen to show he's changed.'

'System works, eh?' said Dicky, and Gilbert hated his casualness about it, and the sarcasm. It wasn't his son who had been in prison.

'He'll want to put it behind him, at any rate,' he said, evenly.

'Well, he can hardly expect to walk straight into a job.'

'I'd thought something menial. At first.'

The 'at first' betrayed him, he knew it did.

'Mortimer tells me in the first quarter his section was up an extra half a percent on estimate.'

'Yes. I'd rather thought it would do him good.'

'Lewis?'

'Yes, Lewis!'

'Can't promise anything, old man—boy like that. But I'll give it some thought. All right?'

'All right,' said Gilbert and turned the Ford into the station. 'Thank you.'

*   *   *

When Gilbert had left for work, Alice went to her room and Lewis sat at the breakfast table.

The night before had felt all wrong. He had come home ready for things to be different, but when his father took him to the church, he could only see himself the way he had been before. He had imagined comfort in being in his own bed again, but his nightmare had come back and there was no sleep after it. It was an evening from before he was sent away and not what he'd planned. He had lost ground. He stood up and looked around the room and wiped his hands down his trousers because the palms were sweating.

It would be different. He would do anything to make it that way and not let all the bad things find him again. He remembered the nightmare and the feeling of water closing over his head, and on waking the way the scars on his arm had seemed to reach out, making themselves felt.

He hadn't cut himself in prison; he hadn't thought of it, except in dreaming. It was a strange, vague memory, a twisted habit a child would fall into, that wasn't to be looked at.

The house seemed hot and closed up to the morning and Lewis went to the French doors in the drawing room and let himself out into the dewy garden.

There was sunlight and birdsong and nothing else except the air on his face, and he felt freedom for the first time, and the beauty of it. The memory of the night before vanished to nothing. There was the damp sunlit morning all around, and it lived and shone and waited for him.

There wouldn't be any need for fighting—the life inside him would make things better. He felt his freedom and his youth and that they were unconquerable and, in that moment, with the light glittering garden all around him, he had faith.

*   *   *

Even faith needs an occupation. The morning had promise, but Lewis only had himself and the house and the garden and woods beyond it, and he didn't leave the garden. He went to the untouched shelves in the house and fetched books to read and cigarettes to smoke, and loved every grass-drenched hot, bright moment of his freedom.

He and Alice ate lunch together. He still had his joy and felt too big and too alive for the room and had nothing to say that wouldn't have sounded odd, so he kept quiet. He would have liked to be friendly to her, but when she looked at him, which was rarely, her brittleness made him want to get away. Her nerves made him nervous too, and they went their separate ways as soon as they politely could.

Afterwards he went out into the garden again, which was hot now, with flying things and dry air.

He walked down to the tennis court and there was a sound of crickets in the grass and the heat

187

came off the ground at him. He found a racket, an old one, and a ball and stood back from the wall to hit the ball at it. The ball didn't have much bounce to it and the racket was pretty much ruined, so he had to hit it really hard to get anywhere. Hitting it hard was good and he took his cigarette out of his mouth to do it better and enjoyed getting a sweat up with it. It was hard work, and mesmeric, and pleasing. The bang of the ball on the brick, and its bounce after, was the main sound, but his brain registered another and he stopped. He heard it again, rustling.

The court was backed by bushes, rhododendrons, thickly layered, going back up to the boundary of the garden, where the woods started. Lewis looked into the dark of them, where the sound was coming from, and saw movement.

'I can see you,' he said.

Kit came out of the bushes. She had summer dust and twigs in her hair, which was very, very short and at first he thought she was a boy. Then he saw the dress. Then he realised who she was.

'Kit?'

'Hello.'

She looked funny. She looked like a beautiful child; she hadn't been a beautiful child before.

'You cut all your hair off.'

He had to say it, it jumped out at you, that she had such short hair, and it made her all eyes and neck and naked ears. She seemed to writhe with embarrassment.

'What are you up to?' he said and she squinted up at him in the sunlight, her face contorted with anxiety.

'Nothing. Heard you were back.'

188

He shrugged, 'I'm back.'

'How are you?'

He gestured, as if to say, 'As you can see', but not saying anything. She squinted some more and stood on one leg. She was exactly the same and too easy to tease.

'You get sent to prison for spying, you know,' he said and she glared and started to walk backwards into the bushes.

He hadn't meant her to go, but the sight of her walking backwards was funny and he laughed, and she made a face and tripped over something, and he laughed again and she slipped away into the dark and was gone. He heard her running.

This was how it would be then, the local freak show, all the kids would be out to have a look. Well, it wasn't anything to him. He went back to the tennis wall, but it was pointless now, so he lay down and smoked some more and thought he'd have to get some work soon or he'd run out of cigarettes as well as going crazy.

*   *   *

In the early evening Lewis went to meet his father at the gate as he had used to as a child. He walked down the drive in the deep shadows of the trees, looking at the low sun on the field ahead of him. His skin felt alive from being in the sun all day and the cool shadows were soft around him. He heard the car before he saw it, and then it came around the big bend, and slowed, and stopped. The windows were down and Gilbert leaned across, his face looking hot from the train and his hat on the seat beside him.

189

'Lewis. What are you doing?'

'I thought I'd meet you.'

'Why?'

Lewis opened the door and got in, holding his father's hat carefully.

'Dad—'

'What did you do all day?'

'Nothing.'

'Nothing at all?'

'I was in the garden.'

'All day?'

'Most of it, sir. Look, I've been wanting to say—'

Gilbert took his hat from Lewis's hands and put it on the dashboard in front of them.

'What is it?'

'I've been wanting to apologise.'

'You've done that. We got your letters.'

'Not just that.'

'Well, what?'

A silence.

'What, Lewis? I told you, I expect things to be different—nothing like it was before—that—' He choked on the words, 'That thing you did to yourself—'

'No! I stopped it!'

'Then what do you have to say?'

'That I came back to—'

'To?'

'To make it better.'

The words sounded empty out loud; they had sounded brave and hopeful when he'd thought of them.

'Well, prove it to us then, all right? Prove it to us.'

'Yes, sir.'

190

Gilbert eased the car down the drive, slowly. He stopped at the house and they both got out. He left Lewis and went inside without saying anything else.

*   *   *

Lewis was used to waiting and having nothing to do and he found it easier to do it lying on his bed. That had been his habit in Brixton—the gym first, trying to get tired, and then lying on his bed, and waiting, and finding the strength he needed to redeem himself. He would lie on his bed in his cell and stay still and let his mind go—making up stories, picturing places he'd read about—except that now he was home, when his mind went, it didn't go anywhere good.

There was no breeze at all and the heat made him restless and he was sweating and he half slept, and he thought about walking back from the station and seeing Tamsin. He thought of her wrists, coming out of her white gloves, and how they had been golden and the forearms golden too, and he thought about the hollow of her wrist where it had gone inside the glove and he pictured the little dark groove there, narrower than a finger, into her palm. He could hear raised voices downstairs. Gilbert's voice and then Alice. His door was a little open and he heard her clearly as she came up to the landing.

'I would say it's personal, Gilbert! I would say cheap-looking is personal.'

Lewis went to his door. He could see her, the back of her, as she stood at the top of the stairs. She was wearing a black evening gown that had a

191

deep V-shape at the back, and her hair piled up, with her pearls sitting on her bare neck. Her gloved hand rested on the banister. He heard Gilbert.

'Alice. It's a question of what's appropriate. If you want every man in the room—'

'Not every man! Just—'

'Enough!'

'Why can't you—'

'For God's sake! Just change. This endless attention!'

She turned, quickly, and she was crying. She caught him looking and he shut the door. He didn't want to know this. He didn't want to see her like that and he didn't want to know anything about her and his father. They hadn't used to argue, it had been all politeness before. He leaned against the door and heard her go to her room and the door closing. He waited and he heard them leaving soon after.

Apart from going down to the kitchen to eat something, he stayed in his room for the rest of the evening; he was more comfortable there.

CHAPTER TWO

Kit lay on her back on the sofa and watched her family upside down and thought about Sartre, and his play *No Exit*, and wondered if her family was her hell and she was being punished for something terrible she couldn't remember doing when she had been alive.

'Kit! Will you take your feet off the sofa? How

many times do you have to be told?'

'OK.'

'And please don't use that expression. We are not Americans.'

Dicky was at the fireplace.

'It crossed my mind to tell him that I wouldn't trust that boy to feed my dog. I've every right to turn him down flat.'

'You certainly have. I think it's the most extraordinary presumption, after everything you've done, and in very poor taste.'

Claire was working on her tapestry. The fading light falling on her from the window made her look faded too. She always seemed to Kit less substantial than other people, like something that had been washed too many times and lost its colour. The only time Claire seemed really to be there was when she was angry; her coldness had some life to it.

'We've all had to bear the cost of that boy's crime already,' Dicky said. Kit tried not to stare at him and tried to keep her loathing to herself. Tamsin was opposite Kit, with a magazine and a sherry and dipping in and out of the conversation when she felt she could influence it.

'They let him out after two years!' said Dicky. 'It's an outrage.'

'He must have behaved himself,' said Claire.

'I wish he'd stayed where he bloody well was!'

Didn't they have anything else to talk about? Wasn't there somebody with cancer or an illegitimate baby? It reminded her of how it had been just before Lewis was put away, every school holidays—Lewis Aldridge, and nothing clever, nothing kind, just judgement and gossip.

193

'You'd incarcerate him indefinitely, I suppose. He didn't commit murder!' She said it furiously; she hadn't meant to speak, and Tamsin glanced up from her magazine.

'Shut up, Kit, nobody's impressed,' she said.

'Actually,' said Claire, 'one doesn't really want a person like that anywhere, does one?'

What a vision, what an extraordinary vision; all the people one doesn't want anywhere, where would they go? Kit imagined vast rows of buildings housing all the people one didn't want anywhere, and wanted to go there immediately. There was a silence. Tamsin flicked through her pages and, after a while, looked up.

'Daddy,' she said, idly, 'couldn't you put him to something in the quarry office, or somewhere? Something it doesn't matter about. Then Mr Aldridge will be pleased and you needn't worry too much.'

'I expect I'll do something like that, it's just a bloody bore, that's all.'

Tamsin sipped her sherry.

'I'll telephone now, shall I? I expect you could see him in the morning.'

She got up and wandered out of the room, and Dicky didn't stop her. Kit watched her go, and heard her pick up the telephone. If she were older, if she were blonde, or appealing, perhaps she could get him a job and ring him up and not be just an unwanted shadow. She heard Tamsin laughing her social laugh and then she came back into the room, smiling to herself, and Kit felt her mean heart and was ashamed of it.

'I spoke to Mr Aldridge. He was awfully pleased. Thank you, Daddy. To forgive is divine, you know,' she said.

'My good girl,' said Dicky, and kissed her, while Claire sewed and didn't look up and Kit continued to sit. 'Good girl,' he said, stroking her cheek.

*   *   *

Tamsin had waited at the bottom of the drive for him and beeped the horn, and Lewis grabbed the toast from his plate and his jacket and ran out to her. The morning was cool and the top was up on the Austin.

'Now don't sulk and try not to be peculiar.'

He did up his tie and smiled, that's what he mustn't be: peculiar. She was so very friendly it was impossible not to be drawn in, and it was easier to be in the car with her too, because she had a cardigan over her dress and there were no bare arms to distract him. Her legs were completely covered, in a full skirt, and the coolness of the morning, and the fact that it was morning, made the whole thing less self-conscious than it might have been. Her charm was the same, though, and the conspiratorial, smiling glances.

The quarry office was twenty minutes out of the village, jerry-built and perched on the edge of the abyss of the quarry. It looked as if a strong wind would blow it in. Probably what Dicky was hoping for, Lewis thought. Tamsin drove in a wide arc to the door and stopped.

'Don't be frightened, you know Daddy's not that bad. I'll wait.'

As Lewis got out, Tamsin put the radio on, it was Fats Domino singing 'Blueberry Hill' and it sounded pretty good, and he would much rather

195

stay outside with Tamsin in the sun than go into the office and talk to her father. He went up the metal steps to the door and knocked and entered.

*　　　*　　　*

There was a man of indeterminable age sitting at a desk. He had glasses and a side parting, slicked down. He looked up.

'Lewis Aldridge?' It was an accusation. Lewis nodded. 'Mr Phillips. D'you do?' He half-rose in his seat and gestured at another door with his pencil, 'Mr Carmichael is waiting for you.'

He said it with such deference Lewis thought he was going to touch his forelock. He knocked on the other door, watched by Phillips, who sat down again and cleared his throat, never taking his eyes off Lewis.

'Come!'

Lewis opened the door.

'Lewis. Phillips!' barked Dicky. 'In here please!'

Phillips leaped out of his seat, like something out of Dickens, and shot past Lewis into the room. Dicky stood by the window in customary hands-behind-the-back pose. It had been a long time since Lewis had seen anyone like Dicky, or maybe there wasn't anyone else like Dicky. His blazer and his ruddiness and the squeak of his shoes as he approached were laughable.

'Gilbert all right? Alice?'

'Very well. Thank you, sir.'

'Now, your father's spoken to me and I've asked Mr Phillips here to find you something. Phillips?'

'In filing,' said Phillips, and Lewis nodded; filing sounded fine, he could do that. Dicky nodded to

196

Phillips, and Phillips approached Lewis and went quite close to him.

'I don't want any funny business from you,' he said.

It was almost funny, the way he said it, but actually not, because of his closeness and the way Dicky was looking at them from across the room. Dicky's presence in the room was oppressive and Lewis remembered how much he had always hated him and then tried very hard to forget.

'No, sir,' he said.

'You'll be on trial,' Phillips went on, and Lewis could smell his breath and his hair oil. 'On Mr Carmichael's say-so. I'll expect you on Monday morning, nine o'clock, and I'll show you the ropes then. All right?'

'Thank you,' said Lewis.

There was another exchange of glances and Phillips left the office, and shut the door. Dicky walked over to Lewis.

'I don't usually employ young men straight out of prison, you know.' He paused. 'I want to make it perfectly clear that I'm doing this for your father because he's worked for me for so long. I wonder if you know what this means to him?'

Dicky took a step closer to him.

'In actual fact, I neither like nor trust you, but should you lose this job, it would be to his detriment. Your—father—wouldn't—like—it, do you understand?'

'Yes, sir.' Lewis concentrated on the windows of the room. The windows were sealed all around, they didn't have catches to open them.

'Let's not imagine this job is any more than it is. This is my company, and I need to protect it. I'll be

197

paying you almost nothing to do a worthless job. What do you think about that?'

Dicky had every right to talk to him that way; he wasn't going to be angry, he would make himself quiet. He had spent two years making himself quiet with people who wanted him to lose his temper.

'I've less than no interest in you personally, Lewis—you're a troublemaker. I've never had any time for these excuses about your mother and so forth, for God's sake, we've all had problems. There was a collective sigh of relief when you finally got put away and I don't imagine—'

They wanted him to lose his temper so that they could beat him or lock him up, or prove that he was nothing—as if that needed proving—but he wasn't going to be angry, he was going to be quiet. Dicky had stopped talking, and Lewis hadn't noticed that he'd stopped. There was silence in the room.

'Go on then. Get on with you.'

Dicky laughed and shoved his arm and Lewis saw that he was close up and staring at him, but he couldn't remember what he had been saying.

There was a blank in his head, like a missed step. He guessed the interview was over. Dicky seemed to be waiting for something. Something other than having his tongue ripped out of his mouth.

Lewis concentrated very hard.

'Thank you, sir,' he said.

*   *   *

Outside the office, Lewis got back in the car with

198

Tamsin. His hands were shaking.

'You were ages!' she said, and started the engine and the car bumped down the track and out onto tarmac. 'Well? How'd it go?'

'What?'

'Did you get the job?'

'Oh. Yes.'

'WEEE!' she cried, and laughed, and waved her hand out the window, 'Well done you!'

She laughed again, and he closed his eyes. He was frightened he couldn't remember what Dicky had been saying to him, or how long he'd been in there. He needed not to be like that. He wasn't going to be like that again. He hadn't been in prison, and he was home now.

She was stopping the car. She pulled over to the side of the road and turned off the engine. He looked at her.

'What?'

He saw her take a breath and, breathing, flex her body very slightly against the seat, as if adoring being Tamsin.

The road was empty and sun poured down on the car, which was dark inside where they were. He waited. He had felt paralysed—and now he was filled with the small darkness of the car and Tamsin, looking at him.

'Would you take the top down?' she said.

He got out, and did, and tried not to stare at her while he did it.

He got back into the car. She didn't start the engine. She took off her cardigan. She took it off very consciously, demonstrating the removal of it, and that she was luxuriating in the air.

'Gosh,' she said.

199

'Hot?'

'Awfully.'

She looked like a girl who wanted to be kissed. No—he wanted to kiss her; it wasn't her wanting to be kissed. Why would Tamsin Carmichael want to kiss him? He tried not to think about it, but she seemed to present herself to him, and she still hadn't started the engine.

She tucked her hair behind her ear, slowly, and he couldn't stop himself staring now; at the hollow between her collarbones and her dress, which was light cotton and covering the shape of her, but letting you know it was there underneath. He kept himself still, and looked at her, and thought about kissing her and tried not to look as if he was thinking about it.

'Do you remember how we all used to play together as children?'

She said it quietly, as if she was about to tell him a secret. He nodded, watching her closely. She leaned a little towards him.

'I remember your mother so well,' she said, looking into his eyes. 'She was a wonderful woman. A beautiful woman—and when I heard she'd died like that, I cried.' Her eyes were wide, looking into him. 'Do you remember how patient she was with all of us? All our noisy games? You were ten when she drowned—I'm sorry, my maths! So I must have been twelve . . .'

She didn't seem to notice what she was doing to him, or perhaps she did, and enjoyed it. He said quietly, 'We don't talk about her.'

'Well, of course!' she said, blithely. 'Your father met Alice that same year! I shouldn't think she could stand the sound of her name! How horrid for you, though.'

He'd had enough. 'Yes, look—'

She put her hand on his shoulder.

She was wearing her short, white gloves and she rested her hand there and it wasn't like her flirting before—he must have been wrong about her flirting, he didn't know now—this was horribly kind. Still, her fingers were light on his shoulder and he felt her all through him.

'Would you all like to come up to the house for lunch and tennis on Sunday?'

Lewis tried to regain some hold.

'Yes. Thanks.'

'Good,' she said, and started the engine.

She seemed very pleased, and didn't speak again except to say goodbye when she let him out of the car.

*   *   *

Lewis went into the hall. The house was silent. He loosened his tie and sat on the bottom step. The kitchen door opened and Mary put her head out and, seeing him there, narrowed her eyes slightly and then shut the door again.

He'd had an interview with the governor at Brixton the week before they let him out. There had been posters on the walls advertising jobs with various skills Lewis didn't possess, and the governor had asked him questions about his schooling and his plans. There had been bemusement that a 'posh boy' was in Brixton in the first place. Well, the governor would be pleased. He was going to a tennis party at the weekend and had a job starting on Monday. It looked as if he

201

was being rehabilitated. Lewis smiled down at the floor, bringing his hand up to half cover his face like he didn't want to be caught doing it. It seemed a risky thing to be doing, smiling, and he wasn't sure he should commit himself. Then he lay back on the stairs and thought of Tamsin Carmichael, and smiled some more, and got up and went out into the sunny garden.

CHAPTER THREE

Lewis didn't go to church with Alice and Gilbert on Sunday; it was bad enough for them to have to put up with people knowing he was back, without him actually being there.

They drove back through the heat and sunshine to pick him up before going on to the Carmichaels', and didn't speak, except for Gilbert saying, 'Do you remember when Lewis played that tennis tournament against the other prep school, which one was it?'

'I don't know,' said Alice, 'I think it was the summer before we met.'

And he turned to her and said, quite sweetly, 'Looking forward to the party?'

'Very much,' said Alice.

'I think it's going to be jolly nice,' he said, 'don't you?'

*　　　*　　　*

At the Carmichaels' house, Preston got out of the car and opened the door for Claire and then for

202

Dicky, and then came around to let out Tamsin and Kit. When she was released, Kit galloped into the house and up to her room, pulling off her dress.

She put on her shorts and splashed her face with cold water and ran down, fast, and out into the garden, grabbing her tennis racket from the stand by the back door. The housekeeper was laying out glasses on a long table on the terrace. Kit got halfway to the tennis court and stopped, skidding, and remembered Lewis. She looked down at her bare brown legs below her shorts and her plimsolls, which were battered. She wondered if there was anything to be done about the way she looked. Maybe she ought to put a frock on. She didn't want to. He wouldn't look at her anyway. She could look at him, couldn't she? She set off running again, and laughed.

* * *

Tamsin stood still in front of the glass and smiled at her reflection. She stopped herself kissing it, as she had used to when just a little younger. She could hear people arriving and wondered if any of them were the Aldridges, and thought of her mother's face when she had told her about asking Lewis specially. She saw her eyes smile and brighten and she opened her mouth as if about to speak, to see the way her lips moved when she did that. Then she smiled at herself, a little shyly, glancing over her shoulder at the glass again as she left the room.

* * *

The gravel in front of Dicky Carmichael's house was covered with cars. The front door was open, with the maid standing neatly by it. Lewis followed Alice and Gilbert into the house, which was dark after the bright day. The polished wood was almost black around them and the sun didn't penetrate. It wasn't a house suited to summer.

They went through the hall and the drawing room and they could hear the people first and then see them through the windows.

'Gilbert—' said Alice and he took her hand, and Lewis saw that they were having to get their courage up, and that it was because of him.

Then they went out onto the glaring terrace where the people stood out harshly against the hot flagstones.

Lewis looked at the big garden and the long terrace and the tables laid out and the people spread out over the grass. It was an enormous bright canvas of familiarity and pleasantness and it was shocking to him. He had become used to quite different views. He was allowed back. He was grateful.

Gilbert and Alice were a little ahead of him and Alice put her hand on Gilbert's arm.

Mary Napper was talking to Harry Rawlins and they stopped talking when they saw Lewis and stared. The people next to them noticed and they stared too, and after a moment the whole terrace paused. It could only have lasted a moment, a few seconds, and Gilbert had expected it and told himself he didn't mind, and smiled around at the faces and waited.

The conversation started up again, but falsely,

204

and Gilbert rocked a little on his heels.

'I wonder where they all can have got to,' he said, smiling affably around, and Lewis hurt for him.

'Gilbert! Alice!' Claire had come out of the house with the maid and came over immediately when she saw them.

'I'm so pleased you could come. Don't you have a drink?' she asked and the maid offered them one, and Lewis pretended he wasn't there.

Gilbert and Alice stood very close to each other and talked about nothing, and then David Johnson came up and spoke to Gilbert and he didn't look at Lewis at all, and Lewis took a step backwards and thought about leaving.

'There you are!'

Tamsin was by him. She seemed to have turned her brightness up for the brightness of the day. He felt separate and strange even to be looking at her. She was wearing creamy white, or white and pink, he didn't really look, but she was light and gold.

'Thank goodness you're here!' she said, and took his hand, quite naturally. 'It's been absolutely deadly.'

She pulled him away and he saw that people stared at them, that people stared because of who she was and how she looked, and the fact that she was holding his hand and was not put off by him, and he was amazed at her. She pulled him fast, almost running across the lawn. There were people on the grass and Tamsin stopped in front of two ladies in hats.

'Mrs Patterson, you remember Lewis Aldridge?' she said.

'Of course,' said the woman, and her friend

nodded, and they walked on and didn't smile.

'You do have an effect!' said Tamsin, delighted, and laughed over her shoulder at him, and he saw that she was excited by people hating him.

*   *   *

The tennis court was some way from the house and it was a grass court and smooth and perfect. Around it were fruit trees with roses climbing through them and past that were the woods. The younger people were near the court and Kit and a boy were playing. Tamsin and Lewis got to the edge of the court and the boy served to Kit and she demolished his serve and laughed, and then saw Lewis and stopped, and the boy hit the ball straight past her, and she didn't notice.

'Come on, infant!' called Tamsin, 'we're playing now. You've had ages.'

She went onto the court and held out her hand. Kit gave her the racket and scowled at her.

'Hello, Lewis,' she said.

'Hello, Kit, wind'll change.'

She frowned some more and looked at the ground and rubbed her face, which was sweaty, with her forearm. The boy came over and handed his racket to Lewis.

'Thanks,' said Lewis and he and Tamsin went out onto the court.

Kit flopped down on the ground to watch and chewed a piece of grass and stretched her legs out.

Lewis could look at Tamsin now and not have to pretend not to. He wondered if she had really got so much more lovely between nineteen and twenty-one or if it was just that all women looked

206

fascinating to him because of not having seen any. Whatever it was, she was gorgeous and she was paying attention to him and he should just enjoy it; there was filing with Mr Phillips in the morning.

Tamsin picked up a ball and struck a pose and looked at Lewis challengingly.

'Ready?'

He nodded.

'I said "Ready"?'

'Yes!'

She laughed, and he laughed too and she served a ladylike serve. He tapped it back to her, careful.

'Don't be polite,' she called, 'I'm terribly good.'

Kit got up from the grass, disgusted with them both. She went up to the house and around the corner to where there was nobody and sat against the wall.

She could hear the party, and the stone was cool on her back because she was in shadow. She shut her eyes up tight. She hadn't imagined he'd fall in love with her or anything like that. She'd thought it would be enough to see him, like when she was younger, but it wasn't. Her loving him had been patient before, and slow, but it hurt now and she didn't know what to do. She felt she knew him, but he was other to her, too; almost impossible to look at, he was so different to her. She could have stared and stared, but had to run away because it hurt too much. She hadn't thought it would be like that and Tamsin behaved as if it was all just normal to play with him and draw him in, and Kit felt helpless. There was a wave of adult laughter as everybody drank more and the talk got even smaller. She could hear her father's voice rising over the others like a clenched fist, and she put her hands over her ears.

*   *   *

Tamsin lifted her hair from her neck and fanned herself and smiled and Lewis tried to work out if her flirting was deliberate or instinctive.

'Come on,' she said, 'hit it to me properly, I shall frighten you with my athleticism.'

He served to her, hard, and the ball bounced near her so that she hardly saw it and she squealed.

'Not fair! You absolute swine!'

She glanced around for a ball. There were none nearby and she looked back at Lewis and said, very deliberately, 'I think it went over here, don't you?'

Then she walked off the court with a little glance over her shoulder at him. Lewis dropped his racket and followed. He didn't think anyone saw them go. He didn't care.

He followed her to where they were hidden by trees and roses, and she walked slowly and stretched out her arms and then stopped and turned and he stopped, too.

They were away from everyone now, and the smell of the roses and heat and the stillness were like a separate place. Tamsin looked right at him and didn't speak.

She was waiting for him to tell her how good she looked.

'You're beautiful,' he said.

'Rubbish.'

'Why do you bother with me?'

'Why wouldn't I? I like to help people.'

He smiled then, it was such a young thing to say.

'Is that what I need?'

208

'You used to frighten me.'

She said it a little breathlessly.

'Did I?'

'Are you a reformed character?'

'Don't I look it?'

He imagined going over to her, and holding her, and how she would feel to him, and she looked into his eyes while he thought about it. They couldn't have held the moment any longer without one of them doing something, and she laughed and took her skirt in her hands and fanned her legs with it.

'I say!' she said.

It was a schoolgirlish gesture, but showed her legs all the same. She was deflecting him. She was tantalising him. It occurred to him he might actually ask this girl out. That would be the normal thing to do.

'How would you like to—'

'There it is!' She was kneeling suddenly and had picked up a tennis ball and showed it to him, as if he cared, and before he could get any further she'd turned away.

'Come on,' she said, 'I don't want to play any more, do you? Would you get us some drinks?'

She went off through the trees and he followed her out onto the grass and towards the house and the people. It was as if he wasn't there, and though he walked next to her there was nothing to say. He didn't know why she had changed suddenly; he hoped he hadn't said anything wrong.

'Ed!' she said, and Lewis saw Ed Rawlins coming up to them both. 'Did you come down today? Just for this?'

'This morning,' answered Ed, and then, 'Hello',

to Lewis.

'Hello,' said Lewis back.

Tamsin took Ed's arm and they went off together.

This was more like it, this was like being home. He wasn't sure where to go. He wasn't about to go following after Tamsin and Ed. He looked up at the terrace. The adults were still drinking and standing in groups talking, although what they all had to say to each other year after year he had no idea.

*   *   *

Alice had walked down the garden and watched some tennis and then come back up through the people. She could spend the whole day smiling and walking. Everyone around her smiled and walked too, so there was just a whole garden full of smiling walking people, gliding past one another.

She felt Gilbert watching her from the terrace and looked at him. He wanted her to come and stand by him and he wanted her to stop drinking. She stared back at him until he looked away and she felt triumphant about it. She saw a maid with a tray of cocktails go by and had to sidestep quite quickly to get her attention. She took a drink and stopped herself from raising her glass to Gilbert on the terrace. She thought she'd smile and walk again—but in his direction, so as to please him. She wanted to please him. She wanted Lewis to please him, but she thought there was slim hope of either one of them doing it, with her stupidity and Lewis having already been ruined by both of them. Alice knew she was quite drunk; she thought she'd

210

get drunker. She wondered how drunk she could be before Gilbert was really angry with her; she wondered if it was possible she was angry with him. She reached his side and stood by him.

'Darling,' he said, and smiled and turned back to Dicky, who was telling a joke about a Frenchman.

Alice smiled very brightly.

*   *   *

Lewis was standing apart from the party with his hands in his pockets, wondering what to do. He saw Alice go up to Gilbert on the terrace, where Dicky was holding court. His father was laughing with the others at something Dicky had said. He thought he might go and tell him he'd walk home. He didn't want to draw attention to himself. He had made an appearance, he'd shown willing and not broken Ed's nose again or fallen over drunk, and it was time to go. He'd call the day a success. He didn't want to eat lunch with them. He could see the servants laying out a buffet and the thought of jostling with old ladies for cold cuts and trifle was appallingly silly.

He started across the garden, slowly, and glanced over at his father and Alice. Lewis could see, even at that distance, that Alice was drunk.

He paused, watching. She was adjusting the strap at the back of her shoe and holding her empty glass in the other hand. She put the glass down on the terrace and started to fiddle with her dress, laughing later than everyone else, and then too loudly. Gilbert picked up the glass and handed it to the maid and then put his hand on Alice's arm. He saw Gilbert look at Dicky and saw his fear

211

of everyone noticing, and felt it as if it were his own.

Gilbert looked up at him suddenly and caught his eye and Lewis had been so absorbed in watching them, he felt caught out. His father gestured him over and he went immediately.

Gilbert held onto Alice's arm and stepped a little apart from the group as Lewis reached the terrace. Lewis saw Dicky noticing and turned his back to him, shoulder to shoulder with his father and blocking Dicky's view.

'Your stepmother is feeling unwell. I want you to take her home.'

He spoke very quietly and looked at Lewis steadily.

'Now?'

'Yes, now.'

Alice watched them talking about her; Gilbert exerting his will and Lewis looking like a child—closed up and frightened—and she wanted to shout at Gilbert for bringing him into it, and at Lewis for being so proud to be trusted.

Gilbert handed Lewis the car keys.

'Just drive her straight home. I'll walk back later. Alice?'

Alice didn't answer. She was looking down.

'Alice? Will you go with Lewis?' said Gilbert.

She nodded, hardly looking at either of them. Lewis couldn't take her arm, like Gilbert had done. He started walking and hoped she'd follow him, and she did.

'Thank you,' said Gilbert.

*   *   *

212

Alice followed him from the terrace and around the corner of the house, and Lewis thought about Tamsin and nearly kissing her. His body felt like it was still there with her, in the roses and the grass, and he didn't want to be here at all. He'd get Alice home and then go somewhere by himself. He hated this; he hoped she was drunk enough to forget it—and then Kit bobbed up next to him, appearing from nowhere at his side.

'Mrs Aldridge? Are you all right?'

Alice stopped, annoyingly, and swayed about.

'Little Kit Carmichael. Such a sweet girl.'

She patted her face.

'Can I do anything to help?'

Embarrassment made him angry, 'Thanks. We're fine.'

He got Alice walking again and Kit let them go, and he was aware of her oddly stricken expression as he left her.

Preston had moved the car and Lewis parked Alice by some rhododendrons while he went to find it. She weaved about and he had to stop her from sitting down to wait. He wished himself anywhere but there.

He brought the car around to the front and opened the door and waited while she got in. He had to lean across her to shut the door.

She was glazed, but her make-up was still perfect. He didn't think he'd ever seen her without it. She was sitting with her hands in her lap and staring straight ahead like a doll. They started down the drive—and it was good to be driving a car, he almost enjoyed it—but then Alice started to talk.

'Like a child! Taken home!' She put on a

mimicking voice, 'She's not behaving properly. She's so difficult. Why can't she behave herself?'

This was all new, her being like this, like the arguments. Lewis paid her no attention. He started to tap the steering wheel to a rhythm in his head.

'What does she think she looks like?' said Alice, her words falling over themselves. 'Who does she think she is? One really can't have people being so very badly behaved, can we? Jesus God! Lewis—God!'

He turned into the drive and stopped the car by the house.

She shouted suddenly, 'Look at me when I speak to you! You're just like your bloody father. Look at me!'

Her eyes were bright and furious and when he looked at her, she looked away and was quiet.

He got out and opened her door for her, staring at the ground. She scrambled out of the car and he didn't help her. She went to the front door and got her key from her bag, but she couldn't open the door with the key and she started to cry.

'Oh my God. Lewis. I'm sorry. I can't. Oh God, I've no excuse at all . . .'

He went over to her and took the key and opened the door and gave her the key back.

'I'm sorry,' she said, and she kept crying.

'Don't cry. It's fine.'

She leaned on him. He took her into the hall, supporting her, and he took pride in it.

The hall was dark and cooler, and she made herself upright and seemed to pull herself together. He took a breath and stepped away from her again.

'I'm sorry, Lewis.'

214

'I don't mind.'

'Really, I—'

'It's fine.'

There was the sound of the clock ticking and the smell of the flowers in the vase on the table and the polished wooden floor and Alice stood there damply, clutching her bag and hat, bewildered by herself.

'Oh, gosh. What a fool. I expect you detest me. Of course you do. You've always hated me. I know that you have.'

There was only one response to her. There had always been only one response to her.

'I don't hate you.'

'I don't feel very well at all,' she said, and went to the bottom of the stairs, holding onto the banister.

'I'm—' she tripped and he went to help her and they went up the stairs together.

At the landing they stopped, and he let go of her arm.

The moment trembled and held still. It didn't move on to the next moment where he would go downstairs again. Instead, she spoke.

'The thing is, I feel so very badly about everything.'

He didn't look at her.

'About what?'

'About you.'

There was silence. He was still.

He felt the crisis, the glimpsing of a truth, but it was a murky sort of instinct, and he wanted to get away.

'Lewis?'

He held up his hand to stop her. She took his

215

hand.

She took his hand and held it. It was wrong that she did that. They both looked at her holding his hand like that. Her hands were small and white and they felt hot from her twisting them together and holding her bag so tightly in the hot car. She gripped onto his hand.

'You don't know how it feels,' she said, 'looking at you and knowing it's my fault. I should never have met him. Or I should have been better, but I couldn't be.'

She looked up into his face and her need was so great he couldn't look away from her.

'You were just this little broken thing and I was too young to mend you, and I'm sorry.'

He felt sick with himself and as if he had forced her to say it. He wasn't her fault. The wrongness inside him wasn't because of her and he didn't want her apology.

And then she undid the button on his sleeve. She pushed the sleeve softly up his forearm, and he wanted to pull his arm away, but the fascination was too much and he couldn't move. She pushed up his sleeve and looked at the scars on his arm and, holding his hand with one hand, traced the whiteness of the thin scars with her fingertips.

She touched his scars so lovingly, it seemed.

'Are you still broken?' she asked.

She shouldn't ask a thing like that. He didn't know the answer. She was undoing something in him and he tried to turn away from her, but he couldn't turn away.

'Are you? . . . I need you to forgive me. Can you?'

She went closer and kissed his arm, she kissed

216

the scars on his arm, and it was as if the world quivered all around them.

'Are you better now?' she said and came up closer; he could feel her clothes lightly touching him and she kissed his arm again, holding his hand.

'Don't do that.'

Alice looked up and her face and her mouth were close to him.

'Don't you want to be close? Don't you? Don't you want not to be alone, just for one moment in your life? For one single moment to just not be completely alone?'

'Jesus Christ!' He pushed her away from him hard, and she went backwards against the door frame.

'Don't!'

She was scared of him, so he went to her and he took her face in his hands and soothed her, and kissed her, and felt her tears on him as they kissed.

There was a moment where they both knew they could choose, but then it started, and his mind was nothing but heat. She held onto him tight from the beginning. She was desperate, and she pulled at him and kissed him, and all he could think about was that he mustn't. She had her back against the door frame still, and as they slid down to the floor she pulled his shirt out of his trousers, yanking at his belt; she couldn't get it undone and he helped her. It was fast and hot, and she was kissing him all over his face and licking him and holding on and digging her nails into him. Lewis closed his eyes and felt his face covered in Alice's kisses and her tongue licking his neck and her hands gripping him, and it was dark and absurd and irresistible. Her skirt was very full and the material got

217

between them and he had to push it out of the way. She pulled at her underwear, taking his hand and pushing his fingers hard inside her, and she was wet and hot and like a dark and clawing thing and he was pulled in and, forcing in, felt horror and lust together. She got herself nearer, wriggling along the carpet and opening up her legs for him, and when he was inside her she started to cry and he hadn't known you could feel such shame and still be hard and able to carry on. She was tilting her hips up at him, driving herself against him, but she was making gasping sobs and he started to stroke her face to console her, not wanting her to be in such pain. She kept crying, though, and got her foot wedged against the floor so that she could force herself up faster and harder against him. He felt the need for her going, as the horror got bigger than the need to do it, and there was too much darkness. As he got quieter, going away inside himself, she was grasping him harder and clinging onto him, and she came then—and cried out loudly with it, her nails digging into his arm, but before she had even finished coming, still shuddering with it, she opened her eyes up wide and stared at him. She pulled herself away, as if she was being burned, and scrambled across the floor. Her hands held onto the door frame, gripping, and she looked at him a second more, before getting inside the room and slamming the door shut.

He was half on his knees on the floor of the landing, his trousers and shirt undone and sweat coming off him, and the blank closed door to his parents' room in front of him. He heard his own breathing and no sound from behind the closed door.

He got up and did up his trousers and his belt and went down the stairs. He crossed the hall and saw his hand reach out to the front doorknob and—like in a dream—saw his father on the other side of it, with his key in the door, but when he opened the door there was just the car and the empty drive.

He went back to the drawing room and took the bottle of gin from the cabinet by the door.

The car keys were in his pocket. They hadn't fallen out while he was fucking Alice.

He went out of the front door and got in the car. He drove out onto the road, holding the bottle in one hand, and drank as much as he could without choking.

*   *   *

The day was hot and sunny; it didn't know what had happened. You'd think the sky would be black and stormy once you'd had your stepmother on a Sunday afternoon, but it wasn't. It was high and blue and empty. The road was twisting and Lewis drank some more and then put the bottle between his legs to steer better. He went fast and couldn't feel the gin at all, and thought that if he could kill himself driving it would be a good thing. The hedges went by and the road straightened out, and he drank some more and went faster and felt darkness. He closed his eyes and drove blind for a while, and fast, and waited, and didn't feel any fear except that it got funny. He opened his eyes and started to laugh, and driving is hard when you're laughing that much, and he thought of all the people at the party and of his father and of himself

219

fucking Alice on the landing; and he laughed so that he had to lean his head on his arm to keep it upright and drank some more, and it stopped being funny again. There was a bend coming up and he went into it fast, and crashing wouldn't have mattered if there hadn't been a car coming around it towards him. He saw the black bonnet of the big car, swinging sedately around the corner towards him, and the face of the driver, staring, and he hit the brakes and hauled the car over and it went up on the bank. A second later and he would have killed himself, and the other man too, but as it was he had time, and the black car swerved and there was a screeching sound from one or both of them, and his car went up on the verge and tilted and nearly rolled, and the other car got by; and Lewis pulled the wheel hard over again, and came to a stop across the middle of the road after the bend, and the engine died. He had spilt some of the gin on himself as the car tipped. He saved the bottle from falling. He wiped the sweat off his face.

After a while he moved the car. He got it as far as a shallow ditch and stopped there. He got out of the tilting car and sat at the side of the road with his head down on his arms. The sun was very hot on the back of his neck and his shirt, and it felt like it was holding him down. His head was crowded. He saw Alice up close to him and her mouth open and trembling as she came; he felt her tongue, licking him, and he heard her shouting at him to look at her. He saw his father's face and his own slashed up arm and Alice looking at the blood on him when she'd bandaged him up, and how she'd hated it. He could smell her face powder as he

220

kissed her tears, he could feel the starched layers of the material of her skirt knotting around his hands and the blank bare skin underneath, and he felt her hands, pulling him. Then, like a shadow over him, he felt his father standing behind him—and he looked up—opening his eyes quickly and straight into the sun, and in the pain he thought he saw the black shape of his father, looking down at him, and thought he was always there, only now he could see him.

He drank some more and couldn't sit up any more and he covered his face—and there was Alice, and her dislike for him. Then he remembered she'd kissed his scars and put him inside her, and he thought perhaps she loved him.

When he could, he drank some more. And then he saw his mother under the water, except this time he saw his own foot holding her down. Maybe that had been the truth of it, he thought, and then he passed out.

*   *   *

Kit had lain in bed in darkness and felt her skin tingling and smarting with the beating her father had given her. The night was hot. When she couldn't sleep, she got up and put her dress on.

She let herself out of the house and walked barefoot down the drive and out onto the road. She thought she might keep on walking and not stop. She was blind in the dark night, but she wasn't frightened like she had been in her own bed.

She walked away from the village on the side of the road and her feet made no sound. The tarmac was cooling off from the day and mixed with the smell of the dew on the grass. She saw a pale owl flying low and quite near to her and stopped to watch it. There was the sound of a car engine and then bright headlights. Kit stepped off the road and onto the verge, into the deep grass, but the car slowed right down and, even though she looked away from it, stopped just near her.

'Hey.'

She looked up. It was Lewis driving his father's car and she thought she was imagining it was him, but it was him. The engine idled in the quiet; he didn't drive on. Kit looked in at Lewis.

'What?' she said.

He leaned across and opened the door and she slid into the leather seats, and her bare feet felt strange on the carpet of the car.

'What are you doing out here?' he asked.

'You're drunk.' She could see that he was.

He put the car in gear and carried on driving, very slowly, and they didn't speak.

Kit sat in the cool dark. He was next to her and he was passive, so she could absorb him without his even sensing her doing it. It was like she was a ghost, and visiting, and she could feel him, and not be noticed.

He stopped the car near the end of her drive and waited. Kit looked over at him and couldn't make herself get out. He was just sitting there and squinting, trying to keep his eyes open. He'd never know, he'd never remember.

'I'm in love with you,' she said and then felt very frightened she'd said it.

He focused on her, slowly, and she found herself looking back at him, waiting.

222

'You'll get over it,' he said.

Then he gestured, a sarcastic, 'get out of the car' sort of gesture, and she got out with her head down.

Kit watched him drive away and went slowly up to where her dark house waited for her.

Lewis got the car through his gate without hitting it and left it on the drive. The door was unlocked and he opened it and saw that his father was sitting on the bottom stair. He was wearing his pyjamas and dressing gown.

Lewis shut the door and looked at his father sitting on the stairs and concentrated on not swaying, and waited.

'You all right?' said Gilbert.

Lewis nodded.

'Car all right?'

There was a silence.

'We'll overlook it this time. We've both got work in the morning.'

He got up and went up the stairs. There was still to be no crisis then, no apocalypse. Things were back to normal.

CHAPTER FOUR

'It's a simple alphabetical system, dockets here, buff files monies in, blue files monies out.'

Lewis watched Phillips, happy in his world, moving around the small office, getting out boxes and stationery. He felt light-headed and he wanted to laugh. He was dangerously close to losing himself. He knew he was still drunk as well as being so hungry.

He had left the house without seeing Gilbert or his stepmother. Gilbert had left him the car and taken a taxi to the station and, after throwing up in the bathroom and waiting until there was no-one around, Lewis had taken the keys from the hall table and left.

'You'll find 1952 from April here,' said Phillips, in his stride, musical, 'and ascending—'53, '54 . . . We've just the one sharpener, it's in my office, all right?'

Phillips left him at the desk in the second office and Lewis looked around him, and out into the deep quarry, and picked up a pencil. He started to copy the column of figures from one file into the next and the morning passed like that, like the same moment over and over again. At one o'clock Phillips's head came around the door.

'That's lunch.'

'Right.'

'Noticed you didn't have any sandwiches. In the car, are they?'

'No.'

'Fancy one of mine?'

'Thanks.'

'I usually head outside for lunch. Bit of fresh air. You won't want to sit with me. I'll leave yours on my desk.'

'Thank you.'

Lewis ate at his desk and Phillips sat on a plastic chair in the low shade of some hawthorns that grew up close to the quarry edge. The sandwiches were potted meat, with jam ones afterwards, one of each.

Lewis finished work and got home half an hour before Gilbert. He and Alice didn't see each other until Gilbert came home. After supper the family sat in the drawing room and Lewis listened to the clock tick and tried to count the ticks, which took a lot of concentration because he had to count very fast in his head.

'Shall we go up?' said Gilbert, and Alice might have answered, but Lewis didn't know because he didn't listen, and he didn't know if she looked at him because he didn't raise his head.

'Lewis, will you lock up?'

His father was beginning to trust him. He could go to work and lock up the house alone, and he could drive his stepmother home when she was unwell.

He heard them cross the hall and go upstairs and their door closing. He got up and shut the garden door, and locked it, and then he went around the room turning off the lamps by their tiny switches.

*   *   *

That was Monday. The days that followed felt wrapped up in something, but not something soft, like cotton wool, something hard like thin wire, and every day it tightened. Lewis spent the days working and the evenings in endless mealtimes with the two of them and the nights in his room. He hardly slept, but lay in stillness, with darkness all around him and trying to find something to hold onto to keep himself from it.

225

'Are you sure?'

'Yes, of course.'

'It's been a week, he's doing so well. You won't mind?'

'No. I said I wouldn't.'

'If he comes with us to church, it'll be done then. People will see that he's come home, and that he's with us, and that will be that.'

'I know! I told you.'

'You seem . . .'

'Gilbert!'

'All right then.'

Gilbert sat on the bed and watched Alice. She was putting on her powder, eyes down, behind a cloud.

'I'll bring the car round.'

'All right.'

He went to the door.

'Alice—' He saw her stop, and wait. 'I believe he genuinely wants to make amends. He's doing his best.'

She began to flick away the extra powder from her face.

'I'll see you downstairs,' he said.

Alice finished her dressing and tried to do it without touching herself, or paying too much attention to her body. She heard Gilbert go downstairs and his voice in the hall, and then Lewis's—as she reached behind to do up the buttons of her skirt—and she tried not to touch her skin with her fingers while she did it. When she was dressed she sat at her dressing table, facing away

226

from the mirror, towards the bed, but she didn't look at the bed, she looked at her bedside table. Her alarm clock and night cream and the book she was trying to read were there, and her watch, waiting for her to put it on. She was thirty-five years old. She thought that she was about halfway through her life. It seemed a very long time to have to wait. She got up and crossed the room and put on her watch.

*   *   *

Alice waited in the car while Gilbert made a speech to Lewis about getting through church. Lewis nodded his head and waited for his father to go, and then poured himself a half-tumbler of gin and drank it fast before going out to join them.

*   *   *

The unmarked grass was neat around the graves. Lewis stood by the car with his father, and Alice waited for them, putting on her gloves.

The family was shaded by the chestnut tree they had parked under. They stood and looked at the sunny church and Lewis's mind faltered at the sight of it and at the idea of going into it.

Alice was in the corner of his vision and he turned his head slightly, until she was gone from it.

'Lewis?'

There was a gap in his head again, and quiet fear at it.

'Lewis? I know this is hard for you. Sundays are hardest of all. Of course they are. Lewis?'

'Yes.'

'Coming?' Gilbert came up to him. He put his hand on his shoulder. 'Let's go in. All right?'

They walked towards the crowd of people in the graveyard. Only a few people stared as they crossed the grass.

Kit stood in the porch with her mother and saw the Aldridges coming towards them.

Lewis saw Kit with her family in the porch of the church and she was watching him. He looked at her and she smiled. He thought he heard her say something—but he knew she hadn't, she was too far away—still, he thought she had said something nice to him and it occurred to him he really was losing his mind, and then Dora Cargill stepped up close in front of him and smacked him in the face.

It was a hard smack and it hurt quite a bit and the shock of it was funny. Lewis smiled, but other people weren't smiling. There was a moment of stillness and then Bridget Cargill came up and grabbed her sister and pulled her away, and Dora started to cry and there was a wave of embarrassment and confusion and Lewis found that, instead of being scrutinised, suddenly nobody was looking at all.

He felt quiet. There was honesty at last, and fairness.

He saw Tamsin turn away from her family and come towards him. People were looking again as she took his arm. Her taking his arm was so kind it was painful to him, and she looked up at him and smiled.

'Shall we go in? Would you like to sit with us?'

He felt a horrible sadness, and shame, and he couldn't say anything to her.

Tamsin whispered, 'Everyone knows Dora

228

Cargill is as mad as a hatter' and then, louder, 'Come on', and they walked into the church together and Tamsin greeted the vicar coolly as she held Lewis's arm and took him up to the front with her.

The hymn was 'Onward, Christian Soldiers', which was farcical, and Tamsin leaned close to him under the cover of the voices.

'You're doing awfully well,' she whispered.

*   *   *

Gilbert's carving knife sliced the flesh of the chicken.

'Walk or fly, Lewis?'

'I don't mind.'

'Nice drumstick . . . Alice, walk or fly?'

'Whatever's easiest.'

Mary brought the vegetables and Alice said goodbye to her and she left for the rest of the day. Alice passed the vegetables around and they heard the front door closing.

'Congratulations, Lewis.'

'Sir?'

'That was very difficult. You handled yourself well. That Tamsin Carmichael is a good girl. Don't you think so, Alice?'

'Yes.'

'We've a lot to thank that family for. Alice?'

'Yes.'

'Anyway. Dora . . . One of the graves was their mother's. It was very difficult. But there we are. It's done.'

Lewis looked at the salt and pepper shakers in their tiny silver rack. He looked at the fluted glass

229

vase, and the pinks in the vase, and at the white tablecloth, and the small lace cloths that were on top of the tablecloth and under the other things. He looked at the silver bread basket, at the latticework of it and at the napkin inside, and at the candlesticks and thin china butter dish.

'I've got a jolly busy week next week. We've had all the quarterlies in, it will be too much going back and forth all week. I'll be staying up at the flat until Thursday or Friday. Will you both manage?'

Gilbert picked up the bottle of red wine. He poured himself and Alice a glass and then held the bottle over the table for a moment, and Lewis found he couldn't take his eyes off it. Gilbert's hand, and the bottle, came towards him.

'Good boy. Well done,' said Gilbert and poured wine into Lewis's glass and it was as if the air snapped, he heard the tension break. He couldn't see properly and when he hit the bottle, it smashed against the wall, and his father put his arms up to shield himself from the glass flying and the wine thrown outwards. Lewis brought his hands down onto all the perfect things and he felt the brittle breaking china and the starched cloth buckling. The table seemed to fracture and the naked wood shone out dark under the cloth. He felt his body ringing with the fast rush of it, and the things were breaking and falling and he saw Alice start back and cringing, hide herself—and then he breathed—and could see properly and realised what he was doing.

Gilbert moved quickly, and stood up and shouted blindly and his rage was tearful, but Lewis had gone, out through the open window behind, and it was pointless shouting.

He sat down again and the two of them sat, and looked at the wrecked table, and then Alice stood up and started to collect broken glass in her palm.

'Why would he do that?' said Gilbert, his voice weak, 'why would he do it? Is there something wrong in his head? Alice?' He looked at her, searching, but she didn't look up. '. . . Alice?' he said.

'I don't know,' said Alice and continued piling broken glass into her hand.

*　　　*　　　*

Lewis didn't know how he could go home again. He knew he would go home again. He had no choices and no chances, and he couldn't remember any more what his plan had been or why he had come back. He seemed to glimpse it dimly, an idea of himself he had made while he was shut away, which now was ruined and he would never be able to do it.

The woods were dark and hot and the sun made glowing patches of light, and Lewis walked and felt calmer and waited to be calm enough to stop walking. He thought of Alice and his father and he wished he could take a knife and cut them from his brain, and stopped walking. He seemed to see the knife that would do it and it was thick-bladed and short, and the picture of cutting the bad parts out of his living head was very clear. He and Alice—he heard water; there was the river. The river was ahead of him and he looked at it.

The trees were not so thickly crowded together. The river wound away into the woods and there were ferns around it, and oak trees, and the bank

231

was short and went down gently. The sight of the river stopped his brain and there was only that, the soft curve away through the woods and the ferns around it and stillness. He walked towards it. It had been a still day, and just then there was a breeze and the leaves moved around and above him and made the sunlight dance over the ground.

There was somebody swimming. He saw a dark, sleek head and bare arms, moving, and the breeze stopped and the heat came back, rising. Lewis watched the dark head in the water. It was Kit.

Kit felt him there and turned and screamed and he saw that her shoulders were bare too.

'Oh! Don't look at me!'

He couldn't see anything, she was underwater and he was thirty feet from her. He turned away.

'I'll come out.'

He heard her come out of the water and bare feet scampering and then quiet. He guessed she was dressing.

'I simply hate Sunday lunch en famille, don't you?' she said.

He saw the wrecked table, and himself going out of the window—and he smiled and the very bad things in his head stopped and left him quiet.

'Can I look?' he said.

'I s'pose.'

He turned around. She was wet still, and half in her dress, which she was trying to do up at the back, twisting around. Her hair was wet and gleaming.

'You look like a baby otter.'

'Excuse me, I'll be sixteen in October. Switzerland and everything.'

She gave up with the dress and smiled at him.

232

He went a little closer to her.

'Everything work out the other night?' she asked with studied carelessness, and he had a picture of that night and Kit sitting forlornly in his car, and him trying to drive, and Alice . . .

'Fine, thanks. You?'

'Oh, you know. Thing is, my father hates me. Yours does too, I think.'

'Mine has a reason.'

'What's his reason? The church and everything?'

'And everything.'

It was no good.

'What?'

She waited, looking at him. She was waiting for him to speak, and he needed to speak and he needed to tell her something of himself.

'Sometimes . . .' He struggled. 'I feel like I'm falling away from everything, like the world's just far away from me. And dark. And I'm dark too. Just recently I don't know if I can get back . . . Have you ever felt like that?'

He was frightened by saying it. Kit regarded him briefly.

'Of course,' she said, and he saw she knew exactly.

It was enough. She didn't say anything else. They walked a little way. The bank ahead of them narrowed and there were trees in the way of the path. Lewis stopped, and Kit stopped too. He looked at her.

'Why would he hate you? Your father.'

'He thinks I'm detestable.'

'You seem all right,' he said and was happy to see she was pleased.

233

She was turned away from him, and her neck and shoulder were tanned against her faded dress with its buttons done up wrong at the back and half open. She made him smile. He thought that she had always made him smile. She was a baby, and so easily pleased, and she was too serious and needed teasing. She wouldn't look at him and he remembered her saying that she was in love with him. He wondered how she could be, and what she'd meant by it, or if he'd heard her wrong. Her shyness seemed to invite something, though, and he needed her attention, so he touched her with his finger on the ribs, poked her in the ribs, until she laughed.

'Don't!'

He loved her laughing and did it again.

'Stop it!'

She tried to hit out at him, and he put his hands up to protect himself from her. She had a look about her, like a fighter, and he had to grab her wrists in his hand and hold them together, and even then she tried to kick him. They were both laughing and it was either fight her or take a fall, so he took a fall, and lay on his back looking up at her. She stood triumphantly over him.

'Yah-boo!' she said and he laughed.

She stood over him for a moment, with the sunlight behind her head. He sat up and Kit kicked the ground about a bit and neither one said anything. She saw an interesting stick on the ground and picked it up, and sat against a big tree to play with it, drawing lines in the sandy ground. The tree was big enough for them both and he went next to her, and lit a cigarette, and leaned back, shutting his eyes to smoke.

It was nice to be with her. It was much better than being alone.

'Dora Cargill walloped you.'

'Yes, she did.'

'She's mad.'

'So I hear.'

'What's prison like?'

'It's all right.'

'Were they mean to you?'

'I kept my head down.'

'Is it like school?'

'Except you learn things.'

'What sort of things?'

'I can make wooden tables. And I can attach wheels to them.'

'Gosh. I should think life as a trolley-maker would be very pleasing.'

'Restful, you mean?'

'Somewhat. Ow!'

She had a splinter.

'Show me.'

She held out her hand. He bent over her, looking.

'Actually it hurts quite a lot. Don't squeeze it!'

'How am I going to get it out?'

She took her finger back and sucked it and it was childish, and not childish, and unsettling.

'I've got a knife,' he said.

'You have not.'

'Yes, I have. I'll do it. Show me again.'

'No!'

'I thought you were so tough.'

'I can be.'

'Here, let me.'

He pretended to reach into his pocket.

'No! . . . You haven't?'

'No. I haven't.'

He sat back against the tree and she went back to her finger, trying to grip the splinter, concentrated. A drop of water reached the end of her hair and splashed onto the dry ground. Her dress was damp and sticking to her. He looked at her bent head, and cheek and shoulder. If she had been a drawing, she would be drawn with few lines, and strong ones.

'Why did you cut your hair?'

'I saw a lovely film with a girl with short hair, and I thought it would be glamorous.'

'Not a boy with very short hair?'

'No, a girl—shut up.'

'It's nice.'

'Daddy was furious. I did it myself, and it looked absolutely shocking and I had to go into the barber in Turville to sort it out. They want me to grow it, but I'm not going to.'

'Don't.'

It was soft hair, and dark, and the fine shortness was beautiful against her neck. Not beautiful like women were beautiful, he thought, just like something very beautiful, something else.

'Why did you burn the church down?'

It was a silly question, and his look said it was.

'Honestly, why?'

'I don't know. It happened. I just had to see it.'

'It was a sight.'

'It was.'

'You should have seen all the fuss.'

'You should have seen the judge.'

'They had meetings.'

'They nearly hanged me.'

236

She laughed. There was a silence.

'They buried my mother there, and she never even liked the place. That wasn't why. I don't know why.'

Kit nodded.

'How is it?' he said, looking at her finger, still held out, and she showed him. He went near to her to look and Kit felt his nearness go through her.

'KIT!'

They both jumped. Tamsin was by the river.

'I've been calling for hours! You know we're going for a drive! We've all been waiting.'

'Sorry.'

Kit scrambled up and she had dirt and bits sticking to her dress and her feet. Tamsin was still in her church dress and she was immaculate and cross.

'Hello, Lewis,' she said, and met his eye, and was charming, and Kit looked at Lewis and his reaction to Tamsin, and saw that he had forgotten her.

'Hello, yourself,' he said.

'Well, come on then, if you're in such a hurry,' said Kit, and went to Tamsin and grabbed her hand and pulled her away. Tamsin threw Lewis a look over her shoulder as she went.

'Bye, Lewis, I'm going to bring you lunch at your very important office next week.'

'Thanks,' he said and watched them go.

*   *   *

The woods were quiet when the girls had gone. He felt much better, but he waited as long as he could before he went home and it was dusk when he came into the garden.

Alice was standing on the grass.

She had seen him come out of the trees from the house and had come out to meet him.

Lewis stopped some way from her and couldn't get to the house without passing her.

'Where's my father?'

'He's inside. Where have you been?'

She wasn't a stepmother asking him, she was a woman asking him, and he didn't answer her. His father's house was behind her with the sky reflected in the windows that were opaque and staring. He wouldn't look at her. She was trying to make him, but he wouldn't.

'Lewis? You're just going to pretend? Are you? You're just going to keep pretending?'

'Yes.'

'Lewis?'

'WHAT?'

'What do you think I want from you?'

'I don't know. I don't. Leave me alone.'

'You act as if—'

'Stop it!'

'Please don't be so—You're so . . .'

She was starting to cry and he couldn't stop himself looking, and when he did he wanted to comfort her and it was unbearable. He went past her and felt as if she was reaching her hands out to grasp him as he passed—but she wasn't, she didn't move—and he didn't look back, but went inside to his room and didn't feel safe there, or calm, but walked up and down and tried not to want to do the bad things he needed to, to release himself and to sleep.

It was early morning when Gilbert knocked and came into his room. Lewis was putting on his shirt and thinking it was very bad that his hands were shaking so early in the day when he hadn't got a hangover.

'I'll be off in a minute. I'm leaving you the car.'

'Thank you.'

'I'll see you at the end of the week.'

'Yes.'

Gilbert didn't leave, but stood in Lewis's room, waiting. He was holding a book in his hands and he turned it over as he spoke.

'What you did yesterday, at lunch, losing control of yourself like that, it worries me. It was frightening. Can you see that?'

'Yes, sir.'

'Lewis . . . Sometimes when things seem overwhelming, we have to remember that we have a choice. I wanted you to have this.'

He put the book on the bed between them and bent down to open it at a marked page, fumbling.

'This sort of thing probably seems old-fashioned to you. But it's always meant a lot to me. We can find solace. If we look for it.'

It was the poem 'If'. Lewis couldn't speak to him. He stared at the page.

'Lewis, this can't go on. What's going to become of you?'

'Dad . . . I'm sorry.'

After a silence Gilbert said, 'Sorry isn't good enough, is it?'

'No, sir.'

The water washed the last of the soap away and Lewis rinsed off his face, and the razor, as his father left the house. He didn't close the razor. He looked at it, he looked at the blade and its straightness, and very carefully he traced a line down his forearm, hardly touching the skin, feeling the whisper of it, gentle on him. He was holding the razor so hard his hand was shaking, but the blade was very light against his skin, barely touching. Then he put the razor down.

CHAPTER FIVE

If you can trust yourself when all men doubt
    you,
But make allowance for their doubting too;
If you can wait and not be tired by waiting,
Or being lied about, don't deal in lies,
Or being hated, don't give way to hating . . .

*   *   *

Alice was in the bathroom and Lewis was on his bed and they were alone in the house. It was Tuesday morning. He could hear the water splashing. She could have been washing herself, between her legs, where he had been. The bathroom door opened and he held his breath as she went to her room, and didn't start to breathe again until the door closed behind her. There was so much of his mind taken up with the not thinking

240

of things that the rest of it was having some trouble thinking at all. They hadn't had breakfast together, or supper the night before. He thought if he could just get through this day, and then the next . . . He picked up the book again, 'If you can force your heart and nerve and sinew . . .'

He got up. Phillips would be happy to see him arrive early; there were definite advantages to sleeplessness. As he came down the stairs he saw a brown envelope on the mat. There were no other letters. He kept his eye on it as he went down; knowing what it was and feeling nothing.

He picked up the envelope: 'Ministry of Labour and National Service'. He put it in his pocket and waited until he had stopped outside the quarry office to open it.

It was a brown notice, with his name in crooked type that fell off the dotted line, 'Lewis Robert Aldridge'. Then, below, 'In accordance with the National Service Act, 1948–1950, you are called up for service in the regular army and you are required to present yourself on Monday the 26th August 1957 between 9 am and 4 pm to the Officer Commanding of the Royal West Kent Regiment, The Barracks, Maidstone, Kent. A travelling warrant for your journey is enclosed.' With the notice was a card, with 'Description of Man' at the top, which made him smile. It said: Date of Birth: 29th December 1937; Height: 6 ft and 1¾ ins; Colour of Eyes: Grey; Colour of Hair: Brown.' Well, he thought, it's definitely me.

He had known he would get his enlistment notice. They'd given him his medical in prison; now that he had been locked up for two years, he was apparently not the unstable delinquent the army had felt him to be when he went in. He hadn't thought the notice would come so soon. He put the envelope in his pocket and went into the office.

*   *   *

He and Phillips were a happy team now. It looked as if shrinking your brain down to a tenth of its capacity and pretending you were a small and unsophisticated machine paid off in the world of filing. Lewis wasn't sure what appalling acts Phillips had thought he would commit, but it seemed that he could delight him simply by being there every morning and getting on with it and going home again at the end of the day. Phillips had checked on him and given him strange glances for the first few days, but now he seemed more genuinely fond of him than anyone else Lewis could think of. Lewis took his approval and shored it up against his crimes. When Phillips dumped the dusty boxes of files on his desk, pointless files— from the 1940s, some of them—he gave him friendly looks that said 'Here we go again' and 'Good lad', and Lewis was reminded of the Kafkaesque nature of his work and of Dicky's words, 'I'm paying you almost nothing to do a worthless job . . .' Well, he was going off to the army soon to do another worthless job for almost nothing, and didn't give a damn either way. The sound of a horn distracted him from 'Unpaid invoices, 1950' and he looked up. Tamsin pressed the horn again and waved and beckoned him out.

*   *   *

'I said I'd feed you, didn't I?'

Lewis leaned against the wall of the building and watched her. She had spread a cloth on the bonnet and was unloading things from a basket onto it, bread and cheese and bottles of lemonade.

'I do think you're mean not coming for a picnic. I'm sure that little man has more important things to do than spy on you. Check gravel and so forth.'

Seeing Tamsin was more and more like being visited from another planet. She amazed him with her blitheness and her confidence and he envied her. He couldn't think what her life must be like, or what her interest in him was, and while he appreciated being able to look at her, he felt no connection with her at all. He would have liked to be able to join in. He didn't know how.

'What do you do, mostly?'

She looked up, 'What do you mean?'

'You and most people. Do you stay at home? What?'

'I try to have fun.'

'Meaning?'

'Lewis—gosh, I don't know. I see friends. I go up to town. There are parties. Theatre sometimes and all sorts of charity things. You know.'

He didn't know, did he, he'd been in Brixton prison—he'd barely heard of Elvis, he had no idea what people did or where they went. There were great chunks of him missing. He wondered if she really questioned her life so little that being asked what she did produced genuine surprise, or if it was an affectation, and she actually had it all designed, her place in the blueprint for society. She handed him a sandwich and he sat down

243

against the wall while she arranged herself in the passenger seat of the Austin and sipped her lemonade at him.

He didn't eat. He looked at the way she sipped, and it was adorable, the way she did it, and he thought she was the sort of girl you were supposed to want. She was the kind of girl people married, were lucky to marry. He didn't want to be her charity case.

'Those things you do,' he said, 'do you want to do them with me?'

She'd been asked out so many times, she didn't pause at all.

'You're sweet, I don't know what Daddy would say.'

'I'll ask him,' said Lewis, and it seemed perfectly simple and the sort of thing people did, and she laughed.

'I dare you!'

*   *   *

He walked over to the Carmichael house, not through the woods, but along the road, to arrive the proper way, and his feet were noisy on the gravel as he went up to the front door. He remembered playing on bikes with the others in the gravel and how they had made tracks through it, loving the skidding, and been told off by Preston and had to rake it all flat. Kit opened the door to him and he didn't recognise her again, because he'd been remembering them all as children, and the sight of her was odd. She lit up when she saw him and he could feel her joy. He wondered what made her so happy.

244

'Hello!'

'Hey, Kit. Is your father in?'

'Library,' she said, and disappeared into the dark hall before he could say anything else. Like a shadow in the shadows, she led the way and knocked on the door.

'Lewis is here,' she said, and went, giving him a resentful glance that made him want to chase her and make her laugh.

He went into the library. Dicky was by the desk.

'Well?'

There was nothing for it. Perhaps he hadn't locked himself out of the normal world; perhaps Dicky would see that his intention was good. He'd given him a job, hadn't he? And Lewis had stuck at it.

'I wanted to ask you, I wanted to know—if I could take Tamsin out one evening.'

Dicky turned to face Lewis, taking a step towards him.

'You think not burning anything down for a few days qualifies you as some sort of beau for my daughter?'

Lewis was taken aback. He thought about it.

'Probably not, but I think she'd like to.'

'You think she'd like to?'

'Yes.'

'If you imagine Tamsin's interest in you is anything other than pity—altruistic pity—then you're mistaken. She's kind to people. She's helped you. Don't get above yourself.'

There was silence.

'I expect you're right,' said Lewis.

There was another silence.

'Now would you mind getting out of my house?'

245

Kit hid around the corner as he came out of the study, but she was too angry just to let him go and she followed him out and caught up with him on the drive. He kept on walking and didn't look at her, and she went along next to him in a rage.

'Why did you let him talk to you like that?'

'You shouldn't listen at doors.'

'Why did you?'

'Because he's right,' he said, still not looking. She could see he wanted to be away from her and it was horrible.

'No, he isn't! And anyway, you should be pleased. Tamsin's not nearly so lovely as she thinks she is.'

He stopped and when he looked at her she knew she looked tearful and mean and she didn't feel pretty or like a girl should look.

'Put away your claws, Kit, it's none of your business.'

She stopped and he walked on. He didn't know he was hurting her, she thought. He didn't do it on purpose.

CHAPTER SIX

There was no let-up in the weather. There was no let-up in the heat, or the dryness, and the summer was empty, with no flowers left in it and just dust, and the fields being cut, and the dark green of the woods. It was very near the anniversary of Elizabeth's death.

He was by the river. He was always there. The sky was white and pressing down and the slow, fat raindrop fell on his arm, and the feeling of it falling and the trickle of it were sickening. The water was very dark, and the woman in it was dead already this time, and it wasn't his mother, it was Alice. She was dead, but she was looking at him, and he still couldn't move in the hot day, and the heat was the thing that woke him. The closeness of the suffocating heat woke him, and when he did wake he was shivering and his face was wet and he thought it was sweat, but it wasn't, he'd been crying in his sleep. He never cried normally, just in his sleep, and he could never remember what it felt like afterwards to cry like that. He wasn't crying now, but he was scared.

He sat on the side of the bed and he wiped his face and thought of Alice, and how frail she was, and that he'd always assumed she'd be there in her strange, brittle tenacity. He put the light on to check his watch. It was three o'clock and the window was black. He put the light out again and got up. He could get a drink. He was trying not to do that. He thought of Alice again, and was frightened.

He went out onto the landing, and wasn't sure if he was dreaming he was doing it, or if he really was doing it. Her door was ajar and he went to the gap. He didn't want to open it, he just wanted to check she was there, but he couldn't see her through the gap and he stood listening to his heart beating and trying not to make a sound. He wasn't going to open the door. He told himself he was being stupid; of course she was there, of course she wasn't dead, why would she do a thing like that? But then he thought of her helplessness, and that she was unloved. He pushed the door open with one finger and prayed she'd be sleeping.

She was lying on her back, across the bed, with her body nearly all uncovered by the sheet and wearing her nightdress. Her mouth was open a little and her breasts rose and fell in shallow time with her breathing. She opened her eyes. He stepped back onto the landing.

He didn't think she'd seen. He waited, out of sight, not daring to go back to his room. There was silence and then he heard her move, her body move on the sheet, and a whisper.

'Lewis?'

He waited long minutes before moving, he waited until he could be sure she slept. Then he went back to his bed.

*   *   *

They didn't see each other in the morning and he left for work before she got up. He understood people's previously mystifying attachment to the world of work—it got you out of all sorts of things.

'1949,' said Phillips, and dumped another box on

his desk.

You are required to present yourself on Monday the 26th August . . . He picked up his pencil. Shooting a gun would be good, but he didn't much fancy the prospect of killing anyone. He'd tell his father he was going at the end of the week. Gilbert wouldn't be impressed; he had been a proper soldier with a just war to fight. Lewis pictured himself in a uniform, saluting, and being given a medal, and imagined Gilbert and Alice clapping and dressed up. Then he thought it more likely that, given a gun and a bad day, he'd find the urge to put a bullet through his own head irresistible, and get himself off their hands that way. He continued writing: '80 lbs aggregate, £5 6s 4d . . .'

*   *   *

Leaving the quarry office, and driving home, was at first actually joyful, with the road twisting down the hill in the sunny evening. There was relief and beauty in the country around him and in being away from his terrible desk. Then came the straighter part of the road, towards the village, and he would start to picture home, and Alice, and what she'd be doing, and he'd find himself driving slower and sometimes just stopping and waiting. He didn't do that now; he made himself drive on and he hardly realised he was home already until he saw Tamsin waiting at the bottom of his drive. He slowed down and looked at her, absurdly pretty and pale against the dark leaves. He imagined her walking out to meet him, waiting for him there, and wondered why.

As he got nearer to her, standing there in her

249

bright summer dress, he felt more a part of the dark behind her than the light she stood in. She raised her gloved hand and waved to him. He stopped the car.

'I thought you hadn't seen me!'

'I saw you.' He left the engine running.

'It's been ages. What have you been doing?'

'Working.'

'Daddy said no, didn't he?'

'Of course he did.'

'Will you come for a walk with me?'

'Now?'

'Unless you don't want to, of course.'

He glanced up the drive, to his home—and Alice—and he cut the engine.

'All right then.'

*   *   *

They walked along the verge a little and stopped at the stile into the field that ran along the road to the station. It was a long, narrow field, with a path worn through the grass up to the woods. The sun caught the trunks of the trees sideways and made them glow against their shadows, but the field was all in light, and golden.

Tamsin gave him her hand and stepped onto the stile. She climbed over, and carried on holding his hand and looked into his eyes.

'Let's go into the woods.'

Lewis felt the look. He wasn't sure he should go anywhere with her.

'All right,' he said, and they walked up the field towards the trees.

He lit a cigarette and looked down as he walked,

250

and she seemed happy to walk in silence for a while. He was far away from her in his mind. They reached the wood, and it was cooler between the trees. She walked with her hands behind her back, glancing sideways at him. He knew she was looking, and he knew she wanted him to think she was attractive, but there was nowhere to go from there and he didn't want to get involved with it.

'Don't you like me any more?'

'You're fine.'

There were trees all around them now. Tamsin stopped and leaned against the wide trunk of an oak tree. He stopped too, half turning to look back at her. She took off her shoes and her bare feet were neat and perfect like the rest of her. She undid the button on her glove and took it off, and then the other one, and she held them both and looked up at him, letting the wave of her hair fall forward. He dropped his cigarette and crushed it under his foot and looked at her standing there. He was beginning to feel angry.

'I think you've gone off me,' she said. 'You used to think I was so pretty, I know you did.'

'What do you want with me?'

'What on earth do you mean?'

'Why are you nice to me?'

'I told you, I want to help you.'

'Help me what?'

'Lewis, you're—'

He saw her falter. He enjoyed it.

'When's your birthday?'

'What?'

'When is it?'

'May.'

'Twenty-one in May. Did you have a party?'

'Course, big one. Why?'

'Lots of friends. At home?'

'Lewis?'

'Was it at home?'

'Yes, it was at home! What are you asking me about it for?'

'I'm talking to you like people talk to each other. I'm having a normal conversation like normal people—'

'But you're not normal people, are you?'

'Aren't I? Why aren't I?'

'Well, really! If you need me to tell you—'

No. He didn't need her to tell him. She had her back to the tree. She seemed small against it and he took a step towards her.

'Have you had a boyfriend?'

'I'm twenty-one, don't you think I've been out with men?'

'You wouldn't want a boy, you mean?'

'You're not a boy.'

'Well, what am I?'

She—laughing, 'I should think you're a problem!'

'I'm a problem. I don't like normal things. I can't do things like normal people. I could take you to the pictures. I could buy you dinner somewhere.'

'Silly, I don't want you to.'

'So what do you want? What exactly do you want, Tamsin?'

'I want to talk to you.'

'Talk to me about what?'

'About things.'

'Plays. Books. What?'

'About, well—gosh, about your problems, I

252

suppose. I want you to feel better.'

'*You want me to feel better?*'

'Your mother—'

'My mother drowned. It was nearly ten years ago. I was pretty much a mess for a while, but I'm all right now. What else?'

'Well—'

'What else do you want me to feel better about?'

'Can we stop this?'

'You don't want to talk?'

'I do, but—'

'Not about that? About what, then?'

'You know people say you killed her?'

She was smiling as she said it; she was leaning against the tree and looking up at him and smiling.

'. . . What?'

'People say you killed your mother. Didn't you know? When you got so wild, running away and drinking, that's what everybody said, that it was guilt for killing her. Didn't you know?'

Lewis was quite still and lost.

'I was ten years old. Sh—she drowned.'

He heard his own voice stupidly clumsy like a child's and didn't know if he was defending himself or making a confession.

'She was swimming and she . . .'

Tamsin laid her hand on his arm and came up close to him.

'Oh gosh, Lewis, I'm sorry, I shouldn't have said anything.'

She dropped her gloves and held his other arm, and her mouth was close to his cheek, and then he understood her. He understood her kindness.

'. . . Lewis?' she breathed, close to his ear.

He put his arm around her waist and kissed her

253

and he was quite cool about making her want it. She kissed him back, gratefully, reaching up to him.

'Oh, don't do that,' she whispered, an inch away from his mouth.

He kissed her and felt still and watchful, and she pressed herself against him as they kissed. Then she looked up and smiled at him, very warm and pleased.

'Now I know,' he said.

'What?'

'What you wanted.'

'That's a beastly thing to say.'

She was insulted and he was pleased to have insulted her, and he felt hard about it and liked it. He kissed her again.

'You don't want me to take you out, do you?' he said.

He could feel her heart beating against him or maybe it was his heart, beating against her.

'. . . This is what you want—'

He kissed her again, and lifted her hair from her neck, and kissed her there, and he kept to the rules and didn't touch her below her neck, but he could feel how much she wanted him.

'No—no—'

'No?'

'No,' she said, holding onto his arm with one hand as she reached up to him.

It wasn't like one of those other women wanting him—this was delicate and her fingers on his arm were finding out what it would feel like, not knowing beforehand. He put his hand onto the top of her dress and held onto it and pulled her towards him, and she shook when he did it and

254

made a little sound, a soft girlish sound that came out of her because she wanted him so badly. A button broke from the top of her dress and fell onto the ground, and he had to remember she wasn't the sort of girl you could just have against a tree, even if she was behaving like it, even if he could have done if he wanted. Then—

'All right. Stop now. That's enough.'

She said it very briskly, and he let go of her. There was one still moment, not touching, and then she immediately got close again, as if she'd never said it, and kissed him and put her hand onto his belt buckle and held it. He wanted her badly too now, and she knew that he did, and she smiled up at him, looking into his eyes and holding onto his belt like that, with her fingers tucked inside and pressing into him.

They kissed and he felt her tongue and her parted lips, and then she opened her eyes and took her body away from him again, but left her hand, holding his belt.

She tightened her fingers.

'We'd better get back,' she said. 'They'll wonder where I am.'

Lewis looked down at Tamsin's hand on his belt.

'Oh, sorry,' she said, and laughed, and gave the buckle a little tug, and then took her hand away, but kept looking into his eyes.

He bent down to her and she kissed him with no shyness at all and pressed herself against him and he was getting taken over. And then she pulled away.

'I said No. Stop it,' she said.

He knew how to behave. He hadn't been going to touch her. She should leave it now, though.

255

Didn't she see that she should leave it now?

She looked into his eyes and she smiled.

'There,' she said, 'kiss me on the cheek like a brother and we'll forget all about it.'

Lewis didn't move. She stood on tiptoe to kiss his cheek. She laughed. Then she kissed his neck, stroked her girlish cheek against his neck, her lips against his ear, a tiny whisper, and he heard a rushing in his head and he lost everything . . .

'WHAT DO YOU WANT?'

He slammed his fist into the tree behind her and the pain was beautiful.

'WHAT—? TAMSIN!'

The woods and the sky wheeled around him.

He was on his own again. There was faltering blackness in his head.

He couldn't see her any more. He didn't know how long she had been gone.

He fixed his eyes on her pale blue shoes lying in the dirt with the white gloves next to them and came back to himself, except that the roaring in his ears was still there, muffled and threatening. He turned away and left her things lying there.

*   *   *

Kit saw Tamsin running down from the woods towards the house. She saw that she was upset, and barefoot, and that her dress was open at the top. She had been sitting on the window seat in the drawing room and trying to draw the kitten that was sleeping there. The kitten wasn't hers, and she wasn't allowed it in the house, but it had come in and she had found it sleeping and passed the time with drawing it. She saw Tamsin come down to the terrace and stop. She saw that she had been crying. She felt dread, but she didn't get up immediately. Dicky came out of the house and met Tamsin on the terrace, and Kit pushed the window open to hear.

'Tamsin? What's happened? Where have you been?'

'Nowhere—'

'Tell me!'

'Daddy—'

'Where have you been?'

'Lewis—'

Dicky grabbed Tamsin's arm and pulled her along with him, and inside, and Kit heard him say, 'Tell me! What happened?'

She got up and went out into the hall. She saw Dicky pull Tamsin into the library with him and the door closed. Kit made herself run away from the door, and out of the house and around to the library window. She went against the wall and listened, controlling her breathing.

'—No, he didn't!'

'Look at you!'

'He didn't!'

'Why were you with him?'

'We went for a walk—'

'Why did you go with him?'

Dicky was very angry and he was shouting, and Kit didn't think she'd ever heard him shout at Tamsin.

'He wanted me to, and then—'

'Then?'

'Well, he—'

'What? What?'

'Well, we were—kissing—'

257

'Look at you!'

'He didn't do anything.'

'You!'

'Stop it!'

'You look like a slut—'

'Don't!'

'What's this then?'

'Let go—stop it!'

'What did he do to you? What did you let him do to you?'

'Nothing, he was kissing me. He kissed me, that's all.'

'You're lying to me—'

'Don't do that! Stop that! You're horrible.'

She heard the punch and Tamsin's cry, and then the sound of her falling.

She couldn't not look. She saw Tamsin on her knees with her hands to her face and Dicky standing over her. Her sister kept her hands to her face, and then Dicky was on his knees and he was crying and apologising and trying to kiss her and stroke her hair. Kit put her hand over her mouth and was sickened by her jealousy. He had never apologised to her. He had never punched her face. Her face wasn't worth punching. She was appalled at herself.

Dicky pulled Tamsin up and took her to the sofa and sat her down. Her fingers were fluttering over her cheek and eye, where he had punched her. He went to the sideboard, near the window, and Kit went back against the wall and shut her eyes and listened as he poured a drink and tried to make Tamsin drink it, and kept on apologising and saying he couldn't stand it. After a while Tamsin said, 'It's all right, Daddy' in a clear voice, quite like herself again, and there was silence.

After a moment Dicky said, 'Better?'

'Better.'

'Good girl. The boy—he took you to the woods?'

'Yes.'

'And he attacked you there?'

'Yes. He hit me, but I escaped before he could . . . ?'

'Yes.'

There was another silence.

'Where is he now?' said Dicky.

CHAPTER SEVEN

Lewis had decided to walk over to the Carmichaels' and apologise to Tamsin. He didn't feel very clear in his head, but it sickened him that he'd scared her and he thought she should know.

He'd started towards her house, but Kit had been there on the path and she had been looking for him. She was out of breath and determined, and holding the keys to Dicky's Jaguar.

She was irresistible and stubborn. She dragged him along the path to the stables behind the house that were converted into garages and when she'd pulled the cover off the Jaguar—like she was pulling the rug off a racehorse before a race—he had looked at her, incredulous and admiring.

'You want me to steal your father's car?'

'He won't notice. It's just for looking at.'

'You're insane.'

'I'll drive it myself then. I will. You can't stop

me.'

Lewis had looked at her hopeful, desperate little face and felt he had no choice about it.

'Where are we going?'

'It doesn't matter, come on!'

*   *   *

The road was clear and light, and the car felt very good to drive and Lewis didn't think about anything except the driving, and Kit played with the radio and tried to find songs she liked. They didn't talk. Kit fiddled with the radio and Lewis felt the ease of being with her. It was the only thing he could be doing, and just right, and the feel of the car going fast and the noise of the engine and the snatches of music above it were perfect.

*   *   *

They went to London. He hadn't driven into town before and they were lost at first and drove around and looked at things and then parked in Soho Square, and he turned off the engine and waited. It was very quiet without the engine noise and the wind going by.

'I've never been out in London at night before,' said Kit.

'I should hope not.'

'Just tea with aunts, and uniforms.'

He lit a cigarette and she pulled down the mirror and got a lipstick out of the pocket of her jeans. She wasn't used to doing it, and although she didn't make a mess of it, it was clumsy, the way she did it, and without vanity.

260

'There.' She turned to him, 'Is it all right?'

She had a black top on and she squashed her hair down—what there was of it—and smiled at him. He found he couldn't say anything. He nodded. She looked down into her lap and then glanced up at him.

'Do you quite like jazz?'

There was only one place to go.

*   *   *

They left the car, and the London night was hotter than the country, and dirty-smelling. Lewis forgot everything except that he was alive and that it was good to be alive, and not shut in anywhere, and the familiarity of the street was not a melancholy feeling, but reminded him of the rush he'd felt whenever he escaped there before, and he thought maybe this was the right place to be.

Kit felt joy at being out with him, and on the streets, and thought if nothing else happened in her life she'd be happy.

They stopped at the corner where the club was, and there was a crowd and Lewis pushed past some people and rapped on a door. The panel slid aside.

'Lewis. Bloody hell!'

They went inside and Tony slapped Lewis on the shoulder as they went down, and Kit held his hand tightly down the steep, dark stair. It was very smoky and there were people standing on the stairs and around the bar. Lewis was walking into the past.

Kit gripped his hand and kept his shoulders in front of her, and stared. It was very busy and the

261

crowd was noisy and moving, and it was the same as it had been, for Lewis, but still shocking because it was so full of energy and heat. Kit pressed close to him and he led her across the room to a table.

There was only one chair and he seated her and looked around for another. He saw then how thrilled she was, and he felt at home and proud to be showing his place to her. He had been twenty-six months in one prison and then two weeks more in a different kind. He was out now.

The band playing was a small jazz band, close together on the stage, and they were playing something hot and fast. There were people near the stage and people listening, or dancing, or just ignoring the music and talking. There was a couple kissing at a table, which Kit was shocked to see and had to look away from because it made her embarrassed.

Lewis put a chair for himself next to her and went over to the bar. Jack was there. Of course Jack was there.

'Hey, Lewis; long time, man.'

'Jack.'

They shook hands.

'You won't be looking for any trouble with that pretty girl around—'

Lewis turned around to look for the pretty girl and realised he meant Kit, who was watching the band with her chin on her hands. She felt his look and smiled at him, before looking away again. She looked beautiful, he could see that she did. If she hadn't been Kit, and he hadn't known she was fifteen, he would have called her a pretty girl, too. She was fifteen, though. He had been fifteen when he met Jeanie. He didn't know how old Jeanie was.

It wasn't the same thing.

'How you been keeping, Lewis?'

'All right, you?'

'Pretty good. Gin? And the lady?'

'No. I'll have a beer. And a . . . Coke. Thanks.'

He took the drinks and went over to Kit with them. He sat down. Kit leaned forward and sipped her drink and then laughed suddenly and said something to him, but he couldn't hear. He leaned towards her and she shouted into his ear over the music. She was talking fast, about whether the band had a singer, and wondering if they were from America, and that they reminded her of another band she had read about; and he couldn't catch everything she was saying, but just listening to her was lovely because she didn't know what he knew, and she saw it all her way, which was a good way to see things.

The set finished and the lights came up a little, and Kit sat back and looked at him, as if he'd given her the biggest present in the world. It wasn't a look he was used to. It made him feel uncomfortable.

'What?'

'Nothing—' But she kept on looking at him.

It was odd how being looked at like that made him feel that he was someone different.

'Well, for God's sake, we are having a heatwave.'

Jeanie was at his shoulder. Her hand was on her hip, and most of the rest of her seemed to be on a level with his eye.

'Hello, Jeanie.'

'Introduce me?'

'Jeanie Lee. Kit Carmichael. Kit, Jeanie.'

Kit held her hand out very politely and Jeanie

263

took it.

'Hello there, Kit Carmichael,' she said, and then she turned to Lewis, 'That's jailbait, Lewis.'

She didn't lower her voice to say it, and Lewis saw Kit's eyes widen.

Then she leaned down and said, 'Happy to see me?'

In a funny way he was, but he glimpsed Kit's face as he stood up and he turned away from the table and spoke to Jeanie quietly.

'How've you been?'

'Missed you, baby.' She had always called him that. He'd been one, hadn't he?

'Yeah, I was away for a while.'

'I heard.' She patted his cheek. 'My boy's all grown up now.'

She was good-looking still.

'Look,' he said, 'she's just a kid, she doesn't know anything.'

'That's easy to see.'

She looked hard, and he didn't know if she'd always been so obvious looking, but he remembered how he'd felt about her. It seemed a long time ago. He was worried about Kit.

'Be sweet, eh?' he said.

'You know I can be.'

He had a picture of her in bed with him, in her flat, and how she had tasted in his mouth and the noise she made when he did that to her. Her, and Alice—and Jeanie bent down to Kit and said in her ear, 'Look after him, honey, won't you?'

She walked away and Lewis watched her go. She met a man at the bar and he helped her on with her coat and they left together.

Whatever shine there had been on the evening

had gone. He waited and felt the flatness and the tension, and he wished he could hide Kit away. He couldn't meet her eye. She should be in her big, safe house, and part of the clean world where he couldn't be. He should never have brought her. He hadn't meant to, he'd just wanted to run away, he hadn't been thinking about her. He was thinking about her now.

'Who was she?' she said, and he could see she was trying to sound casual and he hated himself.

'Just a—girl.'

'Did you used to come to this place quite a lot?' She made it sound so nice.

'Yes.'

'And they let you in?'

'I spent some time here. When it was no good at home.'

'You're so lucky. When I run away I can't go anywhere—the police would bring me back or I'd be kidnapped for a white slave or something. Boys have much more fun.'

He looked up. 'You run away?'

'All the time.' She met his gaze.

'Why?'

'Do you read Jean-Paul Sartre?'

She was trying to put him off, and her precocity was lovely, but he knew that she was trying to put him off, and he still wanted to know.

'No. Why do you run away?'

'Oh. Just existential crisis, ha-ha, or maybe a difficult home life.'

He remembered her walking barefoot along the road after he and Alice . . .

'Why were you on the road that night? The night I picked you up?'

265

'Why were you?'

She was smart. He didn't say, because I'd just fucked my father's wife. He could barely sit opposite this clear-eyed girl with it in his mind.

'Really,' she looked into him. 'Why were you?'

'This is no good. Come on. Let's go.'

He started up and she grabbed his wrist—

'Lewis!'

She loved him. He could see that she did and he was terrified she was going to say it again. He leaned forward to her. She was open to him, her face was open to him, and she was alive and hopeful and waiting.

'Look, Kit. I can only do you harm. I've got nothing you need, do you understand? Nothing.'

'But I know you,' she said, and he thought she was going to cry.

'You've got some little-girl ideas about—I don't know what—but you don't see.'

'But, Lewis, I can see.' Her look was steady and she didn't seem young. 'I see you. You think you're dark, and there's all this darkness around you, but when I look at you . . . you're like a shining thing. You're light. You just are. You always were.'

He seemed to glimpse something, sideways, a way he hadn't seen, obvious and elusive.

She put her hand out across the table and he could see she was being brave to do it. It occurred to him that she probably hadn't held a boy's hand before his, and that he wasn't a boy, not like that, and he had no right to take it. He could take her hand, and he could have her, and let her think she was right about him, and ruin her, or he could let her go. He reached across the table and gently pushed her hand away from him.

266

'Let's get you home.'

'I'm not going home.'

'It's time.'

'It is not.'

'Come on.'

'Just because you've had some absurd attack of spurious conscience?'

'Your vocabulary must exhaust you. It's bedtime.'

'I'm not tired and you think I'm just a baby, to be told—'

'I don't think that!'

She was funny, and broke his heart, together.

'Yes, you do. I'm more grown-up than you are.'

'That's a fact. Let's go.'

'NO!'

She got up and away from him and went over to the bar, and Lewis watched her and waited to see what she'd do. She checked he was watching and pushed through the people and put herself between two men. She smiled at them. One of the men was the drummer from the band, on his break and drinking. He bent down to her and spoke and she nodded and threw a look over at Lewis that challenged him and made him smile. She was playing, and Lewis could have watched her do it for a while, just to see her, but he thought it might get serious, so he got up. By the time he got over there, the drummer had bought her a whisky. Lewis ignored the drummer and spoke to her.

'Come on, don't be childish,' he said, in her ear.

Kit made a face at him and picked up the whisky. Lewis took it from her and put it on the bar.

'Hey!' said the drummer, who was very big, and

wearing a patterned shirt, and didn't know he wasn't really a part of what Kit and Lewis were doing, which was a private game and pleasing them both. Lewis ignored him. He took Kit's arm.

'Let go!' she said.

'Let her go,' said the drummer.

'Let's sit down,' said Lewis.

'I don't want to sit down!'

'She doesn't want to sit down.'

Lewis saw that he'd have to speak to him.

'Just forget it, all right?'

This was a mistake. The drummer squared up to him and got very close. Lewis was bored by him and more interested in Kit's reaction, which was extreme.

'Sorry,' she said, very Surrey, 'you have it', and she handed the whisky to the drummer, who didn't stop staring at Lewis.

'Come on!' she said to him.

'You wanted the lady, go with the lady,' said the drummer and Lewis wanted to laugh, and then there was a whistle and a blast on the trumpet, and the drummer looked up and was distracted.

The rest of the band were back up on the stage and the lights were going down and he couldn't stay and hit Lewis, even if he'd really meant to. He stared at him again and left.

'Lewis!'

'I wasn't going to fight him.'

'Yes you were!'

'You're so easy to tease.'

'No, I'm not. You are. I hate whisky. Are you in love with Tamsin?'

'No.'

'Why did you kiss her?'

268

'She wanted me to.'

The singer came on. She was black and very voluptuous, and she was wearing a white satin dress, and she moved very slowly as if she had to drag her feet along. She reached the centre of the stage by degrees, hips first and feet after, and then she gave a slow smile.

'Help,' said Kit.

The band started to play again and it wasn't like before, it was an old Gershwin song, but not recognisable at first because of the way they did it, with double bass and the piano climbing in and out of the bass, and it was only when she started to sing that they knew it. Her voice was warm and scratchy, playing with the rhythm, and the song was about loving somebody and regret, and people started to dance.

Kit stood away from Lewis and looked at him and held out her hand.

'What do you want?' he said, and she smiled at him.

He took her outstretched hand and let her pull him out onto the floor.

She was in his arms and it was a new feeling, and she felt just right to him. She had her head close to him, but not touching, and when he bent down he could feel the softness of her hair, and her hand was resting on his shoulder. He held her hand to dance and put his other hand behind her, at the top of her back, and then after a while a little higher so that his thumb rested in the perfect hollow at the back of her neck, where her hair stopped and her neck began. His thumb fitted there and he didn't need to move it, or stroke her, to know that she felt it, and he wouldn't have done anyway because it was right the way it was. She was a fine girl and he felt her fineness and his surprise at finding her and he didn't question it at all. He forgot that she wasn't for him and all the reasons she wasn't for him.

Kit felt as if she was holding fire in her two hands and not getting burned.

When they walked back to the car they didn't talk, but Lewis took her hand and held it.

They drove out of London feeling that they were very far apart from each other in the car, and so she moved across and put her head on his shoulder and he drove with one hand on the wheel and the other arm around her.

*   *   *

Kit was asleep when they came into the village and the sun was just up.

*   *   *

She woke when the sirens started, and because Lewis had to pull the wheel over to get the car into the verge, and the car swerved and then bumped up onto grass. A police car was in front of them, and another behind, and the sirens stayed on and there were policemen coming out of the cars and coming fast at them and Lewis was dragged out and cuffed, with his face pressed down onto the roof of the car.

Kit's door opened and Dicky leaned in, pulling her out and away towards his car, and when she saw her father she screamed for Lewis. He hadn't fought until then, but he fought when she screamed and they couldn't hold onto him, and had to hit him in the side and in the head to get him down into the police car. He was still fighting though, because he could still hear Kit.

*   *   *

People came out of their houses to see it and stood staring as Lewis Aldridge got arrested again and Kit Carmichael was rescued from him by her father. They stayed out in the street for a long time talking about it and waiting to see if anything else would happen, but apart from Preston coming down to the village to collect the Jaguar, nothing did.

CHAPTER EIGHT

The feeling of the handcuffs was familiar to Lewis and the time in between wearing them, and in between being locked up, became shadowy very quickly.

In the middle of the day he was brought out of his cell and put into a room and questioned about Tamsin: hitting her and what else he'd done to her, and what he had done to Kit and where they'd been. It was the same room he'd been in after burning the church. He didn't answer very well. He was stunned from being hit in the head and wasn't sure what he could answer because he couldn't remember what had happened, or if he was there because of Tamsin or because of the church or because of Alice. He wasn't sure why his father was standing next to him sometimes and then not there, and why he wouldn't speak to him, but then he realised his father wasn't really there—he was just imagining he was there. There was Wilson, and another policeman who came in and out, and they were talking about him and saying he was insane and asking him stupid things to try to catch him out, and he knew that was what they were doing, but he couldn't follow them anyway. His mind closed up to get away from it and he lost himself.

*　　　*　　　*

Kit was locked in her bedroom, which she was used to. In the drawing room, Dicky sat next to Tamsin when the chief inspector came to see her. She wouldn't press charges against Lewis and she made it very clear that he hadn't raped her. When the inspector tried to get details from her about what Lewis had done, Dicky stopped him. There was to be no discussion about it; she was intact.

*　　　*　　　*

Lewis was let go late in the afternoon. Wilson telephoned Alice to say he was coming home and, after she put the telephone down, she stood in the hall and waited, and pictured him walking back through the village towards the house. She gripped her hands together and stared at the front door and after a long time he came in.

His face was empty and it made her stay very still when she saw it. It was a look she remembered from before he was sent away and she understood why it frightened people, but it didn't frighten her;

272

she had known him for so long and he had never hurt her. He went past her, and up the stairs.

Alice sat down on the chair in the hall. No, she thought, he had never hurt her.

She knew she should go up, but she couldn't go up. She imagined herself helping him. In her imagining he was younger again, he was fourteen, and she was making him better and not worse, but she knew she wouldn't do it and she sat in the hall and waited.

*   *   *

Lewis was in the corner of the bathroom, on the floor between the basin and the bath. He put his foot against the door and took the razor from the edge of the basin. He held it for a while. Only the hand holding the razor was there. The razor, the handle of it and the blade were the only things that were hard, everything else was numb, with no substance and nothing to touch. It was like having no body. It was like being the smallest thing in the world. The blade was beautiful and shining and sharp and he rested his face against it, just to feel the metal on his cheek. Then he put his head back against the wall and held his arm out and there was a rush then, like pressure building up behind a barrier, and his hand started to shake and the rush got faster and he knew when he did it there would be something. He tilted the blade and pressed it into a long slanting cut, and the first thing he felt was his heart beating and the spit come into his mouth with the fear of it. The blade cut into him and the relief as the blood started was everything. He saw the blood start and colour came back, and pain, and his eyes were hot. He was breathing quickly now and he took the blade and felt the desire to do it taking him over, and when he cut again there was real pain and regret and something to hold on to and to fight with. He was aware of the room and the feeling of the tiles at his back, and the pitiful reluctance to do what he was doing, yet still having to do it. He could feel now that he was stupid and wrong to be doing it and that his head was full of pain, and when he cut again it was much greater and he had to do it faster after that to keep up the courage to do it, because he could feel himself now and he was present. When he made the last cut he knew it was the last cut and it wasn't a gradual ending, but a sudden one, like slamming into something hard, like a punch in the face. He was knocked back with the full knowledge of his hurting and of his failure, and he didn't need to do it any more and put the razor down and away from him.

He shut his eyes. He felt the hopes that he'd had, and prison, and his father, and that he was lost.

His hand wiped the blood over his arm as his head rested back against the tiles, but he couldn't feel it, just his loss.

*   *   *

Kit heard her father coming along the corridor to her room. She had known when she thought of taking Lewis away that Dicky would punish her. She had thought it was a fair swap, a beating, for Lewis's alibi, but it hadn't worked and he was being blamed anyway and now it seemed a silly and

274

babyish sort of plan that never could have worked, and she regretted being upset when she thought of it and not thinking clearly. She hoped Lewis would understand. She thought he would. She stood up to face her father.

Dicky came in, and he was carrying his stick, and he stared at her for a moment.

'Give me a reason, young lady,' he said.

He often said that before hitting her.

'I took the car. It was my idea,' said Kit.

He walked over and smacked her on the side of the head.

'I hate you,' she said and he hit her again, knocking her down. 'I don't care,' she said and started to get up.

He hit her with the stick, casually, in the soft part of her body, and then he held her up from the floor by her arm and he did it again. He let her go and smacked her face, and carried on smacking her face between the blows with the stick, but always flat-handed and carefully, so it wouldn't bruise. He had a lot of technique about his violence with Kit, because he did it often and he was cold about it. Tamsin's beautiful face was precious to him, and while he was beating Kit he remembered hitting her and it took some of the pleasure away because he felt ashamed of himself. Kit was good for it though, and her silence was provocative and he liked to carry on until she cried, or made some noise of pain, which often took a long time because of her defiance.

When he had hit her until she lost control of herself, he left her on the floor and went to his bedroom for privacy, and to calm himself.

Alice looked at her watch. It was a Cartier one that
Gilbert had given her and had a tiny face and
Roman numerals. It always made her feel pretty
and like a proper wife. Lewis had been upstairs for
half an hour. She picked up the telephone and
rang Gilbert in London and told him to come
home. She needed him. She needed him to come
and take charge of it, and deal with his son and
take the burden away from her. The house was
desperate, with her and Lewis in it. If she could
make Gilbert come and take control and see what
had happened to Lewis, he might feel some pity
and help him.

*   *   *

Gilbert took Alice's call and said that he would
come home. He sat at his desk thinking about what
to do. He wasn't happy that Alice was there alone
with Lewis, after what he'd done to Tamsin. He
telephoned Dr Straechen in Waterford and asked
him for the name of a psychiatrist. The psychiatrist
had his offices in Harley Street and Gilbert was
surprised because he didn't know doctors like that
worked out of Harley Street; he imagined them in
Victorian hospitals, with bars on their windows.
The thought of Lewis being in a place like that was
appalling. The thought of him staying at home was
intolerable. Gilbert made an appointment with the
man, a Dr Bond, to talk about Lewis and then he
set off for the station. It wasn't the usual train and
when he got to Waterford there was nobody at the
station apart from himself and a woman with her

child, which she was dragging along by the arm and shouting at. She was nobody he knew, and not the sort of person he would know.

He took a taxi home, dreading it. He remembered driving home after work in the autumn evenings just after Elizabeth had died. He remembered Lewis waiting at the end of the drive, and starting to smile when he saw him. Gilbert remembered that he hadn't been able to smile back, or look at him properly, and although he didn't remember Lewis being bad at ten years old, he had been repelled by him so perhaps he had been. He seemed to see Lewis standing there like a little ghost as the taxi turned in—then he saw Alice waiting in the doorway for him and pulled himself together to face her. She had something of the same look, needing him, and he wanted to tell her she had the wrong man.

He paid the driver and turned to her and her smile was eager and close to crying.

'He's upstairs,' she said, 'in the bathroom. It's been more than two hours, Gilbert. I just haven't dared.'

When the bathroom door opened, Lewis didn't look up. There was a moment when Gilbert saw the blood and that Lewis wasn't moving and thought he had slashed his wrists, but then he saw it was the same as before, just this sickening mutilation. It was only the blood and the way Lewis was staring that were so frightening.

Gilbert opened the bathroom cupboard and took out a clean, white bandage. He held it out to his son. There was a pause and Gilbert saw Lewis's eyes flickering, and then he took the bandage obediently and held it. Gilbert was in his dark suit and his tie and clean shirt, and he was still wearing his hat and felt entirely out of place, and protected by his strangeness.

'Dr Straechen has recommended a man in London,' he said. 'I think the best thing would be if you were to go away for a while. Somewhere you can get better . . . Lewis?' He didn't think Lewis could hear him. He waited. 'Lewis?' he said again.

He thought Lewis seemed to nod. He must see it's the best thing, he thought, and he went out, leaving the door open, and went downstairs. He saw Alice in the hall, waiting, and he didn't want to speak to her about it. He reached the bottom of the stairs.

'Is he all right?' asked Alice, which seemed an absurd thing to say.

He needed a drink. He went into the drawing room and poured himself three fingers of Scotch, and drank it standing. Alice came and stood near him, watching him.

'Was it very bad?' she asked.

'Yes.'

'Is he coming out? Was he talking?'

'No. I don't know.'

'Gilbert, I don't think he hit Tamsin.'

He looked at her. 'Don't be silly,' he said, and finished his drink.

'He's never been violent—not like that. Why would he do that?'

'Will you be all right? I'm going over to Dicky's. I don't like to leave you with him.'

'I told you, I don't think he did it.'

'I heard you. I don't know why you're defending him. Have you seen him? Don't you remember what he did?'

278

'Please don't shout at me, I'm just saying—'

'I'm not shouting at you. I'm going to the Carmichaels'. I'll see what I can do there and I'll come back.'

He left then, and Alice stood in the hall. She'd wanted Gilbert to see Lewis like that, but it hadn't been as she'd hoped; he had just been scared.

*　　　*　　　*

Kit's ribs were hurting her to breathe, but she didn't think anything was broken. They had hurt like that before and it was just bruising and went away. Her head hurt, under her hair, where she had hit the floor, and it made her whole head feel full of tears that she couldn't cry.

Her father hitting her and her loneliness were much worse now, and wrong, because of Lewis holding her hand, and the way he had held her when they danced. He was gentle to her and she wanted to tell him her hardest secrets.

Tamsin brought Kit a tray of supper in her room and put the tray on the bed and looked at her curled up on the window seat.

'Oh, you look all right!' she said. 'Have you seen my face?'

'Does it hurt?'

'Not really. How is it the only time he does it to me, he has to make it show? Yours never do.'

Kit shrugged. She didn't trust herself to ask what had happened to Lewis.

'You are feeble,' said Tamsin. 'You should come down and apologise.'

She went out and shut the door behind her. Kit began to cry, but then stopped herself. She took a breath and held it a moment, looking at the faces on the sleeves of the records around her room, imagining they were giving her courage, and then she made herself eat something from the tray. There were sandwiches, and a plate of biscuits, and the taste of them was horrible, but she made herself eat them because she had always thought that part of winning her battle was looking after herself, being someone who still looked after themselves. She ate a sandwich and a biscuit and she drank the water, and after she had eaten she went back to the window and climbed out of it.

*   *   *

She ducked into the bushes at the side of the drive when she saw Mr Aldridge's car arriving. She wiped her face with her hand, and her hand was dirty from climbing out of her window and it left marks on her face. Her legs were still humming inside from being jarred, dropping down onto the hard grass. She kept hidden as much as she could, and she went towards the village and the police station to see if she could see Lewis there, or find something out. She knew she mustn't be seen and she thought she'd try to look in the windows at the back, where the building faced onto the golf course.

There was still heat in the air and her legs were scratched by brambles as she walked, and her head was still beating pain from her father. She knew she wasn't sensible. For the first time in her life she wanted to surrender; she wanted to surrender to Lewis and have him hold her and let herself be weak. She needed to feel that: Lewis holding her.

She wanted refuge.

CHAPTER NINE

Alice waited until she was feeling as strong and as calm as she could before she went up.

When she opened the bathroom door, Lewis was sitting on the edge of the bath. He was trying to rinse his arm off under the tap and holding the bandage at the same time. He looked clumsy doing it and she saw the child in him again. She didn't know if she'd ever see him just at one age. She wondered if that was what being a mother felt like. She didn't think she would ever know.

He stopped when she opened the door, not moving. She turned off the tap and sat next to him on the edge of the bath.

'I know you didn't hurt that silly girl,' she said.

He shook his head and bowed it down so that she couldn't see him. She looked at the pale blood on the tiles, and the blood on his arm that was dark and smeared, but dry.

'Why don't we go downstairs and clean you up?' she said.

Downstairs she put him in the chair by the doors to the garden, and she fetched a bowl with water and disinfectant and cotton wool and took the bandage from him. He watched her and he felt quiet and more himself, but he didn't have any hope.

She knelt in front of him and wiped away the dried blood and was very careful around the straight lines of the cuts and the places they crossed each other.

'This is a bad one, isn't it?' she said.

He held out his arm and kept it still and his fingers trembled while she did it. When she had finished she wrapped the clean bandage around the arm, very neatly, and tied it, cutting the end in two pieces to do it.

'I'm sorry,' he said, and looked at the top of her head as she knelt.

'Don't be silly.'

'What you call just like old times.'

She looked up, and she had warmth in her look, and then her face seemed to break up, and she bent her head to hide from him.

'What am I going to do?' she asked.

'I'm not exactly the person to ask.'

She didn't look up again, so he touched the side of her cheek so that she would.

'I can't bear to look at myself in the mirror,' she said.

They were the same then. She rested her face against his hand and her doing it made him feel strong. He bent down to her and lifted her face and kissed her cheek and she closed her eyes and put her hand on the back of his head to hold him and to keep the feeling of not being alone and being forgiven for a little while longer.

To be so lost, and then to find comfort, was strange for Lewis and he didn't trust it, but it did feel good, that they should be kind to each other, and that being kind to each other—even with what they had done—was a precious thing.

Kit came through the trees, and the trees hid part of her view of the back of the house, and she could see them through the open door, but it wasn't until she came onto the lawn that she saw more clearly. It was the feeling of intruding upon something that struck her before anything else, before she consciously thought how wrong it was that they should be holding each other like that. Alice was kneeling at his feet and it was that, and her hand on the back of his head and their faces touching, that was all wrong. She walked slowly towards them, without knowing she was still walking, and saw that they didn't move and that Alice's eyes were closed. She couldn't see Lewis's face because it was behind, but his hand stroked Alice's hair and Kit thought: it's all right, he's comforting her—but then they turned and saw her and she knew it wasn't all right. They were ashamed and shocked to be seen, and couldn't hide it. Lewis looked straight at her and Kit stopped noticing Alice, because all she could see was Lewis and try to understand that he was involved somehow with her.

He got up and started to come towards her and she didn't know what they could say, and didn't want to say what was in her mind, so she turned away, turned and started to run away. He came after her and grabbed her wrist. He grabbed her wrist very hard and it hurt her and she was frightened. She had never been frightened of him before; it was because of what she had seen.

She pulled her arm away from him and he saw her fear and stopped coming after her. She was almost at the trees and she could have got away, but she stopped—because she had to know.

'You and her? Is it true?'

'Yes.'

There was a short silence and then she was very

283

distressed and crying out with it, 'But she's your stepmother! It's like she's your—she's your—'

'No! She isn't!'

He shouted it because hearing that was intolerable, but she was frightened of him again and he started to talk just to say anything.

'Kit, it was once. We didn't mean to—I—she was—'

She turned away from him, and held on to herself with her arms.

He waited and was helpless, watching her back, as she fought with disgust, and when she turned back to him she was calm, and quiet, and closed up.

'I came to tell you not to worry,' she smiled a small, bitter smile, 'because they won't do anything to you about Tamsin. Daddy hit her. I made you come up to London with me because I knew they were going to blame you for her being hurt, and I wanted it to be impossible. Because you'd have been with me. But it went wrong.'

She rubbed her forehead with the back of her hand, and seemed tired and muddled.

'Your father?'

'Yes. Usually he only does it to me. I've never told. I wanted you to know about it. I don't know why.'

'He hits you?'

'They'll just want to forget about it.'

'When. When does he?'

'Oh, almost all the time.'

She undid the middle buttons at the front of her cotton dress and showed him the fresh marks of the stick on her skin.

Lewis was in stillness, with the world exploding

around him, and looking at this beautiful girl who he had thought was untouched, and he was blinded by the change in everything.

He held out his hand in wonder, in disbelief. He held out his hand to her because she was so hurt. She shook her head.

'I don't ever want to see you again,' she said.

She walked away from him and he stood where he was. Kit was gone into the woods and he was alone.

*   *   *

Lewis stood between the wood and the house, and he could go up to the wood or he could go back down towards the house. He heard a car door slam, and he saw his father come around the side of the house. Lewis's reaction was a child's reaction; he thought his father would be able to help, and he ran down the garden towards him.

'Dad!'

Gilbert had come from talking to Dicky. He had been apologising, and Dicky had made it very difficult for him and, leaving, he had seen Tamsin's face as she closed the drawing room door. The sight of her, with the vicious bruise around her eye and on her cheek, was still in his mind and when he saw her little sister getting away from his son through the trees, he was very frightened and very angry. They met on the terrace.

'What the bloody hell do you think you're doing? Get inside!'

'I have to talk to you.'

'Inside! You're not to leave this house.'

The habit of assuming his father's superiority

285

was very deep in Lewis and he followed Gilbert into the drawing room. Alice wasn't there. Gilbert went over to the drinks cabinet and started to cram the bottles from the top into the cupboard below, fumbling with them. Lewis watched him and kept thinking, like a child does, that if he could explain, then everything would be all right, and his father would do something and there would be fairness. He could see his father didn't understand, and he needed to explain to him.

'You've been at the Carmichaels'?'

'Yes, I've been there and I have never been so humiliated. I was humiliated—for you, for what you've done! I had to let Dicky Carmichael rub my nose in your filth!'

'Tamsin? I didn't hurt her. She—'

He didn't want to get sidetracked with this. He was thinking of Kit, and he needed to help her, and he didn't know how to do it. He was frightened he'd lose himself again and he needed to explain, and not lose the hold he had on what was important. He felt the bandage on his cuts, firm and holding, and he shook his head—shut his eyes just quickly—so that he could think. Gilbert was closing the doors of the cabinet and trying to lock them.

'So bloody lying and deceit are the latest of your sins?'

Gilbert straightened up from the locked drinks cabinet, and Lewis grasped the significance of his trying to hide away the bottles like that; that he was hiding the liquor from him, but Lewis wasn't thinking about drink, he wasn't thinking about anything but Kit, and he was trying to be heard and he wasn't being heard, and Gilbert was facing him

286

and shouting at him and trying to keep him down, like always, trying to keep him down and keep him small and keep him from doing anything.

'We've had violence,' he was saying, and his voice was shaking with his absurd anger, 'we've had drunkenness, we've had a sick form of self-abuse that most people would find hard to imagine, and now you're—'

'I didn't hurt her!'

Lewis tried to keep hold of the thread in his mind and not let his anger break it, but his father was shouting at him.

'If you think I'm going to let you come back into my home and destroy my life with your—'

Then Lewis went for him—and Alice came into the room as he went for him—and he saw his father's fear and felt nothing about it. He put his hand on his father. He put his hand on him and grabbed at his neck, his collar and the lapel of his jacket. His father felt weak in his hand, and his hand felt big as he pushed him down. He had enough of himself left not to carry on with him, but he kicked the drinks cabinet, the front of it, and the wood splintered under his foot. His father went down to the floor and the light, decorated doors broke into pieces, and the smell of the liquor, as the bottles smashed, the mixing, sweet, alcohol smell, came up and hit him, and he left, as Alice pressed herself against the wall.

*   *   *

The air seemed to stick to him as he forced his way through it. He ran the path along the edge of the trees and into her garden. He was pouring sweat,

287

and the quiet smell of cut grass and the still beauty of the house were evil to him. He started to shout her name and ran the length of the house looking for her, and it was nothing to him that as he went, and as he shouted for her, he smashed his fist into the glinting mullioned windows. He shouted for her, but she didn't come. He didn't feel the sagging lead as he hit the windows, but he shouted Kit's name and thought she must come to him.

He stopped, and yelled her name again to the blank house. There was a man, not Dicky, another man, coming around the side of the house and he heard screaming from inside and Dicky's voice shouting, and then he saw Kit. She was looking down, from a window above him, and not moving. He was distracted by seeing her, and the man reached him and threw his shoulder against his chest and got him down. He held Lewis down and tried to force his head sideways with his knee on his chest. Lewis twisted his body and kicked the man hard in the face and didn't think about it, but got up when he could. He saw Dicky come out of the house, but he couldn't go for him because he had a shotgun in his hands. Lewis saw the man he'd kicked was Preston and that he was bleeding, with his hands up to his face on the ground. There was still screaming. Lewis started to run towards the trees. There was a gunshot, but he was in the trees by then and it was just to scare him, not aimed at him.

*   *   *

The woods were very close and dim, like being underwater, and there was a strong smell of wild garlic and the sap from the trees and nettles. Lewis went away from the path, and through brambles and dead leaves that were years old. When he got to where he couldn't see a way forward any more he stopped and rested, leaning his hand against a tree and getting his breath.

He shut his eyes and he saw Kit very clearly. His whole body was numb and light and he kept thinking of Kit and that he loved her, and that now he knew that he loved her.

He saw her in his car, in London, smiling at him, and he remembered her dancing with him and the feel of her. He thought of her leaning against the tree in her damp dress that sunny afternoon, and talking to him, but letting him be quiet too. He thought of the sweetness of her. It was stupid to feel happy thinking about her, but when he saw her in his mind he did, or at least could imagine happiness. He thought that the idea of hurting such a girl was too bad to think about, and that letting a girl like that be hurt was just as bad.

He noticed his right hand was stinging and he looked at it and couldn't understand why it had small pieces of glass stuck into the side of it and the heel of it, where his wrist started, and then he remembered the windows.

He sat down against the tree to pick the pieces of glass out, and the hand started to shake badly and the small cuts burned.

He rested his head on the back of the cut hand for a while and tried to think what to do. It was difficult to concentrate.

Leaving Kit there was intolerable.

Perhaps if he could talk to her, then things would be all right. It was a stupid sort of clarity, but it gave him something to hold on to.

CHAPTER TEN

Kit had stood in her room as Lewis came for her
and shouted for her and she heard the banging on
the glass and Tamsin screaming. She was so
frightened she shook all over, like she did when
her father beat her; she felt the physical horror of
those beatings and made a connection to Lewis
that she had never made. He had always been
gentleness to her. She had thought him gentle and
now she wanted to run from him. She would lock
her door, she would barricade herself in, she would
hide away from him. She was too scared to move
from the window as he shouted for her, and when
he saw her and shouted her name and she saw
Preston trying to hold him and Lewis kick his face,
she was sickened by it. The sickness and fear were
tied together in her mind with sex—the sex he had
with Alice, and the sex she sensed from her father
—and thinking of those things was unspeakably
dark to her, and unbearable.

To Kit, the idea of sex was a vulnerable and new
thing, and when she dreamed of it, or thought of it,
it was sweet and thrilling and it had to do with love
and promises. The idea of Lewis and Alice, and
the fear of him she now felt, belonged to a place
that was corrupt. She thought of the woman in the
jazz club, stroking his face. She thought of Tamsin
running barefoot with her broken-open dress.
Lewis wasn't gentle to her now. She didn't know
what he was.

290

After he had got away into the woods she went to her bed and sat there for a long time.

There were voices and people downstairs and she could hear her father's voice and then, after a while, there was the sound of hammering, metal and wood. She went to the window and saw there were men barring the smashed windows with raw timber battens. The hammering went on for a long time, as the sky darkened to invisible outside her window. It was very loud and relentless and after it stopped the silence rang.

Kit switched on the lamp on her bedside table. She looked around her room at the record frieze propped against the skirting and the faces were dumb. There was no Lewis to think of, there was no song to listen to. All of her loves were empty.

She heard footsteps in the corridor, but it wasn't her father and she didn't get up.

Tamsin opened the door. Her bruise was ugly against her skin and pale hair and she leaned against the door and looked at Kit very coolly.

'What's up, infant?'

Kit felt an infant too, and wanted Tamsin to be kind.

'Did they finish the windows?'

'Yes, isn't it ghastly? All barred in till tomorrow when they'll get somebody in to see about them properly. Why was he shouting for you?'

'What?'

'Lewis. Why was he shouting for you?'

'Instead of you, you mean?'

'Idiot. No, I mean what on earth was all that about?'

'Does Daddy want to know?'

'Have you been out? Did you see Lewis after

291

they let him go?'

'No.'

'What happened when he took the car?'

'Nothing.'

'Well, why was he after you?'

'I don't know.'

'Did you tell him?'

'Tell him what?'

There was silence.

'Does he know? You know, about you being—did you tell him about Daddy?'

'Of course not.'

'Nobody would believe a person like him anyway.'

'I know.'

'Well, good then.'

Tamsin went to the window and looked out, but it was dark now and the woods were hidden. She turned from the window and sat on the edge of Kit's bed and she looked uncomfortable doing it.

'Horrid, wasn't it?' she said.

Kit nodded.

'You know they've sent a policeman to watch the house?' said Tamsin. 'We're safe inside, all of us.' And she smiled at her and was warm and like a proper big sister.

'Why don't you come down and be with us all?' she said. 'We're in the drawing room. It's not supper yet because everything's late. Come on. Mummy will probably let you have a sherry, it's that sort of day, and you're practically sixteen.'

She held out her hand and Kit took it and they went together, along the corridor, down the stairs and into the drawing room. Dicky and Claire were on the sofa and they looked up at the girls as they came in.

'There you are,' said Dicky, smiling.

'Look,' said Tamsin, 'there's your kitten. I don't know how she got in again. I've been playing with her. Look, try her with this, she loves it.'

She let go of Kit's hand and picked up a skein of Claire's tapestry wool from the floor and handed it to her. Kit took it and went to the floor by the kitten, near her mother. Tamsin and Dicky looked at each other, and Tamsin smiled a little and Dicky nodded and went back to his paper. The family sat in the drawing room and waited for dinner to be ready.

*   *   *

Wilson came to speak to Gilbert. Alice went to her room and stayed there. If she heard the things they said about Lewis she would cry with fear, and show her guilt. She lay in bed, like a little girl pretending to have a temperature, and listened to the men's voices coming up from the drawing room, and it didn't make any difference that she couldn't hear the words. They were talking about how to find Lewis, and what he'd done and that he was beyond being accommodated and forgiven now—by his father, and by everybody.

*   *   *

Lewis was hidden in the woods watching Dicky Carmichael's house. There was a man walking past the windows. Bars of light came through the wood and fell on him as he walked.

If Lewis could get to the house and get Kit's

293

attention, she might come out to him. He knew there was no explaining what had happened between him and Alice, especially to her little-girl heart. He had to try.

He waited for the man to go away from him around the house and then he ran across the dark grass to the drawing room.

He could see her now. She was on the hearth rug with a kitten and absorbed in playing with it. She had her legs tucked under her and he wanted to pick her up in his arms, curled up like that, and hold her. He stared at her and willed her to look up.

Tamsin said something to Kit, but Lewis didn't hear it, and Kit got up and walked away from the family. Lewis kept pace with her in the darkness and at the end of the room she stopped by the radio. She bent over it and started searching for a programme. She was about four feet away from him through the damaged window. Lewis glanced to his right, to where the man would reappear in a moment. Kit was frowning at the radio as she tuned it. She found the Third Programme and twiddled the knob some more, and then Tamsin's voice came down the room again and she looked up—and saw Lewis.

She fixed her eyes on him. She had changed. Lewis knew the man would come around the corner, but he couldn't move; he just stood looking at how different she was and thinking that he had made her different.

Then Kit opened her mouth, slowly. She took a breath, 'There!'

Lewis didn't wait; he ran—before the policeman got around the house, before Dicky got down the drawing room to Kit, and put his arm around her, and asked her what she had seen, and held her, as they both looked out into the garden.

*   *   *

This time they did come after him. He hadn't been in the woods very long before he heard movement behind him, and voices. He looked over his shoulder and there were lights, flicking as they crossed through the trees.

He left the path and tried to go quicker, but it was too dark. He couldn't see his arms in front of him or the trees around. It was like being blind, except that when he turned he could see the lights behind him. They could move fast because they could see, and he was like something blinded and couldn't get away as quickly as they could follow him. They hadn't seen him yet, but they were closer. He began to panic. He was running and falling and, when he fell, trying to get along the ground because it didn't seem to make any difference if he was on his feet or not.

There were brambles and tree trunks and ferns and ditches and he didn't know what he was putting his hands on. The people chasing him were closer still and he fell again, against a fallen tree, and forced himself lower to the ground and down further, as flat as he could to the ground, trying to keep still and quiet.

He could hear them coming.

He was frightened of them, but what was worse was that they were human, and comforting because of that. They knew where they were at least—they were part of something and sure.

They were getting closer.

He wished they'd find him, but that meant being held down again, it meant being hit again. He thought of being dragged out and he thought of being locked up, and he covered his mouth to stop from crying and to stop himself shouting out to them and he pushed himself lower into the ground.

A beam of light flashed past him. He could see a fallen tree, weirdly lit undergrowth, and then darkness again, more complete than before. He shut his eyes so he'd be in his own darkness.

They were talking to each other, quite relaxed and determined, and not sure which way to go. They went silent for a moment and Lewis opened his eyes again and there were lights flashing around, but not near him. One of them said, 'Here!'

It wasn't the man just near Lewis, but another, and the man near Lewis carried on walking, and walked past him and his footfalls were heavy and close.

They moved off. They were talking, not always about him, sometimes about other things, normal things, and he envied them again and, when they had gone on, he was quiet and lay where he was.

He wiped his face, and found he'd been crying. To lie with your face in dirt and cry with fear and not even feel it because you were terrified—it didn't seem like there was anything worse than that. And Kit looking at him the way she had. She had been hurt all of this time and he hadn't known, and he hadn't seen her and he was ashamed. He would be locked up and he couldn't help her.

He got up.

He had been losing his balance in total

darkness, but now he could see that ahead of him there was a difference between the ground and the trees and the sky. He went towards where the darkness wasn't so complete. He didn't know if it was the end of the woods or a gap in them—until he saw the river.

The air moved over his skin. The river was shining. It was shining because the sky was full of stars. He looked up at the stars. They gave a light that dimly washed over everything and wasn't white like moonlight, and he could see the woods all around the clearing, and the water ahead.

The ten-year-old in him recognised it first; it's the part of the river with the wreck in it, he thought. He walked over to the edge of the water, where he had stood and watched his mother swimming.

'*Right then! . . . This dashed rudder. I'm going to get it.*'

*　　　*　　　*

The river was still, but he could hear water splashing. He felt water around him mixing with the hot air, and then less air and just water, and he put his hand out, but his hand was on the ground because he was down on his knees; he kept his eyes open and stinging sweat went into them and he felt the sand and the stones against his face. He could hear his own breathing.

*　　　*　　　*

He slept and he dreamed, but he didn't know that he was sleeping, and when he remembered it later

297

it never felt like a dream, but like something that happened to him, with all the clarity and beauty of truth, perhaps more clarity and beauty than that.

Lewis hadn't seen his mother for nine years. He had put the part of himself that missed her away in his mind, and he had put away the part that remembered too, so that when she came out of the trees towards him it was a jolt of remembering her, more than surprise. It had been so very, very long since he had seen her and she walked towards him in her normal way. She was wearing a short-sleeved dress with a green background and pink. He must have been lying down because when she reached him she knelt. He saw her cheek and brown hair, clipped back. He looked into her face. He realised they both had the same coloured eyes. He hadn't noticed before. There was enough light to see her by and he wasn't sure why that was, because it was still night. It must have been all the stars, he thought. The sky was full of them.

She took his hand and her hands were firm, and he'd always loved that they were strong and not fragile. She held his hand and leaned over him, his mother, and looked at him. She was wearing her pearls and they swung forward minutely as she leaned down. She kissed him on the forehead. Then she sat back up and she was very happy and very normal.

She didn't go; she waited with him and he was too tired to keep looking at her, even though he wanted to, and he shut his eyes. She held his hand a little longer and then she slipped her hand away from him, and when he woke up there was a lot of birdsong and a heavy dew and the early sun, just up, was coming sideways through the trees.

The sky was extremely pale blue.

He got up. He was cold and his clothes were uncomfortable from the sweat and the dew and the dirt from the woods. He stood by the water and listened to the birds singing; there were blackbirds and lots of other ones he didn't know. He felt how uncomfortable he was, and how dirty, and then he got undressed and went into the water. The river was icy and he stopped himself from yelling and swam a little to keep moving, and then put his head under and came out and shook the water off and washed his face. He drank some of the river. It tasted wonderful and cold and soft. He hoped it was clean enough to drink and wouldn't make him sick.

He picked up his shirt from the bank and washed it and then twisted the water out and hung it on a tree with the low sun hitting it. He put on the trousers and brushed off as much of the leaves and dirt from them as he could. The bandage on his arm was wet from swimming, but there was no blood coming through.

He felt hungry. He had his wallet in his back pocket, but he didn't think it was a good idea to go into the village, or any village. He counted his cigarettes. There were six, not very many. He lit one and his fingers were wet and soaked into the paper.

He was cold, so he went out to where it was sunniest, drying his hands some more on his trousers, and stood and smoked and thought what to do. The cold made everything bright and clear. He would have to go back. He would have to not get caught.

He put on his wet shirt and started back through

299

the trees. The woods looked very pretty in the early morning and the air was fresh. His shirt began to dry on him as he walked.

CHAPTER ELEVEN

Lewis lay in the branches of an oak tree that was about fifteen feet into the forest and gave him a clear view of Dicky Carmichael's house.

He was hidden, and the branch that he was on was wide enough for him to lean back against the trunk of the tree with his feet up and be comfortable and still be able to see. He was nervous to begin with that he'd be discovered, but he was screened by the tree and nobody came up to the top of the garden, which was unplanted and the day passed with spacing out his cigarettes and watching and thinking. He had to be in Kent for his National Service on Monday. It was Friday.

Not much happened in the early morning. The gardener came and weeded the beds near the house, which was something to look at for a while, and at about ten o'clock Dicky left. Lewis heard the front door and saw the Rolls turning in front of the house, and the back of it as it went down the drive. After that he was more relaxed and, apart from waiting to see Kit, didn't think too much about the house, but let his mind go.

He thought about Dicky. He thought quite a lot about killing him, but also tried to work out how a man like that must think. He kept himself from picturing how Dicky might harm Kit because he needed to stay quiet and keep thinking sensibly, but he let himself think about other things: how Dicky would justify it to himself, how he would keep it a secret. He thought of Kit saying that she had never told anyone, and of how bad her bruises were. She was very proud, and he loved her pride, but it was a stupid pride if she hadn't asked for help from anybody and her father had hurt her for a long time. He imagined her at school and wondered who she could have told and thought if she was like him, then there would be no-one. Telling hard things like that was impossible, he knew it was. He thought she might feel ashamed somehow and he hoped she didn't. She was lovely and mustn't feel that. He wondered what Dicky had done to Tamsin. He hadn't seen Tamsin since the woods and he wasn't particularly interested in her, but she didn't deserve hurting and he hoped she wasn't hurt badly. He remembered her light blue shoes lying in the dirt after she'd run away from him. He had been angry with her then, but it didn't matter any more. She didn't understand him any more than he understood her. He hadn't been clear in his mind. He felt clearer now.

He heard the sound of a telephone ringing and a little while afterwards a van arrived and was sent round the back, and he heard the engine go away from him and then the sound of it in the stable yard. He lit his third cigarette and after a few minutes some workmen came round with the butler and Claire, and started to look at the damaged windows. Some of them were smashed and the lead bent in places. After feeling very conspicuous, and putting out his cigarette against the tree, Lewis realised they weren't going to see him and enjoyed being able to watch them. He

301

regretted panicking and putting out his cigarette. He only had three more and it wasn't lunchtime. He wished he hadn't thought about lunch. He watched the glass being brought round and the panes being cut and fitted. He wanted to see Kit. He wanted her to come out. Then she did come out, as if she'd heard him.

She had a book and an apple and the kitten under her arm, but the kitten ran away immediately she put it down. She came up the terrace steps towards him and then stopped on the grass and lay down on her front and read her book, with her feet swinging occasionally and taking bites of her apple. The workmen carried on behind her and she lay in the sun reading, and she was about sixty feet away from Lewis and he could watch her.

She had shorts on, and a shirt that could have been part of her school games uniform, and her feet were bare. He loved her ears. He noticed the way she held her apple, in her whole hand, and took big bites out of it. He tried to see what she was reading, but couldn't. She was tanned and smooth-looking and every part of her fitted with every other part. She had a practical sort of body, he thought, the sort of body that looked better naked than with clothes; good with clothes, but even better without. He tried not to think about her being naked because she didn't know he was there and it wasn't fair. He shut his eyes. He wanted to stroke the soft backs of her knees. He wanted to find out what her hipbone felt like and put his hand there, and on her back to find out the slope of it into her waist, and the texture of her skin. He wanted to feel her hair again as it went softly into her neck, like a boy and not like a boy.

302

Not thinking about her body wasn't working, so he opened his eyes and tried to think of something else. He thought about what he could do to help her and that made him remember she didn't want his help. Maybe she had wanted it, but she didn't want it now. She knew now, about Alice, and because of it she wasn't going to love him and he had to forget about that. It wasn't a new thought for him, that he wouldn't be loved, but it did seem hard that Kit had loved him and now, knowing, didn't love him any more. He wouldn't let himself think about how things might have been between them if he were better. He knew he wasn't all right for a girl like that. He would have been sweet to her, he would be gentle and quiet with her—but he had to remember she wasn't for him. She wasn't for him, but he needed to help her if he could.

Her house rose up behind her. Everything was different. The house had stopped being something that was good and secure and had become a bad place. It seemed to Lewis that the repairs that were being done to it were like repairs being made to a fortress in a break in the fighting. This was a break though, and the day was warm, and Lewis felt nothing very bad could happen for a while, so he watched Kit some more and loved watching her and let himself feel that.

Claire came out occasionally and checked on the workmen and at one o'clock they stopped and went away. The gong rang for lunch and Kit got up and stretched herself and went down the garden.

There was nothing to look at now and Lewis was warm and let himself sleep. It wasn't a real sleep, it was a half sleep and in it his mind kept going over and over familiar things and changing them and he

303

began rebuilding the picture he had of the world. His mind, freed up with not eating, seemed to lose its edges and he saw that the assumptions he had always made were false, and broke apart when he looked at them. His thoughts ran away, and flowed away, and made pictures.

It was an odd feeling, a looking-glass feeling, that he had, that all his life he had been on one side of the glass with everybody else on the other and now the glass had broken and the thick, broken pieces were at all of their feet.

*   *   *

That morning Gilbert had left for work at the normal time, but he was only at his desk for an hour before leaving for his appointment with r Bond. He took a taxi to Harley Street and found that he was checking nobody was looking as he entered the building.

There was a lift with a metal gate you pulled across to take him to the third floor and he watched the red-carpeted landings passing him. He felt terribly embarrassed giving his name to the receptionist and hated waiting. He looked at the closed door and the brass plaque with 'Dr W. Bond' that was screwed onto it. A woman came out of the door and she held a handkerchief up to her eyes as she went by. She was wearing a suit and a little hat tipped forward and Gilbert didn't know if the handkerchief was just to hide her face, because she didn't want to be seen either, or if she'd been crying. The whole place seemed to be fake; pretending to be respectable when it was full of damage, pretending to be quite open when

304

it was full of shame.

He fidgeted and waited and got angry about waiting. When he finally went in, he was surprised by the size of the room. The big net curtain on the window shone bright white with diffused sunlight and the air was stuffy. He sat opposite Dr Bond, who had the light behind him so that his face wasn't quite clear. Gilbert put his briefcase down.

'This is about your son, isn't it, Mr Aldridge?'

'Yes. Lewis.'

'Tell me about Lewis.'

'. . . What do you mean?'

'He's having a difficult time?'

'Yes. He's—' It was still horrible to say it out loud, 'He's recently come out of prison. He was in prison for two years. For arson. He's nineteen now. When he came home, it seemed at first that he was better. He seemed to want to behave and he got himself a job, or I got him a job.'

'When was this?'

'Just over two weeks ago.'

'When you say better?'

'He has problems. He drinks—'

'How much does he drink?'

'He drinks secretly. He wasn't drinking at first. Then he started to. But I haven't explained.'

'It's all right, Mr Aldridge, take your time, you're doing very well.'

Gilbert felt patronised and irritated and wondered if this man had any proper qualifications. He looked professional enough, he was in his fifties and had grey hair and a neat suit and held his glasses in one hand as he made notes with the other. Gilbert felt scrutinised and judged and he wanted to say: don't look at me, it's my son

305

we're talking about. He had a silly fear the doctor would suddenly accuse him of some mental problem and recommend that he be treated immediately.

'I need to explain. He . . . when he was younger he had a habit of, well, he would—if things went wrong at all—he would cut himself. With a razor. On the arm.'

'I see. Not his wrists?'

'No. It wasn't like that. Here,' he showed him, 'on the arm.'

'You say when he was younger?'

'Yes. We think he didn't do it while he was away. He seems not to have got into any trouble there. Then, just recently he did it again, very badly.'

'Do you know what could have caused him to do it?'

'What do you mean?'

'Well, what might have happened that made him do it?'

'He was arrested. It was when they let him go. He took a girl into the woods and he—hurt her— he didn't, well, it wasn't like that, at least I don't think so, but he—he gave her a black eye and he ran away, he stole a car and he ran off with another girl—her sister, who is very young—and he was arrested again.'

'And then he was released?'

'She didn't want to press charges against him. The family are our neighbours. Her father has a lot of influence. It could have been much worse. They've been extremely understanding. But now he's run away—'

'Let's go back a little. When would you say this behaviour started? What sort of a boy was he?'

306

Gilbert felt impatient again; this was all the sort of nonsense he had expected.

'He was a normal boy. Like any boy.'

'Until?'

'I don't know. He seemed all right. His mother died a few years ago. Of course it affected him.'

'How old was he when his mother died?'

'Ten.'

'How did she die?'

He didn't have time for this.

'She drowned. In the river near our home. Lewis was the only one there. We don't know what happened.'

'I imagine it was a terrible shock.'

'Of course.'

'Would you say it was after that he became difficult?'

'Not really. He was quiet. He got on all right. I remarried. It was when he was fourteen or fifteen that he became unmanageable, with the things he did and the drinking.'

'This terrible event. This drowning . . . Tell me about your wife.'

'I don't see why.'

'It must have been very difficult.'

'Of course.'

'You say he was the only one there.'

'Yes.'

'He never said how it happened?'

'He wouldn't speak. He was quiet. He was oddly quiet.'

'What are you saying?'

'I'm not saying anything.'

'You appear to be saying the events were mysterious in some way.'

307

'I don't know what you mean. Mysterious. It was very sad. Lewis was a little boy. He was a strong swimmer. The water wasn't very deep. I don't know. I wasn't there.'

'You seem upset.'

'I'm not at all upset. My son is missing. He may go back to prison. He's not a child now. He's nineteen and he's violent and he's a drunk and he's harming people, and you seem to want to talk about an unpleasant event that happened many years ago.'

'I don't want to upset you.'

'I would like to keep to the point.'

'Are you all right?'

'Will you, please!'

'Would you like some water? Would you like a drink?'

Gilbert checked his watch.

'A brandy?' said Dr Bond.

Gilbert had a drink, and thought how excellent it was that medicinal drinking in doctors' offices allowed you to break the not-before-twelve rule. He felt a little better. He told Dr Bond about Lewis attacking the Carmichaels' house and disappearing. He told him about the blood on the bathroom wall and that he had seen Tamsin and how shocking that was. He told him about Lewis's blankness and sudden, unprovoked rage.

'We don't know where he is,' he said. 'That was yesterday. He ran away after that and we don't know where he is now, or what may happen to him if he's caught.'

'What are your thoughts?' The question was weighted with significance. Gilbert felt very emotional suddenly, and found it hard to speak.

'I'm very concerned for him.'

'And?'

'I'm very concerned for my wife. My second wife. And for the other family I told you about, my neighbour and his daughters.'

'When you say concerned . . .'

'I fear for them.'

'Would you say your son was a danger to himself?'

'Yes.'

'Would you say he was a danger to others?'

'. . . yes.'

'Sometimes . . . when a person doesn't accept they need treatment, a committal order can be a way of initiating the process.'

There, he'd said it; Gilbert had wanted him to say it, but now that he had he felt sick with himself, and frightened. He looked down at his glass and waited. The doctor's voice was very gentle.

'It's a legitimate route to take.'

Gilbert nodded and didn't look at him.

'You're not betraying your son, Mr Aldridge.'

'. . . no.'

*   *   *

Lewis's sleep was like diving into something. The layers were pushed back, his mind kept dropping, deeper and deeper, and when he woke it was a sudden waking and it was much hotter. He didn't feel peaceful any more, he felt restless. The workmen were at the windows again, and it seemed so dogged and stupid the way they were putting back each little diamond pane he'd broken.

He had always thought he had been wrong. He

309

hadn't been wrong. His heart got faster and he felt weak and strong together. He wanted Kit out of there and didn't know how he could stand it or what he was going to do. He looked at his hand shaking in front of him and willed it to stop and it did stop, and he lit his second-last cigarette with a steady hand.

He smoked and tried to make it enough, so that he wouldn't be so hungry, and watched the smoke, and imagined his father at work in his office and what he might be doing.

As a child, the idea of his father's work life had been impressive—he imagined a leather-topped desk and important papers that needed attending to—but as he grew older he lost respect for it. He remembered one day when he was sixteen he'd got out of bed with Jeanie in the afternoon and gone out into the street. He'd walked away from her flat and down towards St James's and bought a bottle of gin in an off-licence there. He had put it in his pocket and then seen his father coming out of his club after lunch. He had stood on a corner, with the bottle of gin in his pocket and Jeanie in his mind and on his body, and seen his father in his suit and hat, talking to some people. He'd watched him say goodbye and get into a taxi and his father hadn't seen him, and Lewis had gone back to Jeanie's bed and been with her until night-time. He had lain in bed while she slept against him and felt completely alone. He didn't have any idea what his life would be like, and it had terrified him that he didn't, but he knew it couldn't be like his father's, even if he had wanted it.

When he was in jail, and letting his mind go, he would think of the lives he had seen or heard

310

about: businessman, barman, musician, cleaner, prison officer, policeman; but when he looked at the future, he didn't exist. There was no place for him. He was a wrecked person.

The difference now was that all his life he had thought his father and Dicky and Alice and Tamsin and all of the people who managed in the world weren't wrecked people, and now he knew they were. It looked like everybody was in a broken, bad world that fitted them just right.

Kit wasn't, though. Kit was too beautiful and too shaming, and he lost all his thought then.

*   *   *

Gilbert returned to his office after his meeting with the doctor. He worked hard and took the normal train home. When he came into the hall Alice was in the drawing room as usual, by the drinks cabinet with the broken doors. Gilbert couldn't go in to her. He sat in a chair by the door and put his briefcase on his lap, and after a while she noticed and she came out.

'Gilbert?'

'Yes?'

'You're home.'

'Yes.'

'What's the matter?'

He got up and went into the drawing room and she followed him and handed him his drink.

'Did you see the doctor?'

'Yes.'

'And?'

'And?'

'What did he say?'

311

'Oh, he gave me a form to fill in. We talked about Lewis.'

'What form?'

He gestured at his briefcase and took his drink and sat down by the empty grate. She went to the briefcase and opened it, struggling with the lock because she wasn't used to it, and got out some stapled pieces of paper. She knelt there, reading them.

'What's for dinner?' he asked.

'Gilbert—this is to have him committed. You can't have him committed. Gilbert?'

'For God's sake, what?'

'You can't do this.'

'No. We have to bloody find him first. They think he may have gone to London—'

'When he hurt himself this time—'

'It's not just that!'

'I know he didn't hit Tamsin.'

'Have you seen her face?'

'Please stop shouting. You can't do this to him, Gilbert. It will break him.'

'He's broken already.'

'Gilbert—'

'I'm not discussing this with you, Alice. You're not his mother and it's not your decision. Another topic, please, or if you can't find one, why don't you go to your room until dinner time?' Alice stood up and she still held the paper in her hands. 'Well?'

'When we met,' she wasn't going to cry, 'and you were so very sad, Gilbert, I thought I could make you forget her and be happy. But you've guarded your misery, haven't you? . . . You've let it turn black. I've no idea how you can live with me and be

312

so hard and so cold. Did I do this? I used to blame myself . . . and Lewis. But perhaps it's just you. Perhaps this is just you.'

He didn't look at her still, but made an impatient gesture with his hand, and she turned and went out of the room and upstairs, just as he had asked.

CHAPTER TWELVE

When it was quite dark, the Carmichaels' house was lit up like a doll's house. Lewis was waiting until everybody had gone to bed so he could go back to his father's house and try to find something to eat. He would have to break in and not be caught. The family were in the drawing room. He could see the maid and the housekeeper going in and out of the other rooms and doing things. A little later they all had supper and Lewis climbed down to see better. He watched them eat and smoked his last cigarette waiting for Kit to go up to bed. The night was dark and alive around him. He felt frightened for her, and disgusted, and couldn't leave until her light was safely turned off. When her window was dark he started back through the trees.

*   *   *

Kit lay still and quiet in her bed. She had wanted all evening to be by herself and cry, but now she was alone she couldn't cry, but felt small and hard and as if there was nothing left of her. She needed to get used to Lewis not being there in her heart with her any more. She wanted not to think about him, but she thought about him all the time. She didn't know where he was and it obsessed her, not knowing, and it went around in her mind, fearing him, fearing for him, fearing his capture, fearing his return. She couldn't seem to adjust to this new reality. She hadn't known she was happy before, with her loves and her dream world and Lewis in her mind, the way she had thought that he was.

There must be something else for her than this. In a month she'd be in Switzerland. There would be the holidays, though, and she would be back for those. Just like school, home to Daddy in the holidays. It was as if nothing would ever change. She had lost her will to imagine change.

*   *   *

The path home was well worn and Lewis had known it all his life, but felt as if he'd never walked it before. At the top of his garden he stood in the safety of the trees, looking down to the house. There were no lights showing and no sign of anyone and he came out of the woods onto the smooth lawn. He approached the house, slowly, until it stood above him, blocking the sky. He felt the windows watching him and he knew he should move, but he stood still, feeling nothing but the cold blood in his veins. He was home.

Through the long summer the windows had stood open at night to let the cool air in, but now they were locked. All along the drawing room and the dining room they were locked. He went around the house. The side door was locked too, but the

314

kitchen window was just pulled to, and Lewis opened it wide and climbed inside. He stood in the kitchen and felt out of place, like an animal that had got in, something that didn't belong there. He heard his heart beating.

He went to the larder and opened it, and it opened quietly. There were dishes of food, covered, and he took off the covers. There was a rice salad and he ate some of that and then he got a knife and cut pieces of ham for himself and ate them standing. There was bread in the bread bin and he ate some of that too, and didn't bother to cut it because he was going to take it with him. He tried not to eat too quickly, but he took big mouthfuls and the ham was strong and very dry with the bread and he went to the tap and bent down to drink from it. It felt strange to be eating, as if it had been longer than two days. He waited in the dark and listened, and his strength came back. He began to notice the house more and how it sounded and how it felt to be there. He listened and couldn't hear anything except the hum of the refrigerator. The house felt small after the woods, like a pretend thing, with the thinness of its walls and the open night outside them.

It was very dark, and darker still in the hall, and he could only just see the white of the banister as it curved up towards where Alice and Gilbert were. He worried he'd made too much noise with the tap and he waited for a while before doing anything else. His case was upstairs, and his cigarettes, and he needed a shirt and his razor. He had to get them.

He went into the hall and started very slowly up the stairs and kept his eyes on his parents' door as he went up.

When he'd come out of prison he had felt that he had hardly been away, that two years was very short. The three days he'd been gone this time felt much longer.

He watched his father's door as he climbed the stairs. The cold feeling left him and his mind seemed to heat up as it filled with memories and with feelings that crowded behind his eyes.

He was seven years old and shut out of the room. He was ten years old and being sent upstairs as a punishment. He was twelve and sitting on the stairs and trying to be quiet and not knowing where to be in the house because it all felt wrong to him. He was fifteen and going up to get away from them and to drink and to try not to hurt himself.

Feeling all his life playing inside him at once like that was painful and the sad, wrong feeling was very strong. He remembered his mother running up the stairs; she always seemed to run, always getting something she had forgotten and calling up or down to people while she ran. There was no hush about her. The house had been hushed ever since.

At the top of the stairs he stood in front of the door and it seemed to him that his mind was so noisy it would shake the air in the still house and there was no way his father could not hear it and come out. He didn't know if he wanted his father to come or was frightened he'd come because of what he might do. But he didn't. He didn't come out. The door stayed shut.

He went to his room and got the case from the cupboard and put it on the bed. He took his white

316

shirt from its hanger and underwear from the chest of drawers, and his cigarettes and his enlistment notice from the drawer by the bed.

He went across the landing and reached into the bathroom and took the razor and a piece of soap, and knelt down and tucked the razor and the soap into the elastic pocket in the side of the case.

He didn't close the clips while he was up there because of the noise, but went downstairs as quietly as he could and back into the kitchen.

He put the case on the table and took more ham from the larder and some cheese and some bread, and he wrapped them up well in tea-towels and put them in the case too, in the pocket inside the lid.

He couldn't think of anything else. All the feelings were in his head still, and filling his heart, and he wanted to be out of the house for good.

He stood in the kitchen, by the open suitcase, and kept his head down and tried to concentrate. He noticed the dirty bandage on his arm. It was very important to take it off. He forgot about getting out and stopped to do it.

The knot was tight and small, and had got wet and dried again, and he had to use his teeth. When it was undone he unwound the bandage, and his arm emerged. The cuts were healing well and didn't look bad at all, just raised still, and damp, and needing the air to mend them. He looked at his arm and wondered how long it would take all the cuts to heal, for all of the scars to heal completely. He hadn't cut himself for two years in prison, and the scars from before had been fading well until he came home. He couldn't imagine two years ahead. He flexed his hand and felt the tightness of the razor cuts and thought of how much pain he had been in, and how lonely.

'Lewis.'

Lewis turned around. Gilbert was in the doorway of the kitchen. Lewis had the bandage in his hand. He put it down.

'Hello, Dad.'

'Where have you been?' Gilbert's voice was shaking.

Lewis was quiet and still, but with danger too, and they could both feel it.

'Somewhere. I thought I'd go back there.'

'I've been worried about you.'

Lewis didn't think that was probably true.

'Have you?' he said.

'Why don't we sit down and talk about this?'

He said it so obviously, it was silly.

'Phoned already?'

'What?'

'Who's coming for me? The police? Doctors? How does it go this time?'

Gilbert drew himself up.

'You have been—'

'NO!'

He saw Gilbert stop and, stopping, hold his breath and wait. He had silenced his father and now he wanted to get out. He went to pick up his things from the table and Gilbert flinched, and Lewis saw that he was frightened of him.

'What?' he said, advancing on his father, and flooded with the need to hurt him. 'What? What do you think I'm going to do? You think I'm going to hit you? You think I want that? I'd like to kill you—'

He made himself quiet and found words and it was very hard to do.

318

'You've done nothing for me,' he said—and didn't know he was going to say it until he did and then the words came out of the centre of him— 'and all of this time I've been trying to make it up to you. Not any more. You lose your job because of me? I'm glad. You lose this house? Your wife? I hope you do. You don't deserve her and I'm sick of the guilt.'

'Lewis—'

'Why couldn't you have faith in me? Just a little bit of faith in me? All of that locking me up, the threats, telling me I was no good, there was something wrong with me—I was a child, I was a kid—if you'd just have believed for one minute, been on my side—but you couldn't. Yes, I drink, yes, I cut myself; God, didn't you even want to help?'

The violence had all drained away from him and he felt weak from saying it all and like crying, and he had to get out of there. He turned to the suitcase again and closed it.

'You were used to too much love as a little boy. She spoiled you.'

'Well, you put a stop to that.'

He started to the door. Gilbert was trying to speak, he looked down and seemed to struggle, and Lewis knew how he felt doing that, and hated that he pitied this man who had hurt him so badly and for so long.

'It's not a question of wanting to help,' said Gilbert. His lip was shaking. 'From the day she died I just—couldn't look at you, Lewis. You were so like her—and you were so full of your grief. You didn't want my company.'

That was it then. That was all. Lewis felt very

319

cool suddenly and that none of it mattered.

'Must have been awfully difficult for you, Dad. Still. Put it out of your mind. I'll be away again soon.'

He stopped in the doorway, remembering.

'Don't call anyone. Leave me alone. Understand?'

He went out of the house by the front door and left it open and Gilbert watched him go and heard his footsteps fade. He felt weak, and sat down in a kitchen chair.

He sat in the chair and when Alice heard Lewis leave, she came down and stood in the doorway and waited.

'Lewis,' he said. 'Lewis was here, and he—'

He started to cry. He was broken and overwhelmed by his crying. He held on to her, gripping her nightdress in his hands and burying his face in her to cry. Alice held Gilbert's head in her hands and stroked him and closed her eyes. She imagined Lewis walking away into the dark and she was grateful to him, and hoped he wouldn't come back.

CHAPTER THIRTEEN

Lewis slept in the woods by the tree near the water where his mother had drowned. He put the suitcase up in the tree so that foxes wouldn't come.

He went to sleep with his thoughts very busy about his father and trying to think what to do about Kit, and his mind worked on it in the night so that when he woke up he was clear. He knew what he had to do.

When he went to watch over Kit he felt he'd been doing it for a long time, that it was his habit to guard her. In the afternoon she came out with her book again and he could look at her and dream about her, but it was worse this time, and sad, because he knew what he was going to do and he wanted to say sorry and to explain that there was nothing else to do. He didn't think she would see that. He wished he could see another way out of it, but he couldn't. It was a strange and beautiful thing to watch her like that, knowing he was giving up any hope of her, but being in the heat and the gentle moment of it anyway.

When he went back to his place by the river he didn't sleep. He thought this would be his last night free. He didn't know if he'd be locked up again, or if he'd make it to the army, or if there was a difference, and he valued the night and being alone and the feeling of freedom that was new to him still. He hadn't felt it when he came out of prison. He hadn't felt it until now.

On Sunday morning the sun rose slowly after a very black time, and the sky was pale for ages before there was any real light. He was warm enough, except just before dawn and at dawn, when there was a hard chill to the air and a mist. The sun burned off the mist very quickly, but even in the heat and the dryness you could tell September was coming and the light was thicker and not blazing like it had been.

He washed in the river and then waited for the water to be completely still, and when it was still he took his razor and the soap and shaved very carefully, not breathing onto the water, but holding

321

his breath to shave and then breathing out away into the air so that he wouldn't disturb the reflection.

He rinsed off the razor and dried it on his old shirt and closed it and put it back into the case. He wet his hair and didn't have a comb, but smoothed it with his hands and then he got out the clean white shirt, which was folded and not creased, and his clean trousers and dressed. He packed everything away, and took his case with him, and walked slowly back through the woods.

*   *   *

The church bells started to ring as Lewis watched the family come in for breakfast. The sound of the layers of the ringing bells went out over the country and Lewis imagined all the people at their breakfasts, hearing them.

The church bells rang and Tamsin got up from the table and Lewis saw Preston bring the car round and thought for a moment that he wouldn't have his chance, but then Kit and Claire got up too and Dicky was left on his own in the dining room and Lewis knew he didn't have long.

He crossed the grass quickly, and was inside the room, through the open window right by the table, before Dicky started up to shout something—but Lewis took a step towards him and he stopped.

The still dining room and the breakfast things on the table, and Dicky standing there with his napkin tucked into his neck, were all frozen, waiting for something to happen. It was important not to be seen. Lewis went to the door, fast, and closed it, and his moving jolted Dicky into speech.

322

'Get out of my house. Get out!'

He pulled the napkin from his neck, threw it down onto the table and drew himself up. Lewis thought he might call for somebody and he spoke to him quietly.

'You're a big man . . . Kit's what, five-four? Five-five?' Dicky was distracted, and Lewis went a little closer, keeping his voice low, 'That's quite a challenge, beating up a girl like that.'

'How dare you—'

'How's Tamsin?'

'Don't! Don't you dare mention my daughter's name—'

'Tamsin? Why not? I'm not the one who messed up her face. I never touched her.'

He waited. He saw Dicky, between fear and anger, trying to decide what to do. Lewis listened to the beat of his own heart and counted it out, and then he said, 'She was all over me, though.'

This was easy. Dicky began to move, stopping himself from coming towards him; he had forgotten all about getting help, all about everything, except the picture of Tamsin in his head, and Lewis could see that he had him.

'You—'

'For a nice girl, she certainly does have a way about her . . . Sweet.'

Dicky raised a fist—stopped himself—took another step towards him. Now, thought Lewis, do it now.

'Why don't you?' he said, 'Go on, do it.'

Dicky considered his options. Lewis had that vacant look he'd always had, like somebody hypnotised, hidden away—but he was dangerous too, he'd been violent in the past and Dicky wasn't

323

sure.

'Go on, do it,' said Lewis, softly.

So Dicky hit him. His fist went into Lewis's face, hard, and his knuckles cracked and he felt the jolt up his arm and into his shoulder, a flash of beauty as he hit him.

Lewis's head snapped back and he went back a couple of paces, and Dicky recovered from punching him and stepped away, frightened and light on his feet, with his hands up to shield himself. Except that Lewis didn't come for him— or do anything except stay where he was, and blink a little and look back at him with that same vague look.

'Is that the best you can do?' he said, 'Is that it?'

He had blood in his mouth, Dicky saw his teeth were coloured with it, but he didn't put his hand up to check, like a normal person would.

It was hard for Dicky to think straight. His hand was hot where he had punched Lewis, and it felt naughty to be standing in his dining room with everyone in the house and this boy they were all so scared of, ready to take a beating from him. He pretended to be thinking—but then went for Lewis quickly, to catch him off guard, left, then right, like a boxer, like he'd been taught at school, and Lewis went back again. There was no need to be quick about it; the boy didn't even put his hands up. The punches landed just where he wanted them, in his mouth, where he'd said 'Tamsin'; and on his eye, where he'd looked at her.

Dicky shook his hand out, getting his breath. It hurt him badly to hit the boy's face so hard and Lewis was beginning to look damaged and confused, but then he opened his arms wide and

324

came towards him.

'Do it again,' he said, 'do it again.'

'You are insane,' Dicky said, because he'd often wondered—and it gave him a feeling of delight that Lewis was just crazy, and could be beaten like this and then taken away somewhere out of sight and forgotten about.

'Come on,' said Lewis, 'is it good?'

So Dicky hit him again and had enough of the thrill of it not to feel the pain in his own hands at all, but he was getting tired now and not so coordinated, feeling himself coming to an end.

Lewis was getting closer to where he needed to be. The pain was blurring his sight and he went to his knees and couldn't have stayed standing. Dicky stood over him, panting. His tongue felt thick and hot in his mouth. He saw Kit in his mind—on her knees the times he'd forced her down—and thought how he always had to be careful with her, not to let it show and not to break her body; but with this boy, who was big, there was no need to be careful, he could try to break him. He wiped the sweat off his face and looked down at Lewis.

Lewis hadn't much idea where Dicky was and seemed to have trouble holding his head up.

'What? Can't you see me, boy? Over here.'

Then Lewis did hold his head up and he looked at Dicky, and even with the blood and the state of his face, Dicky could see him smiling.

'Go to hell,' he said, and that was an end to it: one kick to the stomach and one to the head, and Lewis went down and stopped moving. It was done.

Dicky waited. He wet his tongue to get rid of the hot feeling in it and swallowed. He straightened his

325

jacket and smoothed his hair and went over to the door.

At the door he stopped, thinking suddenly of what he'd have to say to people. It would be all right, it was only the servants; and if the boy was still there after church, he'd call the police to take him away. They'd probably give him a medal.

Dicky went into the hall and closed the door behind him. He took out his handkerchief and wiped his hands. He left the house and the car was waiting, with the girls and Claire in the back, and he got in beside Preston and shut the door. He glanced over at Preston.

'All right then,' he said and the car moved off.

Dicky hid his hands, which were throbbing and bruised, by his sides. Preston still had the strapping on his nose where Lewis had kicked his face, and Dicky wanted to show him his hands and say, 'Got him!' and laugh about it with him, but he kept quiet and gripped his handkerchief and looked out of the window and willed himself to think sensibly. He hadn't been frightened for long; it was understandable that he'd been scared, it had been a shock to see Lewis standing there in the room with him, and he had looked dangerous to begin with.

Dicky watched the hedges go by, and let Tamsin and Claire go on with their silly conversations in the back. He could barely keep a straight face. His hands were hurting him more and more from where he had beaten Lewis, and everything looked bright and leaping and marvellous to him. He'd left Lewis lying there and he didn't know if he was dead or alive or blinded or broken. He hoped it was very bad.

The church came into sight and Dicky took out his handkerchief and wiped his hands, hiding them down behind his thigh and checking the bruising.

Preston stopped the car by the gate to the churchyard and left the engine running while he got out and let the women out first, and then Dicky. Dicky put his hands in his pockets and went through the people and smiled and laughed as usual, but made sure he got into the church quickly so that he could sit and relish it better. He saw Gilbert and wanted to tell him what he'd done to Lewis, and laugh at him, but found he couldn't meet his eye. He pitied him for his crazy son and his dead wife, and for being so weak and letting Alice drink publicly the way she did. How did the old joke go? One drunken wife might be looked upon as a misfortune, but two . . . He wanted to say what he'd done and slap him on the back and apologise, and tell him Lewis was there for Gilbert to collect, or for someone from an insane asylum to come and scrape him up from the floor.

Dicky got to his pew, at the front, and stood aside for the women to go in ahead of him, and said good morning to the vicar and sat down. Then he let himself think about it again, the way it had felt to beat Lewis, and he had less shame about his excitement than he did when he punished Kit because there was something pure about this violence, and more honourable, and getting excited at violence like that was normal, and part of being a man. He played it in his mind as people came in behind him: hitting Lewis—who was younger, and taller—hitting him in the face and the side of his head, and across his mouth with his fist that was bleeding, and getting him to his knees.

327

'Darling—' said Claire, and nudged him with her elbow.

The organ had started and he'd forgotten to stand up.

CHAPTER FOURTEEN

Lewis felt the sun come through the window onto his head. The carpet against his cheek was a familiar, childhood sort of feeling. He started to move and seemed to fall into the dark and then tilt back into the room and away again. He kept still for a bit and then he felt his teeth with his tongue and they were all there. They felt loose in his head, but his tongue couldn't feel looseness. It felt as if his skull, and everything that had held it together—the cement he'd never been aware of— had been crushed and had shifted. It hadn't broken, though. His teeth were there. He opened his eyes. His eyes were there. He could see. At least, he was sure one of his eyes was there; the other felt very hot, and when he blinked it didn't move. He waited. Then he lifted his hand—which didn't hurt and felt lovely and free—up to his eye. It was very big, it wasn't a hole or a gap or something frightening, it was just too big and sticky. It was full of blood. He tried to blink again and his eye opened and was very blurred for a while, but not blind. The blood had come from his eyebrow, which was split wide. He sat up and waited for the floor to straighten out, then got to his knees and his feet and held onto the back of a dining chair to do it. He had a very bad pain down

328

the side of his face, in his cheekbone, like being hit with an iron bar, and when he tried to touch the cheekbone it hurt so much that his vision went black. He held on to the chair and waited. The door opened and the maid came in to clear, and saw him and gave a sort of yell.

'Sorry,' he said and she went out.

After a second she came back to shut the door on him and he heard her walking away and then some shouting. He wanted to laugh, but didn't want to have to move his face to do it. There was a weird moment when he saw his reflection and hadn't known there was a mirror there, and nearly yelled himself. He looked pretty bad. He needed to spit some blood out, but he didn't want to do so onto the carpet. Then he remembered it was Dicky's carpet, so he spat the blood onto it, and then some more. The blood was coming from his lip, but it felt like it was just running into his mouth from the inside of his head, as if his whole head was blood. He wasn't really hurting now. Except for the cheekbone, which was bright-white pain and very bad, the rest of him felt all right, and different from other fights because his hands weren't hurting. His hands usually hurt. Jeanie had put his hand in a bowl of iced water when he had been fighting once, but he pictured it being in prison, and that wasn't right; and he thought of a knife fight he'd seen in prison when a man had his cheek cut open so you could see his teeth through it; and he remembered punching Ed and how hot the woods had been, with the heavy sun coming through the trees and the blazing fields afterwards, and he started to feel sleepy and wanted to lie down in the stubble fields in the sun and rest. Then the church bells stopped pealing. He hadn't noticed they were still ringing until they stopped, and when they did he remembered everything.

*　　*　　*

He went out of the house by the garden door. Walking was good, and the air on his face was good too, and he went down the drive and onto the road and towards the village, walking straight, but quite slowly, because of not seeing very well and his head feeling full of blood.

*　　*　　*

Kit stood next to Tamsin and sang the hymn and listened to Dicky's big voice singing over them. When the organ stopped, and the ragged voices had trailed away, they all sat down. The vicar started to speak and Kit didn't listen, but looked down at her hands and things floated into her mind: school assemblies, French verbs, Swiss Alps, lakes, and sleeping and loneliness, and that she felt cold after the hot day outside. And Lewis. Lewis. There was the vicar's voice and somebody whispering at the back of the church and a little girl giggling, and then the church doors clattered and opened. Everybody turned to look, and Kit turned too, a little late, and saw Lewis. The people all saw him, and at the sight of him in the doorway there was an intake of breath; there were no words, there was shock.

The people nearest him went back. Lewis walked up the aisle of the church and there was nothing for anybody to say. He was looking for Kit,

330

and when he saw her he moved quickly and reached past her father and pulled her towards him. Dicky shrank back and didn't realise Lewis was grabbing Kit and pulling her out until it was done.

Lewis held Kit around the waist, like a hostage, so that she faced the people. Her back was pressed against him and she saw his face close up before he turned her, but she couldn't read his expression because of the beating, and he looked terrifying and not like himself. She felt very weak and she looked around the faces staring at her with a sense of unreality. They all had the same expression; her mother, Tamsin, Dicky, all of the people she knew, staring at her, held so hard like that in the church, in front of them and no-one moving or saying anything. She looked at their fear and part of her wanted to say, 'It's all right, it's just Lewis', but she was shocked too, and couldn't speak, and she couldn't breathe very well because he was gripping her. He held her, and then she felt his cheek come down next to her and he pressed his face against her head and whispered in her ear, 'I'm sorry. Sorry—'

Then immediately it was much worse, because he grasped her top, pulled her blouse out from her waistband and yanked it up to show her body, and she closed her eyes. She went very soft, like an animal that's frightened so that it can't move, and she kept her eyes closed and felt her body exposed. She understood he wasn't trying to hurt her. Still, nobody spoke and she felt Lewis turn her, display her, turn her round so that everybody could see. His body was hot, pressed against her back, and his arm gripped her and his hands felt big on her and

331

she felt the air on her bare skin as he showed her, and then he said, 'This is not a secret any more.'

Kit felt a wave of sickness and couldn't have opened her eyes, and he was having to hold her just to keep her upright and his arms felt strong.

'He does this—he does this to her. He hit Tamsin.' Then, much quieter, bending down to her again, 'He mustn't do it to you any more.'

His voice was sweet and soft and close up to her.

'Tamsin?' said Lewis, and Kit opened her eyes and saw her sister looking at Lewis. 'Tamsin?' he said again. 'Didn't your father do that?'

Tamsin kept staring at Lewis and didn't speak. Then she looked down to the ground.

'Let go of my daughter.'

Her father's voice was strong and loud and Lewis pushed down Kit's top, pressing it around her.

There was movement near them, people were preparing to react—something would happen. Lewis backed away with Kit, and Kit saw her father seem to grow, and he took a step towards her and reached out his hand. Kit ducked shy of the hand as it came towards her.

Lewis kept on holding her, drawing back, and Kit saw that her father's hand was cut and bruised. Kit saw it. Everybody saw it, and that she shied away from him. Dicky looked quickly round the faces and his look was fearful.

Kit felt Lewis relax his hold on her and a jolt went through her body, like needles, like the blood starting up again and she pulled away from him. He didn't try to hold on to her and she ran out of the church.

Lewis stood alone. He looked at Dicky and then

around—at the faces that all stared back at him—
and then back at Dicky.

Then he went after Kit.

Everybody watched Lewis until he was out of
the church, and then they turned back to Dicky
and there was stillness again. Dicky felt eyes on
him, examining him. He tried to make himself look
at them; he couldn't, and Claire and Tamsin stood
quietly by, unprotesting.

*   *   *

Lewis got out of the church and the day was bright
and still. There was nobody watching any more;
just Kit walking away and the graves and the bright
light. He went after her, but slowly. As she reached
the road she stopped and turned to him. She had
her arms around herself and she was crying.

'How could you? How could you do that to me?'

'There was nothing else! There was nothing else
I could do. I had to protect you.'

'Protect me!'

'I have to go away.'

'What?'

'My National Service. I got my enlistment notice
and it's that or prison again, and I didn't know
what to do.'

'I waited for you! I waited two years, I've loved
you for as long as I can remember. I wanted to be
all grown-up for you—and look at you!'

'I'm sorry.'

'You're nothing but chaos and disgusting. And
God, Lewis, how could you—go to bed with her?'

He felt very quiet. He'd known it would be like
this, but it hurt anyway.

333

'It wasn't that simple,' he said.

'You're not who I thought you were.'

There was quiet for a moment.

'No,' he said, 'I'm no good. And the world's no good either, but you—you're something else. Kit. Listen. You're the only thing I've ever seen that's right. Just the way you see things makes them better—and I thought you'd make me better too, but you can't. And I thought I could save you. But I can't. I can't seem to.'

'No. I'm fine!'

She held her head up and fought back and he wanted to give her a medal and he said, 'You're not fine, Kit. You're just brave.'

She turned away from him. He looked at her back, and how tough she was trying to look, and at her bare neck.

'You're beautiful. And you deserve everything. I wanted to tell you that—and that I love you.'

She didn't turn around. He waited. He had known she wouldn't turn around and that he'd lost her, and he felt tired and hurting again now it was over.

'Well. I've done it,' he said.

The church bells started again and people came out of the church and Kit didn't wait, but walked away from Lewis and away from the people and back to her house.

Lewis watched her go. No beating would have absolved him.

*   *   *

Afterwards it was all very odd because people came out of the church and there was no scene or

334

shouting or police, and everybody pretended they didn't see him and carried on as usual. Lewis wasn't sure where to go or what to do. He hadn't thought that far ahead. He was vaguely interested to see if he was going to be arrested for smashing up Dicky's house—they had been looking for him after all—but nobody spoke to him and there was no Wilson at his side with handcuffs, or anything to show he was even there. He stood in the graveyard as they all went home and he could have been a ghost, for all the notice they took of him. He watched Claire and Tamsin follow Dicky to the car, and thought it had all probably been for nothing. The world had exploded, but Sunday lunch would go ahead as usual.

He saw that his father hadn't left. He and Alice were waiting by the wall of the church and murmuring to each other and not looking at their friends as they passed them. After a while Gilbert came over and they spoke a few words. There was nothing conclusive; there was no reunion and no statement of loyalty. Gilbert asked him if he was all right and wanted to know if he'd be coming home, and Lewis said he wouldn't, but he might spend the night, and that he had his enlistment notice through—and then they went. He was left with not a person in sight. He glanced over at his mother's grave before leaving, but she'd never really been there, and it didn't mean anything.

He walked down the middle of the road, towards the edge of the village and his father's house, and the Carmichaels'. It wouldn't have mattered, except for Kit. He'd thought that if he could shine a light into the dark places of her life, they would disappear, but he had thought wrong.

335

No-one wanted to look.

'Lewis?'

Lewis turned and saw Dr Straechen. The doctor was standing on the pavement and Lewis thought how he must look, in the middle of the street, blood down his shirt and not even able to walk straight.

'Why don't you come with me to the surgery?'

'I'm all right.'

'I think you should.'

*   *   *

They walked down the main street to his house, which had the surgery in the front of it, and Lewis could smell lunch cooking and hear Mrs Straechen moving around in the kitchen behind the white-painted door at the back of the hall.

They went into the consulting room. Dr Straechen closed the door.

'Why don't you sit down? I'll clean you up—that cut over your eye looks rather nasty.'

Lewis sat in a metal chair by the curtain that you could pull across to divide the room. He watched the doctor go about collecting cotton wool and other things. He was grey-haired and his suit was a dark pinstripe and worn to softness. He put the things on the small table nearby and pulled up another chair and sat close to Lewis, looking at him.

Lewis felt very tired. The doctor didn't speak, but watched him, steadily, and Lewis looked around the room. There were framed photographs on the desk of Dr Straechen's sons and of his wife. There were flowers that needed changing and a

336

hat-stand with the doctor's hat and coat hanging on it.

'I delivered you.'

'What?' He looked back at the doctor.

'I delivered you. I'll always remember your mother, the way she was about it. She wasn't very frightened, like lots of new mothers; she was extremely brave, and she kept saying she couldn't wait to meet you. Your father was downstairs, waiting, and he was terribly nervous, of course. It was a good straightforward labour and nothing remarkable, just the sort I like, and your mother, Lewis, your mother was a natural. Now, let's have a look at you.'

He looked, and he wiped the blood away while he looked, and asked which bits hurt.

'I imagine you've a concussion. You may have fractured your cheekbone. I can stitch the eye up for you. Do you remember that day?'

'What day?'

'The day—after the church—when I came to see you at the police station.'

Lewis nodded.

'It was distressing to see you like that . . . I've got two boys. They're older than you, of course. Both married now. My elder son's in Egypt, with the British ambassador there. Younger one's in the City. When they were younger it didn't always look as if things might turn out so well. Each of them had a difficult time in one way or another. But things did work out in the end, do you see?'

'Yes. Thank you.'

'I've always thought you were a good boy.'

Lewis sort of laughed.

'Aren't you a good boy? I mean, I've always liked

337

you.'

Lewis looked down because he was going to cry and he felt stupid about it.

'You know you should go to hospital with this.'

'It doesn't matter.'

'It does matter. Lewis, here—' He put his hand on Lewis's head and rubbed his hair and held the back of his neck, looking at him and making Lewis look back. 'It does matter,' he said.

He had Lewis lie down on the metal bed that was there, like a hospital bed, with a cotton blanket, and he put four stitches in his eyebrow. He gave him some painkillers and Lewis fell asleep almost straight after, and the doctor went away and had his lunch.

*   *   *

The long dining table at the Carmichaels' house had been extended to its full length. Silver and china and linen had been laid at sixteen places during the morning, and flowers had been cut from the garden and put in small vases along it. The flowers were August yellow and pollen dropped onto the varnished table.

When the family returned from church there was a nothing, a silence, a regrouping. Claire and Dicky went into the drawing room where there were more yellow flowers, and Tamsin stood in the hall. Kit went upstairs, but stopped in the corridor on the way to her room and sat in a high-backed chair she had never sat in before. She looked up at a painting of a child with a dog. The corridor to her room was to her right and the stairs to her left and she was nowhere, just waiting.

In the hall, Tamsin took off her gloves, slowly. The telephone rang. She picked up the receiver.

'Guildford 237?'

It was Mary Napper cancelling lunch. Joanna was home unexpectedly. They were sorry. Immediately she put the telephone down, Dora Cargill called to say they were both unwell and wouldn't be able to come to lunch. The Turnbulls' butler called, and then David Johnson and then the Pritchards. Everybody was terribly sorry.

*   *   *

The family sat at one end of the table and the lunch was brought in. It took the housekeeper and the maid to carry the side of beef, which had been for sixteen, into the room. They put it in front of Dicky. Dicky picked up the carving knife.

The maid stayed to finish clearing the extra places at the table and, as she finished, looked up and caught Dicky's eye. She hadn't meant for him to see her looking at him, but, when he did, she didn't look away—not until he did.

The housekeeper came back in with vegetables.

'Just leave them,' said Claire, 'we'll manage', and she put them near her on the table and they went out and closed the door. The air in the dining room was still and warm.

'Do you know,' said Tamsin, 'I heard on the wireless, it hasn't rained since the sixteenth of June.'

'It has been terribly dry, but I had no idea it had been that long,' said Claire.

'The garden looks absolutely flat.'

'We've done our best with it.'

'There's not enough humidity for a thunderstorm.'

'No, it's been very dry, hasn't it?'

This went on for a while between Claire and Tamsin, with Dicky coming in occasionally and all three exchanging smiles, smiles that weren't to do with the conversation.

'It's still hot enough to swim,' said Kit. 'May I go after lunch?'

'They say the reservoirs are drying up,' said Dicky, not looking up from his plate. His hands felt very painful, but he was cutting the food up all the same.

'Well, I hope they're not going to start that water-rationing nonsense,' said Claire.

'Mummy? May I swim?'

'Do you remember in '38, when none of us were allowed baths?'

Tamsin laughed. Kit began to feel desperate. Maybe they couldn't hear her.

'I said, could I swim after lunch?'

Dicky and Claire and Tamsin all stopped and turned to Kit and looked at her. Then they carried on.

'Robins spoke to the boy who comes on Tuesdays for the vegetables and he said . . .'

Kit stood up and they didn't acknowledge that she had stood up. She looked around at them. She thought she might laugh; she wanted to laugh at them for being like the girls at school, for being so stupidly mean to her, but somehow she couldn't. She pushed back her chair and left the room.

She went up the stairs and felt a hot feeling in her chest, and the feeling grew and she knew it was all the tears she had been not crying and not

340

feeling, and she felt desperate and that she mustn't cry them and mustn't think about her family hating her, or what her father might do if he found her alone, or of Lewis and what he'd done and how hurt he'd been and not having any hope . . . She wouldn't think about it and she would be strong, and she would endure it and hide herself and be brave. Brave, but not fine. She got to her room and went inside and closed the door.

She went to the floor by her bed and started to tidy the records that were lying there. She knelt, picking them up, and tried not to think about the world being hard and broken or that she was alone and broken too, and with nobody to help her. There was nobody, and she felt weak and faithless. Her tears were hot and hurt her eyes, and she was angry and clumsy, trying not to feel them and losing her battle.

The door opened. Kit scrambled up from the floor. It was her mother. Claire stood in the doorway, with one hand still on the doorknob, not committing to being there. She looked around the room and her look made the room invaded and shameful.

'You'll be going to Sainte-Félicité early,' she said. 'And you can remain there for two years. I telephoned them before lunch. You will take the train on Wednesday. We won't expect you home for the holidays. At the end of your stay there you'll be almost eighteen. Do you understand?'

Kit looked at her mother and she didn't fail herself.

'Perfectly,' she said, 'but when I'm gone, don't you think it will be your turn again, Mother?'

Claire stared at her. Neither one said anything

341

else. Kit clenched her fists and waited for Claire to go and close the door behind her, and then she sat down on the bed.

She was leaving in two days. Not some time in the future, not weeks; two days and not coming back.

She sat on the bed as the feeling came over her and she surrendered. She pressed her face into her pillow and her tears wet the eiderdown that covered it and made dark marks, and she cried and muffled the sound in the pillow. She gave herself up to it and it hurt. It hurt, but the hurt had relief in it because she was getting out. Because of Lewis, she was at last getting out.

*   *   *

Lewis spent his last evening at home outside the house, waiting, while Alice and Gilbert performed their evening in the lit-up drawing room. He stayed outside, where he felt more at home.

He told himself that the next day would come and that he would be away and he'd look back at this and it would be just something that happened to him, like Jeanie, or school—just something that happened and not everything, the way it felt now.

It wouldn't always be so very bad. It wouldn't always be like a death. His face was still hurting, but he reckoned it was just mending like all the other things that faded away. It hadn't been the absolution he had needed. He didn't think anything could be.

He pictured Kit, all her life, from her childhood—all the bits he'd seen—and she was lovely and light and strong, and he wished he could

342

hold that in his mind all the time. He didn't want to forget her. He had forgotten his mother; at least he hadn't been able to keep her image in his mind.

He walked over to the woods behind the Carmichael house to collect his case when it was dark, but he didn't look at the house. At home, he packed and made sure he was ready to go. He looked around the small white bedroom at all the familiar things: the books on the shelves and the chest of drawers and the crack in the ceiling. It was not a living place.

He sat on the bed and let his head go down into his hands. His mind wasn't raging any more, it wasn't rushing and fighting to hurt itself, but he was sad, and he missed Kit, and he had failed, and just then his loneliness hurt him very much. He was surprised by how much it hurt; he had thought he was already broken.

*   *   *

The night was long. He didn't sleep, but waited until the very early morning and then went downstairs to leave.

As he opened the front door, sudden light filled the hall. Gilbert came down the stairs towards the dining room. It was as if they had met by chance in his office or club; he paused and shook Lewis's hand without looking at him particularly.

'Good luck,' he said, and then he picked up the paper from the hall table and went into the dining room.

Lewis left the house and walked towards the road. He heard the door behind him.

'Lewis!'

343

Alice came running, barefoot in her nightdress, across the gravel towards him. Her hair was loose. She stopped in front of him and glanced over her shoulder, like a schoolgirl out of bounds, and breathless with not knowing how to say what she needed to. They looked at each other, and her face, with all its need and hope, went straight to him, as it always had. He felt something like love.

'If you write,' she said, 'write to the flat. We'll be leaving this house.'

'I won't write.'

'No. Goodbye.'

She kissed his cheek, carefully, reaching up, and he put his free arm around her and held her for a moment.

'All right?' he said, worrying. She nodded yes. He thought she meant it. She went back into the house and he didn't wait, or watch her, but carried on, away and out onto the road.

*   *   *

Kit put on a light blue dress that she had been waiting to grow into and found it fitted. She washed her face and did her teeth in the bathroom and ran her damp hands over her hair and her neck for coolness, and then she went downstairs and had her breakfast in the kitchen. She called her kitten in, and fed her, and annoyed her by lifting her up with her paws dangling to kiss her. She put on her shoes by the kitchen door and went outside. She walked slowly over to the Aldridge house through the woods, and when she got there she cut down through the garden to the front door and knocked. It was Mary who answered the door, and not Alice, and when Alice came neither of them could look at the other. Kit looked at the ground and asked for Lewis and only looked up when Alice said he'd left.

'Gone?' she said, 'he's gone?'

*   *   *

Lewis watched the other people getting onto the train. It wasn't the main commuter train to London, but a local one and there weren't many people. When the train had pulled out he was alone on the platform and he watched the signals changing and saw the stationmaster, after staring at him for a while, go back into the station. It was quiet. There was birdsong and the faint murmur on the line of his distant train. He went to the edge of the platform and trod out his cigarette and kicked it onto the stones by the track. He could hear the engine of the train now, the rhythm of it and the shunting and the metal sound as it came through the valley. Then he saw the steam, a long whitish-grey trail against the clean blue sky, and then he heard a girl's voice and stared down the platform and saw her, the blue of her dress, coming out of the station where the stationmaster had gone. She called something and he couldn't hear what it was. He couldn't believe it was her, but it was her, and she was running towards him. He started towards her too and he could see her clearly now and she was still running, and she was wearing the blue dress that made her look like an imagining of Kit, and not real, until he heard her shout and saw her frown and knew it was her.

'What?' he said and she shouted again, but her

345

voice was a girl's voice and he couldn't hear her. 'What?'

'You are good!' They both stopped—just for a second—'I had to tell you—'

They reached each other then and he got his arms around her and she was holding on to him.

'You said you were no good, but you are.'

He held on to her and kissed her face and couldn't believe she was there, but she was, and smelled so clean and beautiful . . .

'I'm sorry,' he said, 'I'm sorry.'

'No, no, it's all right—'

'I'll be better for you, I promise.'

'No, I love you. I *said*—'

'Oh, you're beautiful.'

He kissed her and held on to her and they kissed for ages, a real kiss with longing to it and heat.

'Come with me.'

'I can't.'

'I can't leave you here.'

'No, it's all right, I'm going away, they're sending me to Switzerland early. I'll be gone and they don't want me back.'

'I'll come there, I'll come and get you.'

They were having to talk over the engine noise now, because the train was pulling in and it was vast and noisy and the whistle blew.

'Wait! Look here—' Lewis started through his pockets, looking for a pencil, and the train towered over them and he didn't have a pencil and he pulled out the enlistment notice, pushing it into her hands.

'I'll be here, I don't know where they'll send me after—'

'Don't worry.'

'I'm not, don't be sad.'

'I'm not sad,' she said, crying.

The train had stopped, the guard blew the whistle again. It was too hard, to have to get onto the train and to be leaving her. They held on to each other and then he got in with his case and shut the door and bent down from the window to kiss her some more, and they didn't let go. Everything about her was right, the feel of her, her strength and her softness, and that she was a baby, but so grown-up. It was incredible to him that she knew him and, even knowing him, would hold on to him and kiss him like that, and he felt her hand on his cheek—the one that was all right—and her arm around his neck, and he kissed her some more and there was nothing in the world but that. They forgot about leaving each other, but the train had started, and she started to walk along with it, and it was funny for a moment, but then not. She started to run. He let go of her. They weren't touching any more. She stopped and looked into him and he looked back, loving the sight of her.

'Look, Lewis!' she said and she held her arms out wide. 'We're saved!'

The train got faster and she was a distant figure very quickly, but he waited until he couldn't see her blue dress any more before he stopped leaning out of the window and went back against the wall of the carriage.

There was stillness and quiet; even with the fast train and the noise of it, it was very peaceful. He felt hot. He undid his sleeves and rolled them up, for coolness, not minding about his arm showing.

*   *   *

347

Kit stood on the empty platform and watched the train disappear. When it was gone she stood a while longer. Her body and her mouth felt the way Lewis had held her and the way he had kissed her and how hard it was and how gentle. She felt a different girl, but the same. She felt cherished. She knew it would hurt later, that he had gone, but now she had nothing but joy. After a while she heard cars arriving and the footsteps of the commuters as they came up to the platform, and Kit didn't want to see anybody else, and she walked away from them and down from the platform by the small steps and into the long grass. She would walk back across the fields, slowly.

*   *   *

Lewis stood against the wall of the train until the guard came through to take his ticket. He was a tall man, old, and he walked with a limp, as if he had braces on his legs, and he looked at Lewis oddly, and Lewis couldn't work it out for a while; he was used to people who knew him looking at him like that, but this man was a stranger. Then he realised how he must look, as if he had been in a war, with his face all messed up and his arm cut to pieces and smiling like everything was just right, like everything in the world was laid out for him. He supposed the man didn't know how you could be damaged like that and be so pleased with it.

He showed the guard his ticket and tried to be polite so that he wouldn't frighten him and then he went and found a seat. He didn't think about it, he went straight to a seat facing forwards, so that he could see where he was going.

ACKNOWLEDGEMENTS

I would like to thank Clara Farmer and everybody at Chatto and Windus for their commitment to this book.

*   *   *

Thanks also to Caroline Wood for her confidence and loyalty, and to Jodi Shields for her belief in *The Outcast* in all its forms.

*   *   *

Love and thanks to my husband, Tim Boyd, my family, and to Becky Harris.